FRAMinds

NIKKI J SUMMERS

Copyrighted Material
FRACTURED MINDS

This book is a work of fiction. Names, characters, businesses, places, events and incidents are either the product of the author's imagination or used in a fictitious manner. Any resemblance to actual events or persons living or dead is purely coincidental. Any trademarks, product names or named features are assumed to be the property of their respective owners and are used for reference only.

Copyright 2021 by Nikki J Summers
All rights reserved. No part of this work may be reproduced, scanned or distribute in any printed or electronic form without the express, written consent of the author.
A CIP record of this book is available from the British Library.

Cover Image: Michelle Lancaster
Cover Designer: Lori Jackson Design
Editing: Lindsey Powell at Liji Editing
Interior designed and formatted by: Irish Ink Publishing

OTHER BOOKS *By*

NIKKI J SUMMERS

Rebels of Sandland Series

Renegade Hearts
Tortured Souls

Stand-Alone

Luca
This Cruel Love
Hurt to Love

Joe and Ella Duet

Obsessively Yours
Forever Mine

All available on Amazon Kindle Unlimited.
Only suitable for 18+ due to adult content.

SPOTIFY

Available to download on Spotify
https://spoti.fi/3qM73NP

The Sound of Silence – Simon and Garfunkel
Don't Wake Me – Aranda
Boy Like Me – New Medicine
Death By A Thousand Cuts – Taylor Swift
Jesus of Suburbia – Green Day
Say You Won't Let Go – James Arthur
Lose Somebody – Kygo, OneRepublic
Perfectly Imperfect – Declan J Donovan
Rampage – Gravedgr
Photograph – Ed Sheeran
Songbird – Eva Cassidy

Puzzle Pieces – Framing Hanley
Sound of Madness – Shinedown
Dangerous Night – Thirty Seconds To Mars
Monsters (feat. Blackbear) – All Time Low
Waiting for the Night – Depeche Mode
Killing in the Name – Rage Against the Machine
Die a Little – Yungblud
Make You Feel My Love – Adele
Party Up - DMX

TRIGGER WARNING
A Message from the Author

Fractured Minds is for readers 18 years and upwards due to the graphically violent and sexually explicit scenes that happen in this book. It also deals with issues of sexual abuse towards a child that some may find difficult to read and may cause distress. There is also bad language throughout. You have been warned!

That being said, I hope you enjoy Finn's crazy, and at times, heart-breaking story!

Love Nikki x

The greatest trick the devil ever pulled was convincing the world he didn't exist.
~ Charles Baudelaire

PROLOGUE

FINN

Fifteen years ago

Twenty-eight, twenty-nine, thirty...

At school, I count the tiles on the classroom ceiling to stop myself from lashing out when I get angry. It calms me down. I don't know why. I think one of the counsellors my mum took me to said focusing on something else when I feel it building up inside of me would help to tackle my anxiety. He suggested using nature. He said it can help to centre us, whatever that means. I'm six years old, but he had no idea how to talk to me. He droned on about the brain and how it works, showed me a video on something called mindfulness, and then made me sit in his window and watch the pigeons in a bird bath in his office gardens for the rest of the session. It was the most pointless afternoon of my life.

Sixty-four.

That's how many tiles there are in my classroom, but I still count them most days, regardless.

However, in our bedroom at home, we don't have tiles. I

wouldn't see them in the dark anyway when I really needed to count. So instead, when I need to, I focus on the wallpaper next to my bed. It's torn and peeling off in places. Not because of anything I did. Well, not really. The damp makes it come off and then we can't help ourselves, we have to peel the rest and give it a helping hand. "We" being my sister, Alice, and me. We share a bedroom. Most days, I wish we didn't, but then most days I pray we lived far away from here, from anywhere that adults could hurt us.

If I had one wish, it would be to have a magic key to our bedroom, one that could only be used by us, so no one else could get in. The kids at school are mean sometimes, but adults are far worse. They pretended to be good in front of others, but they can't be trusted. They hide their evil behind sweet smiles and gentle touches; touches that hurt when no one else is watching.

He told me he'd cut my tongue out if I ever told anyone about him coming into our room. He said Mum and Dad would be mad at me for telling, that Alice would be taken away and that I'd end up in prison and everyone would blame me. So, I keep quiet. I don't tell anyone about what happens when the lights go out and the rest of the world falls asleep.

Neither does Alice.

When I hear the click of the bedroom door handle, my stomach rolls over. I stay facing the wall, trying to ignore the rocks in my tummy, and I remind myself to keep counting. If I count hard enough, sometimes I fall asleep too, and then I don't hear Alice's quiet cries or his grunting. I hate that sound. Last night, I counted one hundred and eighty-nine daisies before he left. I hope it's not more than that tonight.

My sister always whimpers as the bed squeaks from his weight on it, and I squeeze my eyes shut as tightly as I can, pretending to be asleep. If I can't count, I draw pictures in my head of what I'd like to do to him when I'm older.

I'm the lucky one.

He never comes to my bed.

It's only Alice he wants.

One day, when I'm a grown up, I'm going to get my sister as far away from here as I can. We'll live in a treehouse or on the beach somewhere, and I'll make sure she has her own room with a massive bolt on the door. No one else will be allowed in unless she lets them. I'll make sure she's always safe.

But for now, we lock ourselves up tightly in our own heads. We keep the pain to ourselves.

We don't talk to anyone.

What's the point?

No one can help us.

No one really cares.

CHAPTER One

FINN

Present Day

I wake up to the sounds of machines beeping all around me, making my banging head pulsate harder and agitating me to the brink of insanity. It took a few seconds for my foggy brain to kick into gear, and when it did, I realised I was in the hospital. It wasn't just the sounds though, the clinical smell gave it away too. The scent of bleach, illness, and death made my stomach turn. It was the whole package; like a cocktail of catastrophe, the omen of my downfall.

Why did I have to wake up here?

Why did I have to wake up at all?

Lying still, my body felt like a dead weight, as if I'd been strapped to the bed like one of those mental patients in a horror movie. I couldn't move. I could barely wriggle my arms, and my legs were fucking useless. As my brain-fog started to clear, I prayed to God no one else would see me here. I looked like a fucking loser. Really felt like one too.

I tried to lift my arm up, but even the slightest movement

made me wince in pain. Breathing wasn't easy either and I grimaced, trying to remember exactly what'd happened after I got that call. The drugs they'd given me in here really weren't helping my memory. I was numb but drowsy, and I needed to be alert.

The last thing I remembered was going bat-shit crazy with the kind of fury that'd make my best friend, Brandon, proud, but probably shit his pants at the same time. I didn't regret it and I'd do it again if only I could get my limbs to comply with my brain and bloody move.

There were exactly four people, other than me, who knew the truth about what'd happened all those years ago. The truth that'd landed me in this hospital bed. My sister Alice, Brandon, our local copper Tom Riley, and *him*. I'd never meant for Tom to find out like he did, but he was good to me. I guess the reason he turned a blind-eye to a lot of the shit we all pulled around Sandland was because of what he'd found out one night, while coming across me and Brandon arguing in an alleyway. I'd done everything in my power to keep my family secrets hidden, but sometimes shit just happened, no matter how careful you were. I was lucky Tom agreed to keep my secrets for me. It could've easily gone the other way, and I knew Alice wasn't strong enough to face a court case.

When I got the call from Tom, giving me the heads-up that he was out of jail, I knew there was only one thing I could do. I had to hunt him down.

Me.

No one else.

I couldn't involve anyone else in my plans. Brandon and his girlfriend, Harper, were having the babies. I couldn't drag him into this. Ryan and Emily had been through enough with her dad and the trial. And Zak? He was a mate, but I didn't feel close enough to him to share something like this. I knew he'd have my back, they all would, but this was my war. My battle. I needed to fight it alone.

I didn't feel like a winner right now though. But what war had ever been fought and won in one night? I had a lifetime of regret, of feeling helpless and vengeful. The enemy I was fighting would take a lot longer to conquer. He needed to take more hits before his crushing defeat. But I'd do it. I owed it to Alice.

It didn't take long for the Sandland grapevine to go into overdrive. When a notorious armed robber gets out of jail and takes himself off to the local boozer to brag about his time inside, it spreads around the town like wildfire. I knew exactly where to find him, and I didn't think twice about going down there. He'd had enough freedom in my book, being out the few hours that he had. Now, it was time for him to face his past. A past that would never forget what he'd done.

No one was truly happy that he'd been let out early on good behaviour. The honest, hard-working people of Sandland wouldn't give him the time of day. But then again, he always did surround himself with fake friends and no-marks who thought his fuck-the-world attitude was cool;

something to replicate. If they knew the real man, like we did, they'd have never let him see the light of day again. Even criminals had a code of ethics, and he just shat all over it. He had no morals. The man was devoid of any humanity.

I wanted to be the one to serve him a one-way ticket to hell. I wasn't that impotent, useless little kid anymore. The fire of anger that balled into thirsty flames inside of me spurred me on, and there was nothing I or anyone else could do to stop it.

I watched him from the window outside the pub, laughing as if he didn't have a care in the world. Downing pint after pint like he was a soldier returning from war, finally getting to enjoy the home comforts that'd cruelly been taken away from him. People walked past his table and patted him on the back, like he'd done something they were proud of. It made me want to raise the baseball bat I'd brought with me up into the air, smash it against the fucking windows of the bar, and shout from the bloody rooftops how deaf, dumb, and blind some of the people of this town were to his evil. He didn't deserve recognition for anything. He was a dead man walking.

An hour later, he got up, choosing to walk outside and down a side alley to take a piss. He couldn't even use the men's room like the rest of us. But then, he wasn't like the rest of us, was he? He had no soul.

He unzipped his trousers, and as he started to relieve himself against the wall, I crept up behind him and swung the bat, ready to take him out with an almighty blow. Only, my silent nature wasn't quiet enough. I guess being in prison for so long teaches you to hone certain skills; one of them being staying alert to any ambush. I thought I'd been stealthy in my approach, but he flew around as soon as I swung my bat, and when it bounced off the wall next to his head, he barrelled into me and knocked me to the floor.

We rolled around together and he struck a few lucky punches. I got some decent hits in myself, and it felt good to know that my fist connecting with his body made him grunt in pain. But it wasn't enough. *I* wasn't strong enough, and before too long, he was overpowering me.

Eventually, he sat up, straddling my waist and brushing the greasy hair out of his eyes. When he finally saw who was lying underneath him, he cackled with a sinister laugh that made my skin crawl and my blood boil.

"I was wondering when you'd show your face, boy." He leaned over me, and the stench of stale alcohol and bad breath from his questionable hygiene made me screw my nose up in disgust. Hate wasn't a strong enough word to describe how I felt about this man. "Think you can go against me, do ya? Think you've got what it takes to take me on? Bigger men than you have tried and failed. You need to remember your place, lad." He spat onto the floor right next to my head then growled. "And it's in the fucking gutter, along with your whore of a sister."

When they tell you anger can spread over you like a red mist, they're not wrong. Hearing him talk about Alice that way made every ounce of fury I'd kept locked up all these years break free with a force I couldn't contain, and I grunted, throwing him off me, and sending him sprawling backwards onto the floor.

He was a smart fighter though, and he twisted himself to avoid my foot connecting with his head as I tried to kick him. Moving with speed and agility, he grabbed the baseball bat that I'd dropped and jumped to his feet. Then he swung with more precision than I'd used and smacked me right around the head. The thud from the whack to my skull made me falter and a sickness washed over me. I grabbed the wall to try and gain some balance, but he was merciless, and he hit me again, pounding the bat off the back of my head. I don't remember anything after that.

The darkness consumed me.

It always did whenever Uncle Tony was around.

-

I heard shuffling in the room and I opened my eyes to see an older nurse fiddling about with a drip at the side of my bed.

"Wakey, wakey, handsome. You've had quite a knock to your head, haven't you? They did a right number on you, love."

She reached over to touch my arm and I pulled away as sharply as my broken body would let me. I didn't want anyone near me.

"Calm down. I'm only checking your line. You're a timid one, aren't ya? Mind you, I'm not surprised after the state they found you in." Her eyes were kind, but she reminded me of the teachers at school; full of pretence and appearing empathetic, when in reality, they were anything but. That was my experience, anyway.

She fussed around me then went to check the chart at the bottom of the bed.

"You've got a few cracked ribs and a lot of bruising. You need to stay in for observation too, that was a nasty blow you took to the back of your head. Don't worry though, I can still see how handsome you are under all that swelling."

She didn't look up as she flipped through the pages on her chart. Obviously, she thought her shallow flattery was enough to make me feel better. All I could think was, how long would I be stuck in here? I needed to get out. Knowing he was out there, that he could do anything while I was trapped in here, unnerved me more than any of my injuries.

"I'm Nurse Young by the way, but you can call me Constance." She beamed back at me. "So, what was it? Mugging? Fight over a girl?"

I tried to speak, but my mouth was as dry as a camel's arse and I coughed, making Constance jump into action and grab a cup of water with a straw.

"No need to tell me now. Plenty of time for that. I called your parents hours ago, but they still haven't come."

Nothing unusual there.

"As soon as they arrive, I'll show them in. The police are outside though, eager buggers, but I'll send them packing. They can wait for their statement. No one upsets my patients."

She winked and then sauntered towards the door. When she opened it, I could hear Ryan giving a piece of his mind to someone in the corridor outside. I bet Alice messaged him and told him I was here. She barely left the house, and after hearing about our uncle's release, she was even more petrified.

I felt myself tense up, even though it hurt every inch of my body to do so. I could handle seeing the lads... But not her. I hoped to God she wasn't here. What would she think of me if she saw me like this?

Effy Spencer.

An angel in a town full of reprobates and losers like me.

I already felt like I wasn't enough for her. I didn't need my fractured and feeble body to remind her how fucking useless I was too.

"Two visitors and that's it," I heard Constance bellow out over their loud voices, shutting them all up, then she started clapping her hands as if she didn't already have everyone's attention within a five mile radius. "*You* can come back tomorrow. *You* can go in, but don't stay long. He needs his rest."

A second later, I saw Ryan and Emily come in and hesitantly walk up to the side of my bed, standing over me like they were at my funeral and I was in a fucking coffin. Emily's face was tear-stained but she was holding it together, for now, anyway.

Ryan reached forward and put his hand on my arm, then

he frowned and asked, "What happened, mate? Did someone jump you?"

I shook my head, but I didn't feel like opening up about it yet. I definitely didn't want to let Ryan know what had really happened when Emily was in the room.

"Are you comfortable? Can we do anything for you? We could get the nurse back if you need more pain relief?" Emily said, gesturing to the door she'd just come through.

I could tell she was talking for the sake of talking. Nervous rambling. That's what normal people do when they're faced with a situation they feel uncomfortable in or they can't control. I didn't do that. When I felt uneasy or vulnerable, I clammed up, which happened a lot more than people realised.

"No," I managed to croak out through my coarse, rough throat. "I'll be fine."

"You're not fine," Ryan snapped. "We need to know who did this. Was it the Lockwoods? Fuck. Brandon was right. You should've kept the boxing classes going. He knew something like this might happen. We're targets…"

I rolled my eyes and he stopped, giving me the time I needed to get my thoughts together and speak. I wish the answer was as simple as it being beef with the Lockwoods. They were evil, and our history with them went way back. But this time, I couldn't pin my shit on them. This went far deeper than that.

"It wasn't Lockwood." I grabbed for the water but Emily beat me to it, holding it under my chin and positioning the straw so I could drink.

"Thanks." I sipped and then pulled away, letting her place it back onto the side table. "I can handle it. It's nothing for you to worry about."

"But we do worry." Emily smiled at me with pity in her eyes. I hated that. I didn't want anyone's pity.

"So you did know them then? I swear to God, mate, if you think you're dealing with whatever this is on your own, you've got another thing coming," Ryan stated firmly, and then another voice from the door spoke over him.

"He won't face anything alone. He's got us. When we find the bastard, he's fucking dead." Brandon strolled into the room, filling the air around us with his presence. He was imposing, intimidating, larger than life, and the best fucking friend I could ever wish for. He stood on the opposite side of the bed to Ryan, looking like he was here to guard me.

"You know who it is, don't you…" Ryan wasn't asking. He knew Brandon and I shared things the rest of them didn't know about. "It's not helping if you keep this from us. We need to know what we're dealing with." He turned his focus onto me then. "Was this because of your graffiti? Were you in that alley working last night?"

I coughed as I tried to reply, but knowing I was struggling for an answer, Brandon spoke up for me.

"I know as much as you, Ry, mate," Brandon said, using his best poker face. Technically, he wasn't wrong. At that very moment, he did know as much as Ryan about the attack. But he also knew my history, and I was thanking every deity that'd ever been worshipped that he wasn't spilling my secrets. Brandon might know as much as Ryan, but he could guess pretty easily what'd happened. A quick google search on my uncle's release and he'd put two and two together. That was why I'd eventually opened up to him all those years ago. I knew he'd get it and he'd take my secrets to the grave. Me and him, we were cut from the same cloth.

"Fine." Ryan ran his hands over his face and sighed. "I didn't mean to snap at you. I just feel so... fucked off. I don't like seeing you lying here like this, Finn. You of all people don't deserve this."

"We all feel like that." Brandon turned to grab a chair for Harper who was standing behind him, speechless and staring at me, clutching her mobile phone like she was on a white-knuckle ride.

"Are you feeling okay?" I asked her, and she huffed out a laugh.

"I should be asking you that." She sat down and rubbed over her little baby bump, but she didn't smile like she usually would've when she did that.

"We both feel better for seeing you awake and talking." Brandon folded his arms over his chest. It was his way of holding himself back. The Brandon I knew probably wanted to punch the wall right about now, but he'd matured a lot since being with Harper. Even so, I could tell it was taking every ounce of strength he had to keep his arms safely locked down.

"Have you talked to the police yet? Are they putting something in place to protect you in here?"

Ryan frowned and I could see the cogs in his brain going into overdrive.

"I haven't spoken to anyone yet, but it's nothing for any of you to worry about. I got jumped. I was in the wrong place at the wrong time." My attempt at detracting them from the truth was a weak one.

Ryan clucked his tongue and shook his head in exasperation.

"Nice try, mate, but I know you're lying," he said. "And when we find out who did this, they're gonna regret ever going against one of our own. You're our brother. They hurt you, they hurt us too."

I loved Ryan for how strongly he believed in our whole brotherhood. Brandon too. I might've had a shit family life, but my friends were solid gold.

"Oh no you don't!" came a booming voice from the hallway. "Two visitors. I told you that. Can't you count?"

Suddenly, Nurse Constance came bustling into the room, puffing her chest out and flapping her arms around like a mad woman.

Then she stopped dead in her tracks and faced Brandon.

"I know you." She narrowed her eyes at him, sussing him out, then turned to Ryan and Emily. "Come to think of it, I recognise both of you too."

Emily went to speak, but Brandon cut her off.

"I have a unique face. If you knew me, you'd remember. One of a kind, that's me."

"Rocky!" Constance rocked back on her heels and then laughed like her lungs were bagpipes. "You're the big man who fainted when I stitched you up. I'd recognise those tattoos anywhere!"

Brandon's eyes went wide. "You're stitching me up right now. Thanks for making me look like a prize dick in front of my girl."

"You don't need any help in that department," Constance shot back, and we all turned to Brandon to see what his reaction would be. I held my breath, waiting for him to explode, and he did, with laughter.

"Queen of stitches, is that right? Queen of sass too."

She winked at him, then glanced down at Harper.

"You're a lucky girl," she whispered, loud enough for us all to hear. "I can see my stitches worked their magic, he's still a looker."

Harper gave a low laugh and threaded her fingers through Brandon's as she gazed up at him.

"And he's all mine." She sighed.

"Oh, dear lord," Constance groaned, then turned on Ryan and Emily. "And I suppose you finally made your choice, missy? Can't say I blame you. I'm a sucker for a pretty face too."

Emily started to blush and then Constance flew into action.

"Well, that's enough chit-chat. Out. All of you. Just because you're all nice to look at doesn't mean I'm going to bend the rules."

She started to shoo Emily out of the room and Ryan smirked, following her, shaking his head and telling me he'd be back to visit again soon.

Brandon used the distraction to his advantage, leaning down and whispering, "I know what you did. I know why too. You can't do it alone though, mate. You should've called me."

"I don't want you involved," I hissed and then winced at the pain of trying to grimace with a face that felt like it'd been used for darts practise. I glanced at Harper, who was putting the chair back in the corner of the room, pretending she hadn't heard us. "You have your own family to think about now."

His eyes darkened, but he responded right away, speaking from the heart.

"You are my family. I won't let this happen again. From now on, you tell me everything."

I nodded, because I knew that's what he needed to make himself feel better. But I knew I'd do the same thing again when I was out of here. This was my problem to solve, not his.

"We'll leave you for now, but we'll be back later, okay?" Brandon said, strolling with Harper towards the door. But when he swung it open, the bottom dropped out of my world. There, on the other side, looking totally destroyed, was Effy Spencer.

"What the fuck?" Brandon cursed under his breath. "I

thought I told you not to text her?" He glared at Harper who huffed right back at him.

"I didn't."

Emily was standing next to Effy with her arm around her shoulders. Hearing Brandon start on Harper, she shut him down, announcing plainly, "I did. So, sue me."

She gave Brandon a look, daring him to argue with her, then sent a sympathetic glance Harper's way before turning to look at me through the doorway.

"She needed to know. She worries about you too. You know that."

I didn't know how to react. This was one of those times that I was clamming up. What was I supposed to say? *Thank goodness you called her over here so she can see how weak and feeble I really am, after getting the shit kicked out of me by a forty-five year old paedophile?* I already felt like pond scum whenever she was around. I didn't need any help on that score.

I watched her as she bit her lip and hovered by the door, and looking at her made the rest of the world fall away. She was always the only girl I ever saw. But she was too good for me. What would a girl like Effy want with a fucked-up, socially inept loser like me?

The others said their goodbyes, but I didn't answer. All I could focus on was Effy. Seeing her made the pain dissolve into thin air, overtaken by my racing heart and the resounding beat in my ears.

I wished life could be different. That she could be mine. But my life and hers were light years apart, and she didn't deserve to be dragged into the hell that was my world. I loved Effy Spencer with all my heart, had done for years, but I could never let her know. If she came too close to me, she might get burnt, and I couldn't take that chance. I wasn't ever going to let that happen. I loved her enough to let her go.

She came into the room and closed the door, then pulled up a chair to sit next to the bed. All the time, she kept her eyes on the floor. I loved that about her, that she was as shy as I was. On her, it was endearing. It showed how pure she was that she was so hesitant around others, always careful to say and do the right thing. With me, it just made me look like a twat who couldn't string a sentence together.

"I'm sorry if you don't want me here..."

She was the only one I ever wanted to be around, and the one person I had to push away.

"But when Emily rang me, I had to come." She lifted her head to look at me and the shine of tears in her eyes made my thumping heart ache for her. A thousand beatings from my uncle wouldn't hurt half as much as seeing her in pain because of me. It was a stark reminder of why I was no good for her. A lifetime of my crap wouldn't be fair on anyone, least of all her.

"Are you okay?" She went to reach forward, then thought better of it and wrung her hands in her lap.

"I've been better." I kept my head down, focusing on the cheap blue hospital blanket draped over the bed. I couldn't take another second of the pity in her eyes. What woman would want a man that made her feel like that? Surely they wanted a protector like Brandon, or a fixer like Ryan and Zak. Nobody wanted an emotional cripple like me. I knew I had to let her go, and yet, I couldn't seem to make that final cut. It was too painful.

"What happened? Was it a gang? I know there's been a bit of trouble lately with gangs from outside Sandland coming in and causing problems."

I thought about denying it, but getting done over by a gang, outnumbered and overpowered, sounded better than the reality of it all. So, I shrugged and let her make up her own mind. At least her version made me look like less of a dickhead and a coward.

"You know I'm here for you, don't you? If you need anything... I can bring some clothes in. Have they told your family?" She glanced around the room, looking for evidence that they'd been here. Pigs flying past the window was more likely to happen than my parents running down here to see me. They'd probably do a quick phone call to check I was still alive and leave it at that.

"Shall I pop round and get you some stuff? You know, pyjamas, toiletries, that sort of thing?"

"I'll get Brandon to do it. It's fine," I snapped. The last place I wanted her to be was at my parent's house. What if my uncle rocked up and saw her? I wouldn't put it past him. I felt sick at the thought of him even looking at her, let alone being near her. Sick bastard.

"I shouldn't have come."

"No, you shouldn't." I regretted saying it the second the words fell out. The last thing I wanted to do was make her feel worse. "I don't like you seeing me like this," I added, trying to claw back some dignity.

"I just don't want you to feel like you're alone, Finn. Please." The sadness in her eyes broke me, and I closed my own to stem the tears that were trying to push their way out.

"I'm tired. I need to rest." I turned my head away from her and kept my eyes shut tight. When I heard the click of the door, indicating that she'd left, I glanced back towards the chair where she'd sat, and I couldn't stop the tears from falling free.

In my dreams, I was her everything.

In reality, I was her worst nightmare.

Only, she refused to see it. But maybe, after seeing me here, she'd finally walk away.

Why did that thought make me feel like giving up entirely?

CHAPTER Two

EFFY

The moment I took that call from Emily, my heart shattered into a million pieces, and each piece pierced my soul until it hurt to breathe. I thought coming down here would ease the excruciating pain somewhat, but it only made it worse.

He didn't want me here.

He didn't care that I cared.

And yet, when I looked into his eyes, I could see all the pain he held inside him, like tidal waves of dark emotions crashing against his impenetrable walls, desperate to break free.

I don't know why I kept doing this to myself. Going through the hurt and rejection every damn day, only to pick myself up and dust myself off again, ready to endure more heartache. But I did, because he had a way of pulling me back in whenever I pulled away, sometimes without even trying. All it took was a look, a sigh, a silent signal from his soul to mine. You see, our souls were made of the same energy, the same level of intensity. Only thing was, he couldn't see it yet. Or if he did, he was fighting it.

I tried not to show how much it hurt to look at him lying broken in the hospital bed. His eyes were so swollen that you could barely see the emerald-green sparkles that I always got lost in. His soft, full lips were split and the urge to reach out and touch them was all-consuming. I wanted to make him feel better, but he couldn't look at me. Instead, he focused on anything in the room other than me, using his dark hair to shield himself as it fell across his eyes.

When he turned his face away from me to rest, I held in the sob that rippled in my throat. He didn't need my misery on top of his own. His shoulders were already sagging; overloaded with the weight of his troubled life. A life I had no idea about, but I wanted to. I was that woman, clinging onto the edge of the cliff as the rocks fell away, desperately hanging on, but knowing eventually she'd have to let go and hope for the best. Resigning myself to the reality of my fate as I slipped further over the precipice, only to claw myself back to safety, spurred on by the occasional, fragile lifelines he threw my way. The latest lifeline came to me right then, as I stood in the hallway, leaning up against his hospital door. The heartbreaking sound of him crying into an empty room.

I wanted to go back in. I wanted to wrap my arms around him and remind him he wasn't alone. But I couldn't. If I did, I knew I'd destroy any self-respect he had left. It was bad enough that I'd seen him beaten and bloody. For me to witness him so vulnerable would probably destroy him completely.

Instead, I leant my forehead against the door and prayed to God that whoever had hurt him would get their ass kicked even harder when karma finally caught up to them. And I swore that I'd try harder to be the type of friend he needed. Not some love-sick teenager, following him around like a lost puppy, but a rock he could count on. I'd loved Finn Knowles since the first time I'd laid eyes on him in high school. But I could never tell him. I knew that was a sure-fire way to scare him off. So, I accepted whatever place I could hold in his life. After all, being a friend was better than being a nobody.

I pushed myself off the door I was leaning against, even though I felt the magnetic pull trying to reel me back in, keep me in place; mind, body and soul. As I walked back down the corridor to leave, my heart hurt, and it took every scrap of willpower I had to get out of there.

When I reached the exit, I saw Liv huffing and puffing her way up the hospital's entrance ramp towards me. Her eyes were fixed on the floor, her brow scrunched deep in thoughts that kept her oblivious to the world around her. I hadn't realised she'd be that affected by Finn's accident, but when she looked up and saw me, her face fell. A wash of pity and sorrow came over her, and I knew then that it wasn't Finn she was here for, or him she was worrying about. It was me.

"I didn't expect to see you here." I stopped in my tracks and let her walk the final few steps towards me.

"Em rang me. She didn't want you to be alone, and

neither do I. Are you okay?" She tilted her head to look me in the eyes, concern radiating off of her.

"I'm fine. Finn isn't though. He's in a bad way, Liv."

She nodded and her eyes dipped back down again. I could tell she was thinking about what to say next, choosing her words carefully. It wasn't often that Liv was apprehensive over what she had to say, but when she was, she had the same look on her face that she did now. A look of uncertainty over whether her next move was a wise one, and when she spoke again, I could tell she was stalling.

"I know it's not good. I got the low-down from Em, and I'm sorry he got attacked like that. It's really shit."

She spoke from the heart, and as she reached out to pull me to her, I let her. I needed a hug from my best friend.

"Yes, it is," I said in a muffled voice as I buried my face into her cashmere scarf.

"How was he when you went in?"

Reluctantly, I stepped out of her embrace and wiped the tears from my cheeks with the back of my hand.

"He looks a mess. His eyes are swollen, his face is fucked up. He's in a lot of pain."

Liv gave me a sorrowful smile and shrugged.

"I kind of guessed that part. I meant, how was he with you?"

I knew what she was getting at. She wasn't here for the rundown on Finn's physical state, she'd gotten that already from Emily. She was here to see where my head was at... as if she didn't already know.

"He was... Finn," I answered as honestly as I could. "He didn't want me there. That much was obvious. But apart from Ryan, Brandon, and Zak, who else has he got?"

Liv grabbed me by my shoulders a little too tightly, making me flinch and jerk backwards slightly.

"It's not your job to fix him, Eff," she said, taking hold of me again and shaking me.

"But I'd be a really shitty friend if I just walked away." I pushed her arms off of me and started to head away from the hospital doors we were currently blocking. This wasn't a conversation I wanted to have in full view of the whole reception area.

"Friends. Is that what you want?" she called out after me. "Because it's pretty clear to me that's not what this is about." Liv marched to catch me up, and tried to stop me by grabbing my arm, but I needed to keep moving. Those metaphorical walls were closing in, and I had to put some space between me and the impending interrogation she was about to throw my way. "He might be in there hurting, but you're in as much pain as he is, and you shouldn't be. He isn't being fair. You want more than friendship, and he's an emotional cripple who can't get his head straight. You deserve more than that."

Hearing her cruel words, I stopped dead in my tracks and turned around to face her.

"Don't call him that."

"Why not? It's true." She flung her arms out and gave me

a look that told me I needed to wake up. But I didn't like her version of my reality. "He's kept you dangling for ages now. Acts like he's interested then freaks out when you get close. He blows hot and cold all the time, and I feel like a right bitch for saying this when he's lying in a hospital bed, but he's not good enough for you. Find a guy that fights for you, chases you; makes you feel like you're the only girl in his world. One that'll shout from the rooftops that he likes you and doesn't care who knows about it. Don't you want that for yourself?"

"Of course I do. Listen, Liv, I know what you're saying, but now is not the right time. He needs me."

"*You* need you. He needs to help himself. Find the support from the lads, or lean on his family more. You can't save someone who doesn't want to be saved."

I knew she spoke sense, but it still hurt to hear it.

"Life isn't black and white," I spat. "Not for Finn, anyway."

He had a story, a crutch that was holding him back from living freely. Only trouble was, I had no idea what that crutch was. Or was it a boulder? A massive chain around his neck, weighing him down in the gutter like an anchor. Was it dragging me down too?

"Maybe I'm being harsh at a really shitty time." Liv's shoulders sagged and she wrapped her arms around herself. "I'm not known for having perfect timing or tact, but I don't care about that. I care about you."

I went towards her, dropping my anger and ditching the

flimsy wall I'd built only seconds ago.

"I appreciate your concern, really, I do. You're my best friend, but I'm not a kid. I know what I'm doing."

"You're too nice." She sighed, then gave a soft laugh. "You need a fucker like me with balls of steel to stand up and say when you're being made a mug of."

"He isn't making a mug of me."

Is he?

"He isn't treating you right either."

She'd hit the nail on the head.

I'd seen how Ryan changed for Emily, and how Brandon was obsessed with Harper. I'd always hoped that in time, Finn would come to see me as something more than what he saw now. But I had to face facts… That day might never come, no matter how much I prayed for it.

"Fine. Whatever. I really don't want to talk about this now. I've got enough on my mind. It'd be nice to know you have my back at least." I was being defensive, I knew that, and I cringed at how rude I sounded, but I didn't have the energy for this anymore. I was tired and drained of any and all arguments.

"I'll always have your back. That's why I'm here. Just be careful, okay? I know you. I know how much you feel for him. I also know that when he breaks your heart, and it will happen, it'll destroy you. I'm here to let you know I'll pick up every damn piece, one by one, but I'll be crushing his balls in a vice with my other hand as I do. Take care of your heart. It isn't safe with him."

I didn't reply, I just turned and walked the last few steps to Liv's car and got in, feeling numb. In the back of my mind, all I could think about was horses, stable doors, and bolting. You know, that old saying. She said my heart wasn't safe with Finn, but it was too late. I'd given my heart to him years ago. It was lying in the palm of his hand. Now, all I could do was hope there'd be something left when he eventually gave it back.

CHAPTER

FINN

Five years ago

"Show them weakness and they'll walk all over you. No one is ever what they seem. You need to remember that," Brandon said, pointing his fork in my face as we sat in the noisy school cafeteria.

Brandon meant well, and I knew he was trying to toughen me up in his own way, but it was easy for him. He had the strength and the muscle to back him up when shit hit the fan. That wasn't how I did things. I usually found burying my head in the sand was a better option for me, but failing that, I preferred to live in the shadows. Keep myself to myself and avoid the drama, if I could. Silence wasn't weakness. Not in my book. Silence showed an inner strength. I kept my demons under lock and key so the rest of the world didn't have to witness what true evil lurked out there, and what it could do to kids like me.

"I'm not weak." I bit down on my stale ham sandwich, even though my appetite was non-existent, my mouth was *dry, and I was struggling to chew. Sitting here, having everyone's eyes on us, made me feel self-conscious. The others liked the attention. I didn't. I might have been a Renaissance man in name, but truthfully, I didn't deserve the title. What did I bring to the group?*

Brandon sat tall, as always, but I kept my head down, choosing to sketch the skull design I'd been working on all morning, and balancing my sandwich in my other hand. That way, I could block the world out.

They had big plans; Ryan, Brandon, and Zak.

Me?

I was tagging along for the ride.

They wanted to own Sandland, be kings of this shitty little town. Ryan, he had a head for numbers. Zak was all about technology. And Brandon? He was going to fight his way to the top. But I didn't fit in. I wasn't cut out to be a king. I was a follower. A loner. I liked my own company, and I hated being in crowds. After the meetings we'd had in Zak's bedroom, discussing parties and fights we could organise, I struggled to see what my role could be. My only talent was fading into the background, not being noticed, and art.

I watched as Ryan dropped down heavily into the chair opposite us. His tray of food clattering onto the table made me flinch, and he quirked his eyebrow at me questioningly, then proceeded to attack his burger like he hadn't eaten in days. I was about to ask him how his maths test had gone, but he froze, and his eyes darted to the door where Emily

Winters stood, glancing around hesitantly, probably looking for her older brother, Danny. Ryan tried to hide the blush on his cheeks and the way his hands began to shake slightly, but I noticed. He had a thing for Emily, but he didn't want anyone to know. He had too much respect for Danny to ever go there.

"Take this joker," Brandon said, totally oblivious to Ryan's current predicament. He nodded at some kid walking out of the food service area, carrying a tray loaded with a mountain of spaghetti and meatballs. I glanced up from my drawing, not really caring about some random dude I'd never met before. Brandon leant into me, so that Ryan couldn't hear. "He stood by and watched me get my ass kicked a few years ago, back when Lockwood and Yates thought they were someone. The idiot just stood there and laughed while they kicked the shit out of me in an alleyway at the side of McDonalds. I begged that fucker to get help. I thought they were gonna kill me that day. But he shook his head and cackled like a motherfucker at what they were doing. He was glad it wasn't him getting the beating. He didn't have the balls to help me. Now look at him. Shady fucker. Revenge is sweet, my friend."

Brandon winked at me, and I watched as he slid his foot out to the side and the kid tripped over it and fell on his ass. The tray crashed to the floor and he followed close behind, face planting the spaghetti. The noise and commotion Brandon created made every person in the cafeteria stop what they were doing to look over at us. Gasps and muffled laughter resounded in the air as the kid stood up, his lunch dripping off his face and down his clothes. He was a fucking mess. I couldn't keep the shock off my face, but Brandon threw his head back and laughed. He laughed just like this kid had done in the alley all those years ago.

"What the fuck, man?" Ryan glared at Brandon and went to stand up, but a voice made him drop back down into his chair.

"You're a no-good, nasty bully, Brandon Mathers. Why would you do that?" Emily Winters was on her knees, scraping up what was left of this kid's lunch onto the tray he'd dropped, and giving Brandon a look that could kill.

Brandon shrugged as if he'd picked the guy at random, just because he could. He didn't let on that they had history. Why would he? That'd show weakness, and like he said, that's something you could never show.

"I think he'll live." He gestured to the kid, who was a little on the larger side. "He's got enough energy stored up to last him 'til Christmas. Or maybe he can drop by McDonalds on his way home." He said that last part through gritted teeth, and the kid narrowed his eyes at Brandon, and then recognition struck. He snapped his mouth shut, started to mumble something about getting out of there, and backed into a corner to get away from us. He knew why Brandon had targeted him, and he probably realised, in some sick and twisted way, he deserved it.

"One day, someone bigger and tougher is going to come along and teach you a lesson. Bullies never win," Emily said over her shoulder as she followed the kid to try and help him.

"Never gonna happen, Winters. I'm the best. Or didn't you get the memo? I can show you, after school, if you like?" He winked at her and then grinned like a lunatic, but she huffed as she stormed away. She wasn't scared of him. She looked like nothing intimidated her.

"Back off," Ryan snapped, and I started to zone out as the two of them began arguing about what Brandon had just done. I didn't hear a word they said because my mind had switched to a kaleidoscope of heightened emotions I couldn't fathom, watching another girl next to Emily, who was helping the kid clean himself up and calm down.

She had a curtain of bobbed brown hair that she used to hide her face, and she knelt down to take something out of her bag. Without a word, she pulled an apple and a chocolate bar from inside and slipped them into the kid's pocket. He didn't even notice and she didn't tell him. Her act of kindness was a silent one, one she thought would go unnoticed, but I saw.

This girl was beautiful. Stunning even. Her beauty shone quietly, making me feel all out of sorts. It was a beauty that radiated from goodness. I could tell from one glance, one selfless act, that she was everything. Good, kind, honest, unassuming. She made me want to stand up and call out to her, let the whole school know what she was doing and why *she was so fucking awesome. I'd never seen anything like what I'd just witnessed. In my world, people took. They took advantage, stole your trust, your innocence. But not her. She gave. And right now, she was giving me goosebumps.*

"Earth to Knowles. Come in, Knowles."

I hadn't noticed Zak joining us. He clicked his fingers in front of my face and broke through my hypnotic state. I shook my head slightly and stared right back at him.

"What?"

He nodded his head in the direction of the angel in the shadows and laughed.

"Don't tell me you're getting a thing for Danny's sister, Emily, too?"

He threw a chip into his mouth and smirked as he ate it. I swallowed back my answer, choosing instead to keep my thoughts to myself. If he wanted to think I liked Emily, then I'd let him. It didn't bother me. But she wasn't the girl I saw when I looked over into the corner, and I didn't want to share that with him. I didn't want to share her with anyone. I had secrets, and the way I felt when I looked at that girl was another one. A better one. The best kind of secret.

CHAPTER

FINN

Present Day

I woke with a start as I heard the click of the door to my hospital room closing. Feeling like my body was made of bricks, I reluctantly rolled over in my bed to see who was invading my space, and heard a low, whispered voice in the shadows of the morning light.

"What did you do?"

Alice stood against the door, looking as pale as a ghost, and the horror painted across her face made me feel both anger and guilt. I hadn't told her what I'd planned to do that night, when I sought him out. I didn't want her trying to change my mind. She'd fought her battle already. Now, it was my turn.

"I did what needed to be done. Well... I tried."

She sighed heavily and stepped out of the shadows to take a seat by the side of my bed. She had a brown paper bag in one hand and a disposable coffee cup in the other, and once she got closer, I could see the familiar logo and smell the delicious breakfast that lay inside. I didn't realise I was hungry until that moment, and right on cue, my stomach caught up with my brain and growled in protest at being ignored for so long.

"Here," Alice said, plonking the coffee and food onto the side table. "You look like you could do with a decent breakfast."

I took the coffee first, wincing as my arm ached from the movement. I figured a shot of caffeine would help me get through this conversation, and possibly numb the pain, but the sting from my lips as I tried to sip reminded me that it'd take a lot more than a decent cup of coffee to solve my problems. Despite my discomfort, I went to open the bag, but stopped when Alice spoke.

"I don't want you going after him, Finn. I know he's out of jail, but I can't cope with it. I can't deal with any more heartache. Do you hear what I'm saying?"

I heard her. I didn't like what I was hearing though.

"I don't want you playing the hero," she carried on. "You need to put a stop to the crazy, vigilante thoughts you've got going on in that head of yours. If you really want to help me, stay away from him. Forget he exists. I have. It's the only way I can survive the nightmare. He is nothing as far as I'm concerned."

But he did exist. He was still as big, as ugly, and as brutal as ever. And that was something I'd never forget.

"You going after him again, Finn, it's dragging it all back

up for me. I know you feel like you need to get justice, but this isn't the way. You'll never win like this. He'll always be one step ahead of you. One punch harder than you. One fucked-up thought away from destroying you too. Do you think I want to see my little brother go to prison because of that man?"

I'd happily do time if it meant he was out of our lives and our minds.

"No, Finn. I don't," she answered, before I'd even had the chance to gather my thoughts. "I don't want him tainting another inch of our lives. Not anymore. Mum and Dad might be hopeless. They never believed me, no matter what I said. But you? You kept me going, Finn. I can't lose you." I heard her voice break as she spoke the last part, and my heart ached for my silently strong sister all over again. Just as it always did when we were kids.

"You won't lose me. Not ever."

She wouldn't.

If there was one thing I could guarantee in this world, it was that I would always be there for Alice. We shared an unbreakable bond, forged from a broken history that only we could comprehend. One that tethered us in a way most siblings would never know, but secretly, they'd be thankful they never had to experience the horror that we did.

"I will lose you if you keep going down this path you've chosen," Alice pleaded. "It's a dead end. A road to destruction. Anything that leads you to where he is is going to take you straight to hell. If you've got any sense, you'll do what I'm gonna do." The way her eyes implored me to listen made me sit up straighter in my hospital bed. I knew I wasn't going to like what came next.

"What are you gonna do?"

"I'm leaving."

My heart caught in my throat, and an overpowering sickness washed over me. But she carried on, choosing to stare at the floor instead of look at me and see the hurt in my eyes.

"Sandland is nothing but a black hole of memories I'd rather forget. It's a town with no hope, no future as far as I can see. And now he's back, it's even worse. It's unbearable. You're the only thing that's kept me tied to this place, but I can't stay here anymore. Not now. I'm praying to God you feel the same way." She took a deep breath and then raised her head to look right at me. "Come with me, Finn. Let's go somewhere that no one knows us. Start again. Be whoever we want to be without his vileness dragging us down."

I knew what she wanted, and it pained me to see her beg like this. I understood her completely, I always did. But her solution was to run and hide. I couldn't do that. Not anymore.

"I can't." I reached my hand out to take hers and she let me, rubbing her thumb over my knuckles as I dug deep within me to try and think of what to say to make this better. She shouldn't have to leave. He was the one who needed to go. Not her.

"Why won't you come with me? You always used to say you'd do anything to make me happy. Why won't you do this?"

Right then, she'd switched to her child-like façade, the one she chose to hide behind when things got too rough. She was disappointed that I wouldn't see things the way she wanted me to see them, and this was her way of trying to gently manipulate me.

I knew Alice had a lot of her childhood stolen from her. She didn't act or see things in the way most adults her age did. But I couldn't hold that against her. She was a woman-child for a reason. With adulthood came responsibility, with that came expectations, and Alice struggled with all of it. He might have robbed her of her innocence, but the child from years ago still lived inside her today, and she refused to leave the safety of Alice's mind. Like a frightened little girl, hiding behind a cupboard or a wardrobe, she lingered but never fully stepped out because of the fear that trapped her there.

"We're not kids anymore, Alice." She flinched at my words hitting a little too close to home, striking with an honesty she wasn't open to accepting. "As much as I want to move on from what happened and be there for you, I need to stay here. This is my home. My friends are here. I have a life."

"And what about me? What about my life?" She dropped my hand and recoiled back into herself. A coping mechanism she'd honed over the years.

"Our lives were tainted by his evil. Our history distorted to feed his sickness. But we can't let him have the future. I want a future here, Al. If I get rid of him, if I make him pay, we can find a way to move on."

I felt justified in what I'd said. Sandland was my home. He was the intruder. But my words weren't hitting home like I'd hoped. Alice just shook her head as if she were trying to deflect my thoughts from penetrating her consciousness.

"I can't move on. Not here. I've been feeling like this for ages now, but him coming back, it's confirmed things for me. I can't be here anymore. Sandland is a graveyard of misery. If I stay, I'll be the next one to be buried. I'm dying here."

I didn't want her misery to drag her down further. I had to think about what was best for both of us. I wouldn't be able to bear the weight of guilt if anything happened to her. Maybe Alice leaving Sandland, getting as far away from *him* as she could, was the right thing to do. Even if it felt like a cut from a thousand knives to my already battered heart. For her, it was the only solution, and I'd have to accept that.

"Where would you go?" I asked, hoping she'd think about it and start to see some of the obstacles in her way.

"I've got a friend that lives over at Brinton Manor. She said I can stay there."

This was the first I'd heard about it.

"What friend? I've never heard you talk about a friend from there before."

"Her name's Danya. She can't wait for me to stay with her." Alice started to chatter away about this friend of hers, and the infectious way she talked about it made me warm slightly towards the idea of her leaving. Her eyes sparkled as she spoke and she sat taller, prouder. That wasn't something

Alice did often. I was pissed that this was the first time I was hearing about this Danya girl, but I could never stay cross at Alice for long. She had her secrets too, obviously. Like my secret. My Effy.

"Sounds like your mind's made up already. Why Brinton Manor, though? It's a shithole town. Can't you both go somewhere new? Why would you want to stay there?"

Brinton Manor was the town next to Sandland, and we'd all avoided it like the plague. Their issues made ours look like child's play. It was the kind of town even the police steered clear of, mainly down to one factor.

The Soldiers of Anarchy.

They were a gang, much like ourselves, but they didn't bring anything to their manor other than destruction, hatred and terror. They didn't throw parties like we did. They didn't strive to make their town better. All they created was mayhem. They hated us and we hated them, but there was an unspoken rule between Sandland and Brinton Manor. We stayed out of each other's patch. That way, we kept the peace. It was a volatile peace, but it had worked so far. I wasn't quite sure whether that would last if I had to go there to visit my sister though. But that was an issue for another day.

"It's better than Sandland."

"Is it? Last I heard, their streets weren't safe to walk during the day, let alone at night." Alice had been cosseted for the most part by me. I don't even think she knew who the Soldiers of Anarchy were.

"It's not safe for strangers maybe... But I wouldn't be walking the streets on my own, would I? Danya's offered to help me. Finn, she's special. More than just a friend."

I wasn't ready for her to elaborate on what more than a friend meant. She was still my sister, after all.

"If you need to leave, I understand, and I'll do whatever I can to help you. But I can't come with you." I hated letting her down, but it was the only way. "I wouldn't even know how to start again. I'm barely holding on as it is."

"I'd help you. We'd be there for each other. Plus, Danya would help us. You'll love her, Finn. She's so kind and caring and––" I cut her off. I was in pain, and this conversation was making it worse.

"No. I won't leave. I can't," I stated firmly. When it came to Alice, you always needed to make things clear. She had a way of sulking to try and get her own way, but you had to be cruel to be kind. As child-like as she was, she couldn't manipulate me. Not this time. Not now.

"Are you going to stop your crusade?" she said, scowling at me. "You do know it's a kamikaze mission you're on? I want to see him pay for what he did, but I don't think that's a choice we can make. Not in this lifetime. Neither one of us has the strength left in us to take him on. Who wants to fight the devil when they've been broken down so much by him, time and time again? Haven't you learnt yet? He always wins." *He wouldn't this time.* "We have to create our own victories. And getting as far away from this place is the biggest one we could make."

"For you maybe, not me. I'll never give up."

Her head snapped up and her eyes blazed with fury.

"I'm not giving up."

"I didn't mean that." I sighed. "I'd never call you a quitter." Alice was one of the strongest people I knew. She had her faults, but she was one of life's warriors. She'd fought the hardest wars that anyone could ever face; a war within her own mind every single day, just to survive.

"I'm choosing my battles. Making a stand for me. Giving myself a better shot at life. I'm still gonna leave, even if you refuse to follow me." She wrapped her arms around her waist, giving herself a hug for support.

"Good for you. I'll help you make the break in any way I can, but I won't follow you. This is where I belong. I'll trust your judgement on this Danya girl. If you think she's worth it, then I'll stand by you on that. I know you don't trust people easily, so she must be the real deal."

"She is." Alice nodded to herself in agreement. "Do you really believe Sandland is the best place for you after everything that's happened here? No one helped us. Ever."

"We didn't shout loud enough," I said, feeling the weight of regret pinning me down.

"We shouldn't have had to shout at all. Our word should have been enough, but it never was, was it? Mum and Dad ignored us. School turned a blind eye. They all did."

For Alice, it was black and white, but I saw the grey in-between. I could have done more to make them see. *I could have saved us.*

"Not all of them turned a blind eye." I'd never told Alice that Brandon knew, but I'm sure she'd guessed. She knew how close we were.

"You were lucky. You made friends. Good friends. I didn't. Well, not until now, anyway. Danya is everything."

Her eyes glazed over as she thought about the girl she was hell-bent on running to. And who was I to stop her? If my sister could make a grab for a little bit of happiness with Danya, what sort of a brother would I be if I stood in her way?

"I don't want this to be how it ends." I knew my words sounded melodramatic, but I couldn't help it.

"This isn't the end. It's a new start. A fresh start." Alice gave a low smile and I returned it. Knowing my sister would be out of his grasp was some comfort. It would certainly make my vengeance easier if I had one less person to worry about.

"I'll come and visit you, as often as I can." I might have to go in disguise in the dead of night to avoid the soldiers, but if that was the only way, so be it.

"I'll count on it." She grinned and stood, looking torn between staying and hugging me and running as fast and as far away as she could from everything that'd chained her to her misery.

"When are you leaving?"

"Well, seeing as you're not coming with me... There's no time like the present. Danya has a room made up ready." I'd already guessed that'd be her answer.

"And you thought you'd drop by with my favourite breakfast for one last goodbye?" I prised open the bag, hoping the contents hadn't gone completely cold.

"Oh, I didn't buy that. One of the nurses was on her way in with it and she gave it to me. It must've been left at the reception." She shrugged and I thought nothing of it.

"It's probably from Brandon, or one of the others." It was definitely something they'd do. They knew hospital food sucked balls.

"You've got good friends, Finn. Don't let him ruin what you have. Leave him be, and hopefully, when he isn't getting the attention he wants, he'll disappear back into the sewers he came from. He's nothing. He doesn't even deserve your anger. We've both wasted enough of our lives being ruled by him. It has to stop. Promise me, it'll stop."

It wouldn't.

"I'll try my best."

Alice seemed convinced by my answer and leant down to give me a hug as I lay there. I tried not to let on that her gentle squeeze hurt like hell, and plastered on my fake smile. In a way, Alice leaving was a weight lifted off my shoulders. If she was safe with Danya, then I could focus on stepping up my plan. I liked the idea of being a lone wolf. I had a pack, but I wanted to do this my way. If I had nothing, then I'd have nothing to lose.

I watched as Alice walked away, closing the door quietly

behind her, and then I peered down into the bag to find a folded note on top of the breakfast inside. I took it out, expecting to see some ridiculous joke or photograph. When I read what was written, my whole body plunged into a free-fall of violently fuelled adrenaline.

I chose your favourite breakfast. Isn't that what they do on death row? Feed you up before your final curtain call. Enjoy your last meal, because when you get out, I'll be waiting. ~Tony

FINN

The minute I could get out of that hospital, I did. The doctors and nurses put me off for days, and to be fair, I wasn't in the best shape to get out of bed and walk away. But as soon as I could, I left. Signed myself out and took the pain meds they gave me, even though I had no intention of ever taking them. I wanted to feel every ache, twinge, and sting, because then I wouldn't waver from the path I needed to take.

He hadn't sent me anymore messages since the fucked-up breakfast, but I knew he'd be watching. He couldn't help himself. In a way, I hoped he was. If his eyes were on me, then maybe he wouldn't notice Alice slipping away. If I could be that distraction for her, I'd be happy. At least in some way I'd have done what I'd always promised to do; help and protect her at all costs.

I hadn't even been home a day and my parents were already getting on my last nerve. I hated this shitty council terrace house. It was rotting from the inside out, and it wasn't just the mildew and rising damp that was the problem.

Nothing good had ever happened here. Nothing worth a damn ever resided here, not even us. But God help anyone if they peered beneath the cracks of our doomed existence. Our life was like a Monet painting; best viewed from afar.

My mum currently felt the incessant need to drone on about how proud she was of Alice for moving out, never stopping to think why she'd left late at night with two overstuffed holdalls and nothing but the change in her pocket. I knew my mum's not-so-subtle digs were aimed at me and the fact that I still lived under their roof. I didn't want to, and it was at the top of my to-do list to find a sofa I could crash on, or a park bench maybe? We lived in the crappiest part of Sandland, but she'd still berated me the minute I left the hospital and came home. Apparently, my getting beaten up had brought shame to her door. Her shining reputation and what the neighbours thought took precedence over what I actually felt. Funny, because when her brother went down for armed robbery, she didn't blast him. No. That mantle was solely reserved for me.

Did I care?

Not one fucking bit.

As for my dad, he was either shadowing Mum around the house, waiting for her to give him guidance on what he should do next, or polishing his pointless, prized fishing trophies. The single thing he loved most in the world, apart from Mum. He was obsessed with fishing, but he'd never taken me. He said it was his chance to get some peace, why would he want to invite the craziness along to join him? The pair of them irritated me beyond belief, but they didn't notice. They never did. My parents were too wrapped up in their own world to ever care what happened in anyone else's, especially their children's.

I don't know why they ever had kids. We never did the things that normal families do. We didn't have days out or go to swimming lessons. They never came to any school events, plays, or parent's evenings. Don't get me wrong, they loved each other, but there wasn't room for anyone else in their lives, even us. We were the product of their relationship, and yet, we were always the outsiders. It was always them and us. Or rather, them with *Uncle Tony*, and us.

He was my mum's brother. A constant in our house since I was five years old, and my parents thought the sun shone out of him. He bought them bottles of beer and wine most nights. Plied them with free cigarettes, and on the odd occasion he could get it, a joint to really knock them out. He kept them up into the small hours, joking and laughing until they fell into bed in a stoned or drunken stupor. They didn't realise he did that for a reason. They were both so pissed-up, they didn't hear a thing that went on after the lights went out, or was it that they just didn't care?

One particular day, just before he was put away for armed robbery, it looked like the tide might be turning for *Uncle Tony* and his little arrangement. Dad had noticed bruises on Alice's legs. She usually hid them pretty well, but on this day, Dad saw. He confronted Tony, said Alice appeared nervous, scared even, and had said he was the one to give her the bruises. He wanted to know exactly how it'd happened, and I sat in the corner of the living room, praying he wouldn't find a reason to wriggle his way out of this one.

We'd tried a few times to tell them how Tony hurt us, but their minds blocked out what we were really saying. They obviously wanted to believe it was all made up to get attention, or simply a heavy hand to two children who, funnily enough, wouldn't say boo to a goose. Not once did they listen, truly listen, and hear the desperation when Alice or I tried to tell them. Our subtle clues only hinted at what went on, because in all honesty, we were too scared to say it out loud. It was too much to put into words, so you can imagine how horrific it was to live it day-in, day-out.

"She's always been clumsy. Can't go a day without breaking something or tripping over. Look at her now, all jumpy..." Tony gestured to where Alice stood quaking in the corner, opposite where I sat. Of course she was skittish, she didn't know when he'd strike next.

"Those aren't bruises from falling over, they're finger marks. I can see––"

"You see what you want to see," Tony snapped, cutting Dad off. "Did she tell you what happened? If it wasn't for me, it'd be a lot worse. I caught her outside, climbing the ladder. Stupid cow was about to fall and break her bloody neck. Yes, I grabbed her, and maybe a little too hard around the thighs, but it was only 'cos I was stopping her from landing on the

concrete and spending the rest of her life in a wheelchair. Isn't that right, love?"

I stayed in the armchair, watching as Uncle Tony's eyes turned to steel behind my dad's back and he dared Alice to try and challenge him.

"You said he hurt you." Dad turned the interrogation back to Alice, but not in a concerned, fatherly way. His words were like darts, pinning her to the wall and shredding her will to fight into tatters. "Is this another one of your sick jokes? You can't go around accusing men of things like that, Alice. He hurt you for a reason. I've a good mind to give you the belt myself for causing trouble like this. You should be thanking your uncle, not making up stories."

Alice swallowed nervously, and plastered herself against the wall in fear. I could tell she was seconds away from bolting. Once again, any effort we made to expose him was futile. He always managed to twist our words and turn our parents against us.

"I... I..." Alice couldn't even get a sentence out. Her eyes darted from the furious face of our dad, to Tony's smug smirk. He shook his head slightly as if to say, 'Not this time, Alice. You won't beat me.'

"Say sorry, right now. Apologise to your uncle," Dad shouted, causing Mum to barrel into the living room to see what all the fuss was about.

She took one look at Alice and then turned to face the men of the house and groaned.

"What has she done this time?"

"The usual. It doesn't matter though, she's going to say sorry, aren't you, Alice?" Dad threw her a vicious glare and she recoiled further into herself.

Alice looked petrified, like she was about to throw up, and I wanted to speak up for her, but I couldn't find the words.

"I... I'm..." She didn't look at anyone else in the room as she stuttered and cowered in the corner. Instead, she hung her head in shame.

I felt it too.

The shame.

When was all this going to end?

I had to find a way for us both to leave, run away before he ended us completely.

"I'm sorry. I said the wrong thing. I didn't mean to cause trouble."

"You certainly did and you have. But it's not the floor you need to apologise to, young lady. Look at your uncle and give him the apology he deserves."

I felt sick. I didn't want Alice to have to go through the agony of looking at him and uttering any sort of kindness. But she did. Like the fighter she was, she took a deep breath and lifted her head, held her hands against the wall behind her to keep her upright, and she glared right at him.

"I'm sorry I told my dad you hurt me."

It was an apology, and each adult in the room smiled at

her admission. He grinned and bristled with pride like he'd just been knighted by the queen. But I understood the meaning behind her apology. She wasn't sorry for what she'd said, only that she'd said it to our dad. The truth still stood; he had hurt her. But she knew better than to trust an adult in this house to ever make it right.

What happened later that night cemented her regret even further. It was the last time she'd ever complain and put herself in the firing line.

The sound of the doorbell ringing pulled me out of my daydream, if you could call it that. Maybe nightmare was a more fitting description. Dreams were a welcome distraction from the horrors you faced in real life. Dreams were what'd kept Alice and I going during the darkest times. Dreams were all we had most days back then.

Dad glanced up from his place at the dining table, but carried on polishing his trophies. He had no intention of getting off his arse to answer it. His casual, flippant attitude bothered me and I pushed my way past him, eager to escape the tension, but I stopped when I heard my mum holler out that she'd get it. There was the usual muffled chatter after that and I thought nothing of it. Neighbours were always popping round to moan about something going on in this street. But then, Mum called out my name, and something told me this wasn't going to be good.

Fuck.

All the lads knew I preferred not to meet them at my

house.

Who else would take the chance of coming here and running the gauntlet of my family?

I dragged myself into the hallway and stopped dead when I saw who it was.

"Finn, why haven't you introduced me to Effy before?" Mum beamed, looking between the two of us, but if she expected a cosy visit, she'd be sorely mistaken.

Effy stood there, fidgeting with the buttons on her pea-green coat and looking awkward, out of place, and totally stunning. Her bobbed brown hair was wind swept and her cheeks were flushed red from the cold outside. It only made her look more adorable, and I had the sudden urge to pull her away to somewhere more private, where I could warm her up and lose myself in the way she always made me feel. But I kept an impassive expression glued to my face, ignoring my mum's question and coming straight to the point.

"What are you doing here?"

"That's no way to welcome a guest!" my mum chastised, but I blanked her out.

Effy's eyes widened slightly and I could see her hands were shaking, but she did a great job of righting herself. Despite what my brash greeting had evoked in her, she took a deep breath and replied, "I wanted to make sure you were okay. The others couldn't tell me anything, so I thought I'd come and see for myself."

"See," my mum sneered. "Effy has manners. Unlike some

people I could mention."

I blocked my mother's pointless contribution to the conversation completely. Like I gave a fuck what she thought. All I cared about was Effy, and it had been brave of her to come here today, I'd give her that. I wasn't the warmest guy to be around. I knew I gave off negative vibes like a porcupine on acid, but she never seemed to give up, and deep down, I was glad. If we'd been in any other place, I'd have felt differently about being around her. But I didn't like her being here. I felt embarrassed about her seeing parts of my life that I preferred to keep hidden. This house was no place for a girl like Effy.

"Well, as you can see, I'm fine." I lifted my arms up as my mum clucked her tongue in annoyance. Then I dropped them by my sides like an idiot as we stood there gawping at each other. Mum cleared her throat and made some announcement about having to change the bed linen, but I didn't acknowledge her. The less time Effy spent here under the scrutiny of my parents, the better. I needed to get her out, even though her presence calmed me.

"Don't just stand there like a fool, invite the girl in for a cuppa," my dad suddenly piped up from the doorway behind me, and I knew from the heat in my face that I was blushing.

"It's okay, Mr Knowles. I can't stop," Effy replied, sounding disappointed with her answer. She spun round to open the front door and make her escape, and in that moment, the idea of her leaving made me jump into action. I couldn't let her go like that. I'd been an arsehole and done nothing but show disdain that I really didn't feel. Not for her, anyway.

My Effy.

The girl I spent every waking moment thinking about.

The girl who gave me a reason to smile, on the rare occasion that I did.

"I'll walk you out," I said as my legs sprang into action and I followed her out of the door. I closed it behind me, not wanting Mum or Dad to eavesdrop on anything I had to say.

"Thanks for coming over. I'm sorry I was a dick in there." I thumbed towards the door behind me, not wanting to take my eyes off her for a second. The way her breathing came in short shallow pants, trying to calm herself, made my heart beat faster. Her eyes bored into mine, searching for something, anything to give her hope, and it made my body shake with nervous anticipation. She was so close, and the overwhelming urge to touch her was becoming unbearable to fight.

"You weren't a dick, Finn. I get it. I caught you off-guard and you didn't want me here."

There is nobody on this God-forsaken planet that I want to spend my days with more than you, Effy. But if you really knew me, you'd run in the opposite direction faster than your legs could carry you.

"It's not that I don't want to see you, it's just..." I sighed, not able to find the words to express how pointless it all was. I couldn't bear to see the hurt in her eyes, so I glanced back at the house, wishing we were anywhere but here.

"You didn't want your parents to see me." She thought she'd hit the bullseye, and yet, it was so much more than that. This house held secrets that I never wanted uncovered. It kept broken parts of me that no one would understand. I couldn't make sense of it myself.

I shrugged, once again letting her come to her own conclusions.

"I didn't want *you* to see my parents."

"That bad, huh?"

"Worse."

I stared at the ground, shuffling the pebbles from our path to give my feet something to do. I heard her huff and I looked up at her. She was doing that thing again where she wrapped her arms around herself like she needed a hug but knew she'd get nothing from me, so she took care of herself. I didn't like that. It made me feel guilty for being such an emotional fuck-up. So, I decided to give her something else to loosen the frown lines on her face.

"I've been working on a new piece at the asylum chapel. I thought maybe you'd like to come and see it one day?"

The asylum chapel was an abandoned building in Sandland that Ryan had claimed for himself. I knew it held a special meaning for him and Emily, but for some reason, he'd let me use it too. He was quite happy to let me loose with my imagination, to turn the drab grey, flaking plaster on the old walls into something magical, mythical, ethereal.

Watching her face light up, I knew my words had done

the trick. Straight away her shoulders dropped and she smiled a full, genuine smile that made my stomach flip over.

"I'd love to. I love your art."

She meant it too. Every time I saw her when I was working, she'd look at my art like it was something that'd come from heaven above just to make the world a better place. She'd listen to me when I told her what'd inspired me, and take it all in, letting my work affect her in a way most artists can only dream of. It was as if it touched her on a deeper level, a level similar to my own. That was one of the many reasons I loved this girl. She saw me even when I was trying to hide.

"It's a bit darker than my other stuff, but I think you'll get it."

You always do.

"I think I will too." She nodded and started to kick the stones on the path like I'd done only moments ago.

"I was kind of going for a dystopian fairy tale. A whole twisted Alice in Wonderland. Not Wonderland though." My words made her snort out a laugh.

"God forbid."

"I like to make art with an edge." I grinned, knowing I didn't need to explain that to her. This was the girl who said my industrial wasteland graffiti, with spiked flowers, mechanical trees and a dark, desolate landscape was awe-inspiring. She'd see the positive in anything.

"You're not like anyone I've ever met. I like your edge."

Just then, a gust of wind blew her hair up, covering her

face and making her struggle to get it under control. I couldn't stop myself from reaching forward to help her, tucking stray strands behind her ears. Feeling my touch, she froze, and I could tell she was holding her breath. The way her eyes shone with longing, glancing up at me through her long lashes, made me brush my thumb gently down her left cheek. Her skin was as soft as velvet and I took a step forward. I wanted to know if her lips were that soft too. Would she taste as good as I'd imagined? Better probably.

"Well, well... What do we have here? Has little Finn got himself a girlfriend?"

I stopped.

The hairs on the back of my neck stood to attention and the yearning I'd felt only moments ago was replaced by total and utter revulsion.

What the fuck was he doing here?

I dropped my hand from Effy's cheek and glared over her shoulder at the devil who lurked behind her. Was he destined to destroy everything for me? For a split second, I had a glimpse of what a normal life could be like. The girl, the feelings, the kiss. But no. I couldn't have that, could I? Not when he was hell-bent on maintaining my place in the pit of despair he wanted me to frequent for all eternity.

He stood at the gate, dominating everything with his presence and turning what was a perfect moment into something twisted and vile. As always, he haunted me like a fucking demon. He always would. But I'd be damned if I let him within an inch of my Effy.

CHAPTER Six

EFFY

The moment Finn heard the voice coming from behind me, he froze and then backed away like I'd given him an electric shock. Fear and tension rolled off of him in waves, and I knew whoever stood at the foot of the path was bad news. Finn was always nervous and guarded, but not like this. This was another level of terror and alarm in the many facets that made up Finn Knowles.

One minute, he was brushing my hair out of my face, and I felt sure he was about to kiss me. The way he'd stroked my cheek felt so intimate, so tender, that I couldn't stop the butterflies in my stomach from flying free and taking control of every part of me. But then that husky, gravelled voice had broken through our moment like a hammer crashing down and breaking the already thin ice of our relationship. And now, the Finn my soul had wrapped itself around only moments ago was locked away behind those high walls of his. Walls that felt impenetrable to a five-foot-four clumsy girl like me who was scared of heights. Who was I kidding? I liked a challenge, and if I had to climb Mount Everest to help him, I would.

In spite of Finn's adverse reaction, I turned around and smiled at the unwelcome visitor. He was tall and so well-built that the buttons on his thick overcoat were bursting at the seams, trying to break free. His face was ruddy from the cold, and his dark hair was slicked back and greying slightly at his temples. If he had a dog by the side of him, which he didn't, I'd have imagined a British bulldog called Bullseye standing faithful to his master with a string for a lead. In short, he did not look friendly. His eyes crinkled with wicked intent and his smile was crooked and insincere. I went to hold my hand out and introduce myself to him, but Finn cut me off.

"She's not my girlfriend." His words dripped with venom and harsh brutality, taking me from elated to gutted in a nanosecond. "She was here to see Alice, but Alice is gone. She doesn't live here anymore."

I dropped my hand before this man could take it in his and glanced back to where Finn stood, furrowing my brow in confusion.

What was going on?

I could sense Finn was agitated, panicked even, but why was he letting this man have such an effect on him?

The man took a step forward, and the way he leered over me in such an intimidating way made me move away from him instinctively.

"No Alice, huh? That's a shame. I was looking forward to

catching up with my favourite niece."

Not the answer I was expecting.

"You're Finn's uncle?" I said, more as a statement than a question.

"That I am. Has he never mentioned me?" Finn's uncle dipped his head in greeting like he was an old-time gent and smiled, then quirked his eyebrow at Finn. Finn didn't return the pseudo warmth that was thrown his way by his relative though. He folded his arms against his chest, causing his muscles to flex and my heart to skip a beat.

"I'll let Alice know you dropped by." Finn's words were meant for me, but he didn't look my way. Instead, he clenched his jaw tightly and I could see a nervous tick develop as he held himself together. I wanted to walk away, let him carry on this façade, but something snapped inside of me.

"If you need me. You know where I am." I gave him a look, trying to tell him that whatever was going on I wanted to help, but I needn't have bothered. His uncle gave a whistle and wiggled his eyebrows suggestively, and Finn decimated any self-respect I had left with his next words.

"If I needed anything, the last person I'd go to is you. Don't come here again. Alice is gone and I'm not interested. You're a fucking nuisance. Just fuck off."

His uncle gave a loud chortle as the heat of shame crept over my face. My throat constricted, feeling like it was closing up and making it difficult to breathe or swallow. If I didn't move away from here, I knew I'd do something to embarrass myself. I couldn't let either of them see the tears that were about to burst free, and even though I knew deep down this wasn't Finn talking––not the real Finn––it still stung like hell. A lifetime of disappointment hadn't hardened my armour or made me stronger for the fight. My skin wasn't thick, but bruised to the point that the pain was simply compounded. What was one more knock, one more cut to the thousand I already held in my heart?

"Say what you really mean, son." His uncle obviously found my discomfort amusing, and the way he leant against the gatepost showed he was enjoying the show and waiting for more.

"I always do. And I'm not your son," Finn bit back, then lifted his chin defiantly. "There's no one home, only me, so *you* may as well fuck off too. Not that you were welcome here in the first place."

"You know I'll be back. My place is with my family. In the arms of my loved ones. It's a shame Alice left. I know how much she loved our cuddle time when she was little."

His uncle winked and Finn lurched forward, but I put my hand on his chest to stop him from doing whatever he was about to do. He gritted his teeth, then tore his hate-filled glare from his uncle to stare at my hand covering his rapidly pounding heart. A thumping beat that matched my own. He didn't say a word, but he didn't need to. Finn always spoke loudest in the silence.

Thank you for understanding.

This isn't about you.

It's... complicated.

"You never were right in the head, boy." His uncle cackled, breaking both of us out of our silent bonding. I heard his slow steady footsteps from behind, heading towards me, and I braced myself, reluctantly dropping my hand from Finn's chest. He came to a stop right by me and grinned down, saying, "You had a lucky escape, *love*." I turned to glare at him and recoiled. His teeth were rotten and I moved away feeling violated at being so close to him. "If you want my number though, I'll see you right. I know how to take care of a lady." He winked, looking me up and down and licking his vile lips. I stumbled backwards, desperate to escape this lecherous creep.

It was on the tip of my tongue to tell him where to go, but I was beaten to it.

"Get out of here," Finn growled over my shoulder, but he didn't push me away.

We both stood rooted to the spot as his uncle huffed and smirked, then turned on his heel and left, muttering that he'd be back to collect what was owed to him.

We watched him saunter down the road like he didn't have a care in the world, and I went to step forward too, but Finn grabbed my arm and pulled me into him, so my back rested against his chest. The warmth from his breath as he whispered into my ear made my goosebumps resurface.

"Let him go first. I don't want him to follow you." He took

a few deep breaths as he held me against him, then he said, "Maybe I should walk you home? It's not safe in this part of Sandland."

As tempting as that sounded, he didn't need to worry about my safety.

"I came in my car. It's parked just down the road. I'll be fine." I tried not to show that his fake but still hurtful words from earlier had affected me, but I was a rubbish actress and he knew it.

"I'm sorry. I didn't mean what I said. I just didn't want him to think that... I don't like the thought of him––"

"You don't have to explain. I think I get it."

I didn't.

And the way his face twisted in pain, I guessed he was praying I didn't either.

I watched with sadness as the boy I'd seen earlier, who spoke with pride about his artwork at the abandoned chapel, began to shrink in front of me, folding into himself and appearing smaller, fragile even.

"I should go." I stepped back, holding my breath and waiting for him to say something to stop me, but he didn't. He nodded, with heavy resignation visibly pulling on his shoulders, and he let me go. Any fight he might've had was long gone. For it to disappear that quickly, he must have very little reserves to call upon, and something told me his uncle was the reason for that.

I clicked the lock of the little wooden gate closed, leaving

Finn where he stood on the path, and made my way to my car. Each step I took felt like I was wading through quicksand. I half expected his uncle to jump out at me and spill more bile into my ear, but the road was empty now. Eerily so.

Opening my car door, I could feel the all too familiar sensation of regret; like my heart was filling with concrete, becoming heavy and hitting my stomach, making everything seem gut-churningly hopeless. I started the engine and checked my mirrors before I pulled out, and there, with his head in his hands, his elbows resting on the gate and leaning forward like his world had just come to an end, stood Finn.

"You're breaking my heart," I whispered to myself in the safety of my car, and the tears I'd kept at bay fell freely.

I wiped them away and pulled off. When I came to the end of the road, I indicated right, deciding to take the long way home. I needed the extra time to gather my thoughts and pull myself together.

I drove through the industrial estate, keeping my eyes ahead and regulating my breathing. It wasn't enough, so I clicked the radio on, and *James Arthur* singing, *"Say You Won't Let Go,"* made me bawl my eyes out all over again as I sang along to every word.

As I pulled up to a junction, I noticed a familiar graffiti tag on the side of an old building. Ahead of me was one of Finn's masterpieces, and what I saw made my skin go cold and realisation blare within me like a siren. There was a little boy holding a blanket, about to wrap it around a little girl that sat cowering on the floor, wrapped up in barbed wire that pierced her skin and made her bleed. The boy wanted to protect her, make her safe, but his blanket wouldn't help when she was already trapped within the grip of the fierce spikes. Finn's work was always a reflection of how he felt, and what was happening in the world around him. And I knew right then that this was his sister, Alice, and Finn, in all his innocence, was trying to save her.

Dear God, what had happened to these two to make them like this? I prayed it wasn't what I thought it was. But in my heart, I knew. There was a reason Finn Knowles kept people at arm's length. And it wasn't because he was cold or unemotional. He had too much emotion, he felt too hard, but he was hurting. He kept people away to protect himself, because anyone he'd let in had hurt him and his sister, and like a wounded animal, he couldn't trust anyone. Not even me.

CHAPTER

EFFY

It was days later, and I still couldn't shake the feeling of dread that'd set up camp in my stomach thinking about what'd happened to Finn. What could still be happening right now.

Against my better judgement, I'd given him space. I hadn't called, text or tried to see him. But I'd asked about him every single day to Brandon, Ryan, and Emily, hoping to find some small grain of hope that he was okay. Trouble was, they knew as much as I did. Finn didn't want to share what was going on, and nobody, not even Brandon, had the power to get through to him.

By day five, I couldn't take it any longer and I decided to do something to try and ease my desperate, painful thoughts. If I couldn't see Finn, I could visit the next best thing, and maybe get a deeper understanding of the whole situation. Find out more about what made him tick.

Sandland Asylum was a rundown, creepy, eerie-looking building that stood on the outskirts of town. The grey walls and pillars that ran around the front of it were crumbling, decaying even, like they were giving up from the strain of having to carry the burdens that these walls held. An empty, desolate place, and if bricks could talk, they'd whisper tales that nobody wanted to hear. Stories that would keep you awake at night. Kind of ironic that Finn liked this place so much. His tale was as secret as the ones locked within these walls.

The security here wasn't great and I was able to slide through a hole in the fencing that was doing a really rubbish job of keeping people out. When I got to the front doors, I could see the padlock to secure this place hung open, and I took it off, placing it carefully on the floor. The door itself was old and heavy, and it didn't have a lot of give in it. Sliding my body through, I winced, praying my coat wouldn't snag on a nail or anything and trap me here. But I made it through and sighed when the door jammed itself shut again behind me, locking me into the foyer.

There was a huge ceiling above me, and long ago it would've looked impressive, but now the coloured glass was shattered, dirty and covered in bird mess. I was thankful it was a dry day too, because I'd probably be wet through, judging from the holes up there.

I squinted, peering around me, and I noticed there was a corridor up ahead. So, I stepped forward, picking my way over the uneven flagstones and holding onto the wall to steady myself. I kept my eyes on the floor, but as I lifted them to look down the corridor, I gasped.

The walls were painted to look like an underground tunnel, and if you looked closely you could see creatures hiding behind the twisted roots that appeared so lifelike you could almost see them moving and spiralling through the dirt. Roots that grew like menacing fingers, invading from the world above, trying to make a grab for the magic that lived below. This was Finn to a tee. A perfect representation of him. He was the creatures that lived down below, hiding in his world, trying not to get dragged away by the roots of life that were clawing to get to him.

I swallowed down my sadness at the thought of it all, and took a few steps forward, running my hands over the paint as I did. I was in awe of his work. I was in awe of him. Nobody had an imagination like Finn Knowles. He was one of a kind.

I smiled as I got farther along, noticing his take on the Mad Hatter's tea party hidden in a larger opening of what looked like a rabbit's warren. The Mad Hatter wore his top hat with the price tag sticking out of it, but he wasn't a cartoon character like the books. He was a boxer dog, sat in an armchair like the king of the castle, sipping tea from a cracked teacup. I laughed to myself, guessing this was a representation of Brandon. The boxer. He was crazy most of the time too, he loved drinking tea, and this suited him perfectly.

Right next to him, the March Hare sat, rolling his eyes at the Boxer Mad Hatter, and I assumed that was Ryan. Then there was the dormouse, asleep at the end of the table on what looked like a laptop. Zak.

"This is brilliant," I whispered to myself, and moved closer to see what else I could find.

Further down the warren was the White Rabbit, holding his pocket watch, and as I looked closer, I noticed that the watch didn't have numbers on it. The clock face spelt out the words, 'Enjoy the Silence.' So I guess that was Finn. The silent one.

Right next to the White Rabbit was Alice. But she didn't have blonde hair like in most of the portrayals of her character. This Alice had shorter brown hair. I tried to recall what colour hair Finn's sister had and I was sure she was blonde, but maybe I'd gotten it wrong? I hadn't seen her in years, not since she left school just as we were starting. She was older than us, and Alice Knowles was an enigma, much like her brother.

I traced my fingers along the warren as it twisted and turned, but just as I came to the Cheshire Cat, grinning in the shadows, I heard a voice that made me jump out of my skin.

"What are you doing here?"

I turned, flushing pink with embarrassment at being caught. Finn stood in the middle of the corridor, his chest rising and falling rapidly and his eyes boring into mine.

"I wanted to see what you'd done," I said, trying to get my nerves under control. I was shaking so badly but I didn't want him to see. I didn't want to look guilty. "You told me about this the other day, but after I left, I wasn't sure the invitation to come together was still open." I was giving him a chance to tell me it was, that he'd wanted to invite me but hadn't gotten round to it. I was always making excuses, but I was getting confused about who they were for. Me or him.

He sighed and looked at the world he'd created then back at me.

"It would've been nice to give you the proper tour." His shoulders dipped slightly, like some of the tension was easing up, and then he folded his arms over his chest and smiled. "What do you think?"

I stepped closer to him so I was adjacent to the Hatters tea party and I pointed at it.

"Does Brandon know you've made him the Mad Hatter?"

Finn threw his head back and laughed, and just like that, all the tension I felt before disappeared. I loved it when he was like this. Care-free. Relaxed. Himself.

"Nobody has picked up on that yet." He shook his head and rubbed over his bristly jaw.

"It's pretty obvious." I quirked my eyebrow at him, smirking. "A boxer. The tea. Even the way he's sat with his legs like that. It's so Brandon. You got them all pretty good," I said, tracing my fingers over the other two characters.

"You get me," he whispered to himself.

"I do."

We stood staring at each other for what felt like an eternity, neither one of us saying a word. I wondered if his heart was beating as fast as mine. If he felt that tug that I did. I didn't know what to do or say next. I was stuck in this spell.

Finn's spell. And I never wanted to leave.

Finn broke the ice, glancing down to the floor and biting his lip before saying, "The new piece I'm working on, its round the back of the building. You can't access it from down there." He pointed down the corridor behind me. "You have to go back out the front. Do you want to see it?"

Stupid question. I would literally watch paint dry if he asked me to.

"Sure," I answered, keeping my excitement in check.

He turned and we both headed back towards the door. I had made the ridiculous decision to wear my boots with the heels today, and when he looked back and saw me picking my way through the rubble haphazardly, holding onto the wall for support, he put his hand out to me. My heart thumped hard in my chest as I reached out and took it. His big hand felt warm and soft wrapped around mine. It felt… perfect.

Suddenly, it didn't matter if he was leading me to the Sistine chapel to show me what he'd done. I didn't care. Every part of me was focused on him and how holding his hand––such a simple, silly act––felt like everything. It made me feel like I was floating across those flagstones, not stumbling like a bloody fool.

"You okay?" he asked, glancing down at me and squeezing my hand.

"Mmmhmm." I nodded back, keeping my eyes on the ground. Words meant thinking, and I wasn't capable of that at the moment. Not when my brain was flooded with endorphins from being connected to him in this way.

He pushed the door open and held it with his shoulder, so I could walk through.

"Thanks." I smiled up at him, and he smiled back as I stepped out onto the front step of the asylum.

And then he peered over my shoulder, looking off into the distance behind me, and his face dropped as well as his hand from mine. Every tingle, every spark of warmth I had felt turned back to dread.

The Finn from inside was gone.

His walls were back in place.

And my heart felt like it was being ripped from my chest once again.

CHAPTER Eight

FINN

He was here.

The fucker had followed me here, and now he stood staring at me and Effy from across the street.

He had an evil smirk on his face and he appeared to be chuckling to himself. No doubt thinking up some sick way to get back at me. To get to me through her.

I should've been more careful. I should've noticed that he was following me. I needed to up my game.

"What's wrong?" She was frozen to the spot in front of me, her eyes holding the sadness I hated seeing in them whenever I let her down. Her body was tense, like she was preparing herself for the onslaught of rejection she knew was coming her way. I felt like a complete bastard.

"You need to leave." I put my head down and stuffed my hands into the pockets of my jeans, walking towards the fence where her car was parked and steering her away from the building and the evil glare of my uncle.

"Why? I want to see your work." She jogged alongside

me, her little legs struggling to keep up with my long strides. "You said its round the back. Can't we––"

"You need to fucking leave!" I shouted, and she flinched at the loud tone I used and stopped still. Her arms crossed over her chest and she took deep breaths, glaring at the floor, trying not to react to my anger. I wanted her to though. I wanted her to fight, just not here where he could see. If he knew she was my weakness, he'd use her. Hurt her. I couldn't let that happen.

"Fine. I'll leave. But you need to stop pushing people away, Finn. People who care about you. The way you're acting right now, it's bullshit."

"It is bullshit. Everything is bullshit," I screeched, hoping he could see the act I was putting on for him from across the street where he stood. I was playing the part of the guy of who belonged to no one. The guy nobody cared about, even her.

Effy's eyes blazed with fury, and I felt the weight of regret sink deep into the pit of my stomach. I was losing her. But what choice did I have?

"One day you're gonna regret being such an arsehole to me," she said and spun around, charging towards the fence where her car was parked.

"I already do," I whispered to myself and watched as she got into her car and drove off.

When I turned to look at him, he was laughing and clapping his hands together like he was in the audience at an open-air theatre.

I couldn't help it. I stalked over to where he was, ready for round two. I might not have my baseball bat, but I had enough anger to fuel my fists and enough rage stored up from years of pain that I was ready to unleash. But he didn't stay around for the encore. He turned and left like the coward he was.

CHAPTER Nine

FINN

With a heavy, broken heart, I made my way back home, barging through the front door and running up the stairs, taking them three at a time so that I could get to my room faster and hide. I didn't want to see anyone. I needed to be alone. But even alone I couldn't shake the demons that had their grip on me, or the gnawing pain of regret.

Why was this ache in my chest overriding the pain in my body and my mind?

It seemed as if I was always destined to be this monumental fuck-up.

I didn't want to be.

In fact, if I had my way, I'd be saying to hell with it and telling Effy exactly how I felt. Maybe, if I could sort out the virus currently destroying my life, I could make that dream a reality.

Maybe.

My life revolved around that bloody word and I'd had enough.

FRACTURED MINDS

I paced my bedroom, biting my nails in an effort to numb the pain, but it didn't work. I knew what would though. I needed to see her one last time today. Make sure she was okay. After the way I'd spoken to her, I needed to apologise. It was the least I could do.

I grabbed my black hoody off the bed and pulled it on. Then I marched over to the door, willing myself to stay focused, but I stopped when I remembered what I had in the top drawer of my desk. I back-tracked and then came to a halt, staring at the dilapidated chest of drawers with half the knobs missing. I bit my lip, fighting an internal debate on whether giving this to her was a good idea or not. The irrational part of my brain won out, it always did, and I opened the drawer, grabbed the paper and slid it into the front pocket of my hoody. It was a peace offering. I'd made it for her and she deserved to see it.

Thirty minutes later, I found myself standing outside her house, staring up at the huge sash windows with their gentle warm glow that came from inside. Even her home looked inviting, as if it'd welcome you in and make all the bad things in the world go away when you were safe within its walls.

I'd made sure that I wasn't followed this time. I would never lead him right to her door, but despite that, I still felt on edge. It was so cold that with every pant of my breath a cloud of steam formed like I was fuelling my own path to misery. A steam train on a track to self-destruction. A runaway with no way of stopping, especially when her garage door started to open, and her dad suddenly spotted me loitering like a goddamn loser.

"Are you okay there? Can I help you?" he called out, rubbing his hands together and then blowing into them to warm them up.

"Is Effy home?" I was surprised I found my voice and it sounded so clear. I appeared confident even though I was anything but.

"Yes, she's home. I'll just go get her." He thumbed behind him and smiled, then disappeared back into his garage, leaving the door open and my heart hanging by a thread. I'd expected him to tell me to sling my hook and stay away from his precious daughter. Seems the reputation of the Renaissance men hadn't proceeded me. Thank God.

I walked forward and stood to the side of her garage, but I made sure I was standing directly under the security light so I didn't look shady to anyone passing by. Not that they had much foot traffic here. This wasn't like my part of town where people were always hanging around. Here, they went everywhere by car. Probably walked their dogs that way too, or used a treadmill to exercise them. I huffed out a grin and was just about to reach for my mobile phone in my back pocket to give me a distraction from my racing thoughts, when I heard her front door open. I moved from the side of her garage and made my way up the steps to where she was waiting.

When she saw it was me, her eyes went wide and I

noticed her hesitation as she took a step back, did the obligatory self-hug that she always did, and then bit her lip.

"I hope I'm not disturbing you," I said, hanging my head and struggling to make eye contact with her.

"Of course you aren't," she huffed out with a gentle laugh. "I was only watching TV. You're the last person I expected to see here though." She gave me a stern yet apprehensive look, like she wasn't sure what my next move would be. I wasn't surprised. I hadn't been very predictable or approachable lately.

She eyed me curiously and then her expression turned solemn. "Is everything okay, Finn? After your outburst earlier, you worried me."

Sure. I'm fine. Nothing to worry about. Only a paedo uncle stalking my every move while my heart shatters into a million pieces over you. But I'll live. I always do.

"No. I... I just.... I didn't want to leave it like that. I felt-" I couldn't finish my sentence. How the hell was I supposed to put into words how I felt? I couldn't. So, I decided I'd let my art do the talking for me. "I wanted to give you this."

I reached inside the front pocket of my hoody and pulled out the folded piece of paper. Carelessly, I thrust it towards her like it was a bomb about to detonate. Truth was, the only explosive device around here was me. I felt like I was about to burst from the pressure that being here evoked inside me. So many feelings, so many emotions that I'd tampered down over the years were bubbling to the surface, and I was powerless to stop them.

She stepped forward and took the paper from my hand, her fingers brushing gently against mine as she did, and a spark of electricity shot down my arm and forced me to pull back in shock. She gasped, probably because she thought my reaction was a negative one. It wasn't.

"What is this?" she whispered, blushing shyly and moving closer to the light on her porch as she unfolded it.

Usually, whenever I'd given her something like this, I posted it through the door, or left it on a brick wall somewhere, hidden from the rest of the prying eyes of Sandland. This was the first time I'd stood in front of her and put myself on the line.

When she saw what was on the paper, she gasped again, only this time she covered her mouth with her hand, and I saw tears well up in her eyes.

"Oh my God, Finn. This is… it's beautiful."

I could see the paper shaking in her hand as she held it and took in what she saw drawn there. I hadn't gone for the usual portrait, and I'd spent a lot more time on this one than I had on the drawing of her dog that I knocked out in ten minutes with an old pencil whilst I leant against her neighbours' fence a few months ago. This one had colour and depth. This was how I saw her.

I'd sketched her looking down, a side profile with her gaze cast to the floor. That way, I could show the delicate upturn of her nose that I loved, shade in the glow of her cheekbones, and the way her hair fell so beautifully over her face as she tried to hide from the world.

Or was it from me?

I loved that she had a quiet confidence. A gentle beauty that radiated from within. And I felt honoured that I got to see it. Sometimes, it felt like her smiles were only for me. She was mine, in my head and my heart, anyway. But in all her understated elegance was a beauty even my pencil couldn't capture. So, I'd used washes of colour around the outside of her face to symbolise what she meant to me; how she made me feel. Blue for the calmness her presence always gave me. A tranquillity and peace that was always lacking at any other time in my life. Lavenders to symbolise her grace and poise. She wasn't like any other girl in Sandland. She danced to the beat of her own drum, lived by her own well-crafted, caring and respectful principles and never failed to make others feel uplifted whenever she was around. And finally, purples, the colour of royalty, because this girl was noble, regal and a million miles out of my league.

"I'm speechless," she whispered into the cold night air and stared at the drawing in awe.

I willed her to look up at me, to make the next move, because I didn't have a clue what to say or do in this situation.

"I can't believe you made this for me. It's the most beautiful thing anyone's ever given to me." She looked up at me then, but the warmth I expected to see flickered and died, leaving behind confusion and hesitation.

She didn't trust me.

And I couldn't blame her.

"I love that you've given this to me, truly I do, but why have you come here, Finn?"

Because I can't ever seem to let you go.

"I felt bad. I said some awful things to you earlier."

And those words will haunt me just as much as any of my nightmares do.

I stuffed my hands into the front pocket of my hoody, so she couldn't see me wring them together nervously.

She smiled to herself, taking a step towards me and blasting another brick from my wall of insecurities. But as she got a bit closer, she hesitated, and her smile faltered.

"I can't ever read you, Finn. One minute I think we're getting somewhere, and then it all changes. I know you're not a bad person. You have a good heart. But you don't make it easy. Not for me. Not for anyone."

I understood what she was saying. It hurt to hear it, but it was the truth. Being around me wasn't a walk in the park. I knew that. It's why I kept myself hidden away most of the time.

I hung my head in shame but willed myself not to back down or turn and run away. Something was happening here, something worth fighting for, and I had to man-up and see this through.

"I think you know by now I pretty much forgive most of the crap you pull." She sighed, giving me yet another lifeline.

She forgave me.

"I don't mean to pull crap…" I answered, a little too defensively, and in an instant she jumped in to explain herself.

"I know you don't, you just… ugh, you confuse me, Finn. I never know where I stand with you."

"Well, right now, on your porch freezing our tits off." It was a lame response, but I was going for the humour angle to deflect from the fact that I could not stop shaking and my face probably looked the shade of a beetroot.

"I didn't mean that. You know what I meant."

"I don't know what you want me to say," I responded, bypassing my brain and answering straight from my gut.

"I don't want you to say anything, just tell me what's in your heart. What do you want? You obviously came here for a reason and it wasn't just to give me this."

She held up the drawing and I felt a wave of embarrassment wash over me. Had I made a dick move giving her a picture like that after being such an arsehole today?

"I don't know if I can do that. Talking isn't easy for me." This was make or break. I hated these games but I couldn't seem to stop them.

She huffed and took a step back, trying to break the spell we were both under, but I wouldn't let that happen. I had to do something, so I moved towards her, closing that distance she'd created and held her gaze with mine, willing her to see what I couldn't say.

I want you, Effy Spencer. I've always wanted you.

My attempts to keep you safe are shit ones, but they come from a place of... love.

"I get that talking isn't your thing." She sighed again. "I really do, but we aren't moving forward. This... whatever it is that's building between us, well, it isn't, is it? Building, that is. It's like waking up in Groundhog Day, wanting to get to the happy ever after but then stalling before the story even starts, if that makes sense. Damn it, even I don't know what I'm talking about." She turned to leave, taking every scrap of dignity I had, and when she looked over her shoulder and said–– "When you figure out what it is you want, come and tell me. I'll be waiting. I'll always be waiting" ––I reached out to grab her arm and pull her back to me.

She didn't resist. She wanted me to stop her. She wanted more too.

And so did I.

I leant my head down to rest my forehead against hers, feeling the warmth of her breath as it mingled with mine.

"I'm counting on it," was all I could manage to say. My senses were too wrapped up in what it felt like to breathe her in as my air.

We stood like that for a few seconds, the world around us falling away, and all that mattered was being close, being connected. When she spoke next, I felt the cracks of my heart slowly easing, healing, and reaching out for her as the one true lifeline I'd always clung to.

"Kiss me."

FRACTURED MINDS

She spoke so softly I wasn't sure if I was dreaming it, or imagining this moment in the way my mind wanted it to go. But when she tilted her head up and her lips skimmed mine, I knew this was it. This was the moment when it all changed for us, and I couldn't stop it. I wanted it to change. Usually, I hated feeling out of control or losing power, but this wasn't a loss. It was me clawing back my life, trying to put right what had been taken away from me. My right to happiness.

Slowly, so as not to scare her away, I pressed my lips to hers. The softness I'd always dreamed about was now a reality, and one that I was falling headfirst into. I would never recover from this.

My lips moved against hers, finding a rhythm, feeling, tasting, loving. And then she opened her mouth to mine, and our tongues started to dance together. I breathed out hard through my nose, revelling in the head rush that this kiss was giving me. I didn't care that we were standing on her porch in full view of the street. I grabbed the back of her neck, threading my fingers into her hair and I took life from her through this kiss. Life and hope.

She placed her hands on my hips and I held her head in my hands, wanting to deepen our connection, get lost in a kiss that I never wanted to end. But happiness had always been fleeting for me, and when she pulled away and caught her breath, touching her lips like she couldn't quite believe what she'd done, I knew the spell had been broken. Reality came crashing down like the unwelcome third party, and I braced myself for her to say it had all been a mistake. When she stayed silent, I beat her to it.

"I shouldn't have done that."

Her subtle flinch didn't go unnoticed.

"Yes. You should. I asked you to. Remember?"

"I can't do this," I said, stepping back.

"Why not? What's wrong with me? Fucking hell, Finn, stop doing this to me. You're making me feel like such a loser."

She covered her face with her hands, so I moved closer and pulled them down to look at her. This was heading in a direction that I didn't want to go. I had to steer us back on track.

"You're not a loser, and there's nothing wrong with you. You're perfect."

Her eyes sparkled but I could tell she was still keeping her guard up. I couldn't blame her. When had I ever given her what she needed? That confirmation that she was safe with me, that her feelings and emotions were safe. I hadn't. I'd been a prick and I knew it.

"Then why don't you ever want me?"

That spike in my chest twisted again, making it hard to breathe.

"I do."

"If you wanted me, you wouldn't keep doing this to me."

It was my turn to run my hand over my face and sigh deeply at what a monumental fuck-up I'd made of everything.

"I know. I'm sorry."

"When are you going to let me in?" she said with such sincerity, I wanted to take her in that instant and run away from this place forever. Make a new life with her where none of the bullshit could get to us. But I had unfinished business that needed taking care of first. Wrongs that needed righting.

"I will let you in. I promise. But first, I need to exorcise all of these demons living inside of me. I'm not good enough for you, Effy. Not yet, anyway."

"You are a good guy, Finn. I hate that you think you're not."

"A good guy?" I huffed on a laugh and shook my head. "I'm trying to be. But I can be better. I want to be better, for you. Please. Just give me time."

"Time." She smiled sadly. "All I've given you is time. And I keep asking myself, will time ever be on our side? Will it ever work out for us?"

The way she looked at me, pleading with me to make this right made me step back into her and cup her face, holding it in my hands and softly running my thumbs over her cheeks to soothe her worries. There was never anyone else for me but her. There never would be.

"It will work out. I just need to get rid of the darkness inside me. Be the man you want me to be."

"You already are the man I want you to be. I don't want you to change."

A tear that'd welled up in her eyes spilled over and trickled down to where my thumb caressed her. I wiped it away. I hated that she cried because of me.

"It isn't about changing, Eff. I have issues, problems I need to deal with. I promise you, I'm almost there. I'm so close, I can almost taste it."

I didn't want to let her go, but she reluctantly pulled away and wiped the back of her hand over her eyes. Then she wrapped her arms around herself and I could see her try to stand taller. She had walls just like I did, only her walls were of my own doing.

"I don't know what it is that's got you feeling this way. I'm guessing you haven't had the best home life, and you don't have to tell me anything, but I hope you know, there is nothing from your past that could make me feel differently about you. Nothing."

She smiled at me to let me know she was sincere and ripples of something eased my burning, tight chest. Whatever it was, I didn't know. Love, maybe?

"I don't deserve you." I sighed.

"Yes, you do. We both deserve each other. We deserve happiness. The future and the here and now are what matter, Finn."

"And that's what I'm fighting for."

It's what I'm always fighting for.

"But you don't have to fight alone. You have me."

"Do I?" I asked hopefully.

"Yes." She didn't bat an eyelid when she responded. This girl would go to hell for me if I asked her to. She was my ride or die.

"Even after I've pushed you away?"

"In spite of you pushing me away. You push and I push back harder. That's how we work." She gave a low laugh to herself before grinning at me, and I grinned back.

"I hope you know what you're letting yourself in for, because when I come for you, Effy, there'll be no stopping me."

"And that's what *I'm* counting on," she whispered back and glanced down at the floor, a cute blush spreading over her already flushed cheeks.

I had to get my shit together. I couldn't wait to make her mine any longer, not after that kiss. I just needed to make sure that when I did come for her, there would be nothing and nobody standing in our way. This was the real deal for me.

-

I headed home, feeling a glimmer of hope beginning to shine a light through the cracks of my pretty dismal life. Maybe guys like me did get the girl after all?

I hoped so.

I headed into my street and cursed the dim street lighting in this part of the town. Half the lights were broken or damaged but nobody cared enough to do anything about it. I decided then and there that I needed to find a new place to live. I'd bitched enough about my parents' place, but I'd never done anything proactive to change it. If I was going to make things right in my life, one of the areas I had to start with was my home.

I opened the front door and felt the warm staleness waft over me as I stepped inside. Mum and Dad were talking loudly in the kitchen, and even though I wanted to head straight to my room to avoid them, I didn't. I needed a drink.

"It's a weight off my shoulders, anyway." Mum smiled to herself as I walked in and went to the fridge to grab a can of Coke.

"He'll see her right." Dad nodded to himself.

I closed the fridge door, leant up against it and popped open the can, sipping as I shifted my gaze between the two of them. Against my better judgement, they'd reeled me in, and I took the bait.

"Who will see who right?" I asked, looking bored with this conversation before it'd even started.

"Tony."

I froze when my mum said his name. Fingernails down a chalkboard would've sounded better and probably given me a less visceral reaction too.

"What about him?" I croaked out. The Coke was doing nothing to wet the sudden dryness in my throat.

"He's moved to Brinton Manor. Got a lovely little two-bed, right by where Alice is staying."

I slammed the can on the counter next to me, making the liquid fizz up and spill over the top, but I just shook the drops from my hand and turned my heated stare on my mum.

"What the hell do you mean, close to Alice? Does he know

where she lives?"

"Of course he does. His place is right around the corner, on Spires Lane." Mum frowned at me, like I'd made the most ridiculous statement. I mean, why wouldn't we tell dear old Uncle Tony where his beloved niece was? I couldn't fucking believe her, and I was equally pissed at myself for the fact that Alice had been put in danger yet again.

"You told him where, didn't you?" I shouted, really losing my shit. "Why? Why would you do that?"

"He's her uncle," she snapped back. "He has every right to know. Why wouldn't we tell him?" She looked to my dad for back up, but she couldn't bring herself to look my way. I would say she felt guilty, but it was more likely she couldn't be bothered to argue with me and wanted me gone.

"He has fuck all rights, Mum."

"Watch your language," Dad barked back, ever the guard dog with a bark no one took any notice of and a bite that didn't exist, not when it came to his brother-in-law, anyway.

I moved my glare from Mum to him, and wished to God I could tell him exactly why he was such a fucking awful father in every way that counted. But I'd never betray Alice in that way. It was her truth to tell, not mine.

"I'll say whatever the fuck I want," I spat. "I can't fucking believe you."

"Now listen here, son..." He waved his finger at me as if he had authority in my life. "We overlook a lot of your crap in this house, but that stops tonight––"

"You're damn right it's gonna stop. I'm out of here. You have no fucking clue what you've just started. But I'll tell you this... I am fucking ending it." I pushed off from where I stood and marched across the room.

"Always talking in riddles, and that's when you *do* decide to bloody speak." Dad laughed at his cruel jab at my anxiety.

It was the last straw.

I couldn't be in this house or in their presence for a moment longer.

I stormed out of the room, grabbed my coat from the foot of the stairs and left, slamming the front door shut. They may have thrown Alice to the wolves, given her up like she was nothing, but she wasn't alone, and I would make damn sure nothing happened to her. If that meant I needed to pay a visit to Brinton Manor, then so be it.

CHAPTER Ten

FINN

I walked for what felt like hours, using my mobile phone to track where I was headed. I didn't know Brinton Manor all that well, and I didn't want to spend any more time than I had to walking around the place.

As I turned a corner, I saw the sign indicating the boundary where Sandland ended and Brinton began. 'Welcome to Brinton Manor' the official road sign said. Behind it, spray-painted in amateur graffiti that stood six foot high and looked like the work of a seven-year-old, were the words, 'All who come here, abandon all fear.' They didn't need to warn us. Nobody ever came here because they wanted to. It was hardly a tourist attraction.

There were broken bottles, glass and other shit littering the pavements and the gutters. The roads were full of potholes and sprigs of grass grew through the walls of the desolate buildings and along the street. Nature was trying to survive here but dying a death under the weight of industrial Britain. Because that's what Brinton was, an old industrial town that'd been shafted in the nineteen-eighties and never fully recovered. Old buildings that used to thrive producing steel and other products had become barren, unused and rundown.

We'd never used any of the buildings for our parties. We never wanted to. Brinton wasn't the kind of place people would choose to go to for a night-out, and we weren't about to change that any time soon.

It was dark, and the street lights here were even worse than in my part of Sandland. At least some of them worked where I lived. Here, it was a ghost town. I glanced down at my phone, noticing that the indictor for where my uncle lived was getting closer. Not long now.

I shoved my hand into my pocket to check I still had the Stanley knife safely tucked away. I hadn't spent much time planning what I'd do when he opened that door. Dwelling on it would only make me nervous. Instead, I focused on my surroundings and tried to regulate my breathing. Anything to keep me calm and help me prepare for what I was about to face.

The streets were dead, and all I could hear was the screeching of a car's brakes in the distance, car horns blaring out and then shouts and bangs. If you closed your eyes, you'd think you were stuck in a video game. Open them and the reality was far worse.

As I neared the end of the road, I saw an underpass looming up ahead. There was no other way to get out the other end, only high walls on either side. If I wanted to keep going, that was where I was going to have to go. Turning and leaving wasn't an option at this point, but when I saw shadows moving in the darkness of the underpass, I felt the nerves kick in.

Someone was waiting in there.

More than one person.

And like a lamb to the slaughter, I was joining them.

I put my phone in my back pocket, hoping the light from the screen hadn't notified them of my approach.

Keep your head down, Finn. Walk past and be on your way. They don't know you. Stay quiet and this will all be over soon.

I heard the banging of metal on metal. A rhythmic, menacing beat. Then the sound of gruff male voices and barking of a dog; a mean, vicious bark. That dog was defending its territory and it saw me as the enemy.

There were fluorescent lights at the end of the underpass that flickered on and off, and when the shadows began to move and I finally stepped out into the murky light of the street, I felt my legs fill with lead and my heart thump in my chest.

There, in front of me, stood five men, all dressed in black with black bandanas covering the lower part of their face. Each one holding some kind of pipe or bat, and every one of them looking like they were about to take me out.

A Rottweiler stood to the side of them, snarling at me and baring his teeth. I had no chance. Five against one? Even Brandon couldn't win with those odds.

They moved as a unit, like a shadow army, taking a step closer to me. They had swagger and an air of intimidation that had me rooted to the spot. I knew their names, but I didn't know which one was which, only that they were the reason I hated this place.

The Soldiers of Anarchy.

They didn't stand for anything. Didn't do anything other than cause fear and mayhem in the town they were brought up in. A town that had chewed them up, spat them out, and now, they were getting payback.

I'd heard some people argue that they kept the peace on the streets, but that was bullshit. They created the problems they professed to 'clean up.' They were the virus, not the cure.

I stayed still, trying to gauge how this was going to play out. Going any further would mean pushing past them, and I wasn't about to cause any kind of confrontation.

I looked at them and they glared back at me. I could feel my fingers getting twitchy, ready to reach for my knife. If they were going to mug me and try to steal my phone, I wouldn't go down without a fight. I might not be a brawler like Brandon, but I had some skills.

The one in the middle pulled down his bandana and his snarl turned to a smile as he looked at the men either side of him. Then he took a step forward to make himself stand out from the others.

So, this was their leader?

Adam Noble.

The main soldier and the meanest one, by all accounts. Nicknamed the psycho by anyone who knew him because he had no morals. He didn't care about anyone or anything, much like the rest of them, but his reputation was the worst. Last time I'd heard his name mentioned in a conversation was because he'd bitten a guy's ear off for looking at him the wrong way. And that was just for starters. Uncle Tony would fit in really well with this crew.

"Well, well, well..." he said, pointing his bat in my direction and giving me a manic grin. "To what do we owe the pleasure, Mr Knowles?"

How the fuck did they know who I was?

"Oh, don't look so surprised. We know you. We know all about you. Looks like you've wandered down the wrong street though, *mate*. You're not welcome here." He tapped the bat against his leg and gave me a look of warning, narrowing his eyes as if to say, 'take that step, I dare you. I'm in the mood to wash these streets with your blood tonight'.

"I just want to get past. I don't want any trouble." I kept my face neutral and my hands in my pockets, so they couldn't see me shaking.

"No, you're not the one who causes trouble, are you?" Noble smirked. "You leave that to your man, Mathers. So, what are you doing here? In case you didn't notice, I'm giving you the chance to fuck off. Take it." He meant it too, and nodded his head to tell me to run.

"I have something I need to do first," I said, holding my

nerves and trying to stay calm.

Breathe in, breathe out. They won't hurt you. They don't want a war on their hands, and that's exactly what they'll get if shit goes down tonight. On second thoughts, a war would probably be exactly what they wanted. It'd give them something to occupy their time. Basically, I was fucked.

"You have no business here in Brinton. Not without our say so, anyway. Get... The fuck... Out." His grin turned menacing, and he started to move towards me, they all did. Instinctively, I backed up, but I tried one last time to make them see sense.

"I can't do that. I have to see someone. Someone here, in Brinton."

"Where are they?" Some blond guy standing to the left of Adam Noble lifted his chin as he asked me. "Maybe we can help you?"

"We ain't doing shit for him, Colton. Shut your damn fucking mouth," Noble barked, making the rabid Rottweiler next to them cower at his anger.

So that was Colton King. The Joker. He had a twisted sense of humour and a talent for fucking shit up. He was ruthless, manic, according to the stories I'd heard, and slightly insane. He'd flip out for any reason, and sometimes for no reason at all. Maybe he was more of a threat than Adam *The Psycho* Noble?

Story was, King's father died in suspicious circumstances. At the funeral, King supposedly wore a T-shirt saying, 'Do I look like I give a fuck?' and spent the day getting wasted. Then he went back to the cemetery after the wake and pitched a sign into the dirt over his dad's grave that said, 'Soul for rent.' Ask anyone and they'll tell you, even to this day, they have no idea why he did that. Maybe his family was more fucked up than mine?

"If he's here to stir shit up for someone, it might be fun." Colton shrugged his shoulders and started swinging the metal pipe in his hands, banging it off a faulty lamppost to the side of him and cackling in a crazy way to himself.

"We don't do shit for them." Noble pointed in my direction. "They can handle their own."

"If I needed help, I'd have brought it." I puffed out my chest in an effort to show some degree of confidence.

"We aren't fucking about," Noble the psycho snapped. "You aren't getting past us. So turn around and jog the fuck on." He held his bat up now, brandishing it to show he meant business. The rest of them followed suit.

I had two options here.

One, I could ignore them, charge my way through, and probably get the shit kicked out of me, yet again. I'd end up with another trip to the emergency room and it'd put me out of action for a few weeks. But that'd leave Tony free to do whatever the fuck he wanted. I couldn't risk that.

Or two, I did what they said. I left, planned my attack better, and came back. Maybe in the daylight, when they'd crawled back to whatever rocks they all lived under. As much as I wanted to take option one, I had to be smarter.

Maybe there was another road I could take to get to Spires Lane?

"Don't even think about trying to get round us and go another way," Noble said, reading my mind. "We have eyes everywhere. If we see you, we will kill you."

"I call shotgun on that ride." Colton laughed, and the others grunted out their own fucked-up responses.

And me? I took a few more steps backward, keeping my eyes trained on the bunch of lunatics in front of me, not trusting them for a second.

"That's it, Knowles. Run back to your little crew and tell them all about how the big bad wolves of Brinton made you shit your pants. If they want a war, they can bring it themselves."

"This is nothing to do with them. It's about me. Only me," I hissed, pointing my finger at them and gritting my teeth. I needed to make sure they understood that this didn't involve my friends.

When I was satisfied that they'd heard, I turned and walked as fast as I could out of there, leaving behind their catcalls and shouts of what a pussy I was. Tonight was not my night, but I wouldn't give up. I had a target. I just needed to get the soldiers out of my way first.

Trying to keep my shaking hands under control, I dug my phone out of my pocket to call Alice. I had no idea if she knew about her new neighbour yet, but I had to make sure she was pre-warned.

"Hey, Finn. You okay?" she answered, sounding carefree. She didn't know.

"You need to leave Brinton Manor, Al. It's not safe," I said, cutting straight to the chase.

"You've said that before, remember? And I didn't listen the first time. I'm fine. Danya knows the area, and they know her."

I had no doubt who the *they* were that she was referring to. The fact that they knew this Danya girl––that being a good thing in Alice's eyes––didn't fill me with a whole lot of confidence.

"He's there," I told her, and the line went quiet. I thought she'd hung up. "Hello? Are you still there?"

"Yeah, I'm here. What do you mean, he's here? Here where?"

"There. In Brinton Manor. He's got a house on Spires Lane. Mum told him where you are." I heard the quiet gasp down the phone.

"Why the fuck would she do that? I told her not to tell anyone."

And if you believed that, you'd believe anything.

"Because she thinks he isn't just anyone."

"Fuck." I could hear noises in the background, then mumbling, like Alice had covered the mouthpiece to speak to Danya without me hearing. I carried on walking at a steady pace, and I covered my other ear so I could try to hear what they were saying.

"We'll leave, now," Alice stated. "Danya has a cousin up north that could put us up."

"Okay. That's good." I nodded even though she couldn't see me. "Will you text me when you get there, so I know you're safe?"

"Of course I will. Listen, I have to go. Finn… Stay safe, and please don't do anything stupid. Hopefully, when he sees he isn't getting the attention he wants, he'll leave and never come back."

Or move onto another victim. That is blood I do not want on my hands.

I sighed.

"Whatever. Be safe, sis."

I hung up just as I crossed back into Sandland. The twist in my gut eased up, and I wasn't sure if it was because Alice was running or because I was on my own turf. Either way, the winds were changing. They had to.

Firing off a quick text to Zak, I asked him if it'd be okay if I crashed at his place. He replied instantly, letting me know that it was cool and he'd make up the airbed in his spare room. I knew Brandon would question why I hadn't asked him, but he had Harper, and with the babies due soon, I didn't want to bring any stress to his door. Tomorrow, I would get my shit together. Drive that piece of crap out of the area and get my girl. Tomorrow, it would all go right for me.

CHAPTER
Eleven

FINN

The buzz from my mobile phone jumping around on the floor beside the airbed woke me up and I reached out my hand, blindly slapping against the carpet with my eyes still closed, trying to find it. I hadn't slept well last night, too much swimming around in my brain. But now, I was groggy and felt like my head was a lead weight, I was that tired.

The door to the bedroom creaked open and I squinted against the light streaming through the blinds. Zak stood there, holding a mug of coffee and a look that told me he wasn't going to buy my evasive answers to his questions this morning. I suppose I needed to tell him something plausible. I was freeloading off him, after all.

"You okay, man?" he asked, placing the mug on the floor next to me and passing me my phone.

"Yeah." I sat up and ran my fingers through my hair, trying to calm the tufts that were sticking up all over the place. "Thanks for putting me up."

"Not a problem. You know you're always welcome. Stay

as long as you need. It's nice to have the company."

I nodded my thanks.

"Finn, I know shit is going down. I don't know what shit exactly, but I want you to know, if you need anything, even just to talk, I'm here. Okay?"

Again, I nodded, picking up my coffee and sipping it. Zak sighed and gave me a smile that didn't reach his eyes. He was obviously hoping for more from me, but he didn't push it, he just turned around and left. I held onto my phone and waited until he'd closed the door before I tapped in my code. I had a bunch of missed calls and text messages. The first was from Alice.

We're here. We're safe. I'll call you in a few days. Don't worry about me. Just stay away from him. Please. Alice x

I didn't respond right away. I didn't know what else to say that hadn't already been said. There was another message, and I hoped it was from Effy, but it wasn't. This was from an unknown number. When I opened it, I saw a link to a video, a message that said, 'You need to watch this,' and a cartoon meme of The Joker laughing that'd been sent straight afterwards. I shouldn't have clicked the link, I knew that, but I wasn't in my right mind. It could've been a virus. But the sticker and the message got to me, and against my better judgement, I opened it. What I saw next would live with me until the day I died.

The video was grainy and unfocused at the start. There were muffled voices, echoes, and laughter that sounded distorted, like in a horror movie. But then the view became clearer when whoever was blocking the camera moved backwards and into focus.

A man, wearing nothing but a pair of black jeans and a white balaclava over his head, stood in front of the camera. Why he'd covered his face though, when his whole chest was painted in identifiable tattoos, was ridiculous. But he wasn't bothered about being recognised. The mask was for effect. To look menacing to me, and whoever else was in that building with him.

The video was being recorded in a warehouse of some kind. There were broken windows situated high up around the dirty, crumbling walls, showing that the place was derelict. A perfect setting for what was about to go down.

The guy held a metal baseball bat in his hand, and when he started to swing it around, four other men came into shot. Each one wearing the same jeans and balaclava disguise. All of them with distinctive tattoos on their chest, arms and back. Every one of them with a weapon.

The video flickered like there was interference, and then the main guy spoke, his words distorted by a voice changer that sent shivers down my spine.

"Welcome to the game of consequences, Mr Knowles."

He stood centre of the screen, with his legs wide, swinging his bat to and fro like he didn't have a care in the world.

"Let me tell you how your game is going to work. We are

going to set you some tasks. You can choose whether to carry out those tasks or not, but like the game says, there are consequences. If you comply, things go well for you. If you don't... Well, let's just say we have something that you might be interested in."

The guy stood to the side, and behind him, strapped to a chair and looking like he'd already taken a pretty bad beating, was my Uncle Tony.

"He squealed like a pig when we caught him. Spilled all of your little secrets within minutes, Mr Knowles. I'm guessing you'll want those secrets to stay hidden. All the stuff about Alice... and you. See, that's where we come in. Play the game and your little problem goes away. Choose to forfeit your turn and all the filth that came out of his mouth just now goes viral. Everyone will hear. Is it becoming clearer now?"

I swallowed nervously, not bothered for a minute about my uncle in that chair, but scared shitless about what these sick fuckers would expect me to do, what they could do, and who they might tell. This was blackmail at its finest, and they had me right where they wanted me.

"This is how the game works. We text you. Give you a mission to complete. You submit the evidence of its completion to us by our deadline and it's all good. You live to see another day. Uncle Tony here doesn't though. If you fail to meet our deadline, there will be consequences for you. Comply and that consequence falls on his head." He pointed his bat over towards Tony, who sat slumped forward in the chair, snivelling and whimpering.

"Do you want to know what your first challenge is?" The five of them stood in a row in front of the camera, but the speaker stayed in the middle, standing slightly forward to give him an edge.

"You have until sunrise tomorrow morning to add your own artistic touch to our town sign. The one on the wall that reminds everyone what we stand for here in Brinton Manor."

All who come here, abandon all fear.

"Repaint it. Make it look good and we won't make your past come back to bite you in the ass." One of the men held up bolt cutters and started snapping them open and closed. "We'll also use those on your dear old uncle here." The main guy pointed at the cutters. "Relieve him of a few unwanted body parts."

Tony started to thrash in the chair behind him and grunt like the animal he was.

"It's your choice, Mr Knowles. Take a photograph of your work and send it to this number before sunrise. If we like it, you get to live another day, and Uncle Tony gets the snip. But don't get too comfortable. We're starting you off with an easy task. They will get harder. What you need to remember is, we run this game. We say when and we say how. Try to trick us and you will regret it. This is your waking nightmare, one that you will never be free from. Not until *we* set you free."

The video cut out and so did my heart. I threw the phone down on the airbed and just stared blankly ahead, blinking and trying to make sense of the head fuck I'd just watched.

They'd kidnapped my uncle.

They knew what he'd done.

And now, they were using that to blackmail and control me.

The Soldiers of Anarchy were going to destroy me, but not before they'd ripped me to pieces like their fucking Rottweiler would a toy. They had the conscience of a rabid dog too. They wouldn't care what this did to me. This was fun for them. A distraction from their own shitty lives.

But what choice did I have?

I didn't.

If I wanted this to end, I needed to see it through.

I dragged myself off the bed, my head in a daze and my body shaking. I was moving on automatic pilot because I didn't know what else to do. Without even noticing what I was doing, I freshened up as best I could, while everything I'd seen on that video played on repeat in my head like a sick horror movie. Then I headed into the living room, hoping my deathly pale complexion didn't give me away.

Zak was typing at his laptop at the table in the corner. I had no idea what he was working on, and I was too consumed with my own shit to care. Like a zombie, I sat down in the chair opposite him and concentrated on breathing and not letting on that I was consumed by fear.

"I'm heading over to Brandon's in a bit. They've got a problem with their internet and they've asked me to take a look. Do you wanna come or do you have to go to work?" he asked, without stopping or looking up from his screen.

"I don't have work," I responded, keeping my voice as even as I could. "They laid me off after I landed myself in the hospital. Said they needed to make cut backs, but I'm not stupid. They didn't want me there." I didn't care. I'd hated that job at the call centre. It was fucking draining on the soul. I couldn't even imagine trying to drag myself into that place with all the rest of the shit going on in my life at the moment.

"I'm sorry to hear that." Zak glanced up at me now. "Are you okay for money?" This guy was solid gold. He'd given me a roof over my head and now he wanted to put money in my pocket too.

"I've got savings." I shrugged, wishing I could sound more grateful, but I felt numb to the world around me. "I've been doing some work on the side for a guy I met through the call centre. He runs an online art website."

"Oh yeah?" Zak sat back in his chair and put his hands behind his head, giving me his full attention.

I don't know why I'd never really told anyone about it. I wasn't the type to brag or make small talk though, and the opportunity to tell someone had never come up before. I didn't really want to talk about it now, but I owed Zak a conversation at least.

"Yeah, people send in photos of themselves," I explained. "Their dogs, pets, anything really. Then we cartoonify it or cartoonize it, whatever the word is. I've done a few for him.

It's good money."

Zak cocked his eyebrow and nodded his approval.

"Sounds cool. You should use this time to look into something better to do, maybe doing that full-time would suit you more? Make the most of your talents. You were dying in that office anyway."

I smiled in agreement, but all I could focus on was since that night, when I'd found out he'd been freed from jail, every part of me was dying. Even more so now I had the soldiers breathing down my neck. I had enough to think about without trying to give my life a complete overhaul. I needed to focus on one fuck-up at a time. I was struggling to even have this conversation. My mind was all over the fucking place and I couldn't concentrate.

"So, Brandon's? You coming or staying here?"

I doubted Zak cared either way, and I had a shit load to prepare for if I was going to get this street art done tonight.

Who was I kidding?

It was never an if; it was a when.

But I also knew, if I didn't go it'd look suspicious, and I didn't want any of my mates asking questions about me or probing into stuff that I didn't want them to know about. Not now. Now, it was my turn to protect them. I couldn't let them find out about this. I had to dance with these devils all on my own.

"Sure. I'm in."

In body, anyway, but my mind? That was long gone.

"You look like you've lost weight, mate. You need to come down the gym with me and I'll get you bench pressing enough to build those muscles back up." Brandon fake punched my chest and grinned, flexing his own muscles.

He meant well, and in his usual, subtle way, he was trying to lighten my dark mood. He could sense something wasn't right with me today, but he knew better than to address the problem head-on. But lifting weights or training in the ring with him wasn't going to help me. Not this time.

"For God's sake, give him a break," Harper piped up from across the room. "You look great, Finn." She smiled, then turned and glared at Brandon. "Not everyone is obsessed with muscles like you, you know."

He huffed out a laugh and strode over to her, wrapping his arms around her from behind and stroking her baby bump. When he nuzzled into her neck, he made her giggle.

"It's not just muscles I'm obsessed with," he grunted low.

I turned away. I loved that my best friend had found his soulmate, but I didn't want to stand there like an idiot, watching them make out. It was bad enough that I didn't have what they had, but I didn't need salt rubbing into that wound.

Brandon and Harper were settled. They'd bought an apartment in town not far from Ryan and Emily, and they had the babies on the way. They'd made it; and just walking through their door, you could feel the warmth and love in the place. If Brandon had his way, the apartment would be full of steel, chrome, and pictures of Bruce Lee, but Harper had done a really good job putting her stamp on it. She'd made it into a proper family home, something Brandon deserved after the life he'd had.

They'd both asked me if I'd paint something special for the nursery, and I had. I was proud of the fairy garden that I'd created, spanning all four walls. Being in a brighter headspace when I'd done it had been refreshing. A welcome break from the darkness I usually injected into my work. Knowing that those little girls would wake up every day to a magical world I'd created gave me life. The fact that they'd find new things hidden every single day made it all worthwhile; a fairy behind a flower, a mouse peaking from a toadstool, the hidden messages written on tree trunks and petals. I'd put more energy and thought into that mural than any other piece I'd ever made. Even I'd forgotten half of what was hidden in there.

I jumped when I heard, "Put her down," bellowed from the doorway behind me, and I turned to see Ryan and Emily walking through the door, chuckling at Brandon and Harper's display. Moments later, my heart crashed hard against my chest as Effy appeared. Seeing her put my whole body on high alert, and the fear I was harbouring from the text messages I'd received this morning began to fade away now that there was a new emotion to get under control. I was excited, nervous, tense, and apprehensive all at once. I never knew how to be around her when we were with the others. I didn't like sharing my moments with her. I liked it better when they were in private.

I pretended that I was too engrossed in one of Harper's Rodin prints on the wall to mask the fact that I wasn't expecting to see her today and I hadn't prepared myself mentally. As always, she took my breath away and made me stop still in my tracks, wondering what a girl like her would ever see in someone like me. And then I remembered the kiss. Our first kiss. And I felt the flame of my cheeks burning at the memory. Did she feel the same? Did her heart race for me like mine did for her?

"How are you doing, Finn?" Emily came to stand next to me as Ryan slapped me on the back and went straight through to Brandon's kitchen. Probably to steal from his fridge like Brandon had done for years at Ryan's dad's.

"I'm okay." I shrugged, keeping my focus solely on the wall and not on the girl that stood out like a beacon in a room of darkness.

"The bruises are fading. Do you still feel pain when you move?"

I went to answer that I was okay, just like I'd said before, but Ryan piped up, "Quit fussing, woman. He's fine."

Emily didn't like that and she spun round to challenge him.

"Woman? What are you, a caveman?" She narrowed her eyes at him but laughed as he banged on his chest with his fist and winked back at her. Here was another couple that had it all, as far as I could tell. I really didn't need any more reminders about how tragic my own life was, but I guess fate had other plans for me.

Emily patted my arm, then moved to the other side of the room to talk babies with Harper. Ryan and the others were hunched over Brandon's laptop discussing the wifi. And I just stood there like a fool, ignoring the elephant in the room… my crippling anxiety and hopeless social awkwardness.

Effy shuffled on the edge of the group just like I did, and to my surprise, I found myself talking first in an attempt to settle her nerves.

"I didn't think you'd be here." Not the best opener, but I was impressed with myself for making a move. So was she, if the light in her eyes was anything to go by.

"Harper asked me and Em to come and see the nursery. Is my being here a problem? I thought after last night that…" she stuttered over what to say to finish her sentence and it made me ache for her, to see her falter like that.

"Of course, its fine." I stepped a little closer so the others couldn't overhear. "I like seeing you." I whispered the last part, but she heard me and smiled as her eyes darted down to the ground. When she bit her lip, I wanted to reach forward and tug it free. I wanted to do a lot of things.

"I was going to text you, after… you know… but I didn't want to bug you," she said, blushing. I loved that she'd thought about me.

"You would never be bugging me." I reached forward and

touched her, but pulled away again. I didn't feel comfortable doing it in front of the others, but the way she stood and her whole vibe had me buzzing. It was getting harder to ignore how she pulled me in. Magnetic forces had nothing on the attraction I felt for Effy Spencer.

"So, a few of us are going to the cinema tonight. Just Em, Ryan, Liv, and me. I thought maybe... if you weren't busy... or you wanted to... you might come with us? With me?" Her face shone as she spoke. The hope and light in her eyes was distracting and infectious. And like a cruel motherfucker, fate was giving me the middle finger yet again. Flashing the prospect of a future in front of my eyes and ripping it to pieces as it laughed at me.

My heart literally dropped from my chest and shattered on the floor. What the hell was I supposed to say? I couldn't go. I had blackmailing psychopaths to deal with. Fuck. Why did shit like this keep happening to me? When was I ever going to catch a break?

"I can't." I was the one to stumble over my words now, and I winced at the pain in my chest when I saw how hard her face fell. "It's not that I don't want to... I just can't."

She nodded to herself and took a step away from me. I could sense her walls going up as her body stiffened and she tried really hard to keep her emotions in check. From the pained expression on her face, you'd think I'd just stabbed her in the back. Maybe I had?

"I get it," she said without looking at me. "It's too soon.

You have *stuff* to take care of that's more important." She used air quotes as she referred to my *stuff* and I knew she thought I was bullshitting again. I couldn't blame her.

"It's not more important, it's just important that I take care of it now," I urged and wished to God that I could tell her there was nothing more I wanted to do tonight than sit in a warm cinema with my arms around her, but I couldn't. I had to go to shitty Brinton Manor and spend my night creating art so that this town didn't find out how dark my past really was. "I have business to take care of. It can't wait."

"But I always will." She sighed and ran her hands over her face. "I'm sorry. That wasn't fair."

"No. It was, and you're right. I'm the one who should be sorry." And I was. So sorry I felt like cutting myself open right in front of her to show her how it blackened my soul to keep hurting her like this. My body and my mind were a fractured fucking mess and she didn't deserve any of it.

"When is it going to be our turn?" she said so softly I almost didn't hear her. But I felt it, the pain as she spoke, because it mirrored my own.

I felt a jolt of anger and then I wanted to kick my own ass for putting her through this. She was hurting because of me, and after the morning I'd had, I wasn't in the right headspace to deal with this or find a way to put things right. I had to get out of there, get my shit together, and do what I needed to get done.

Like I always told myself, Effy deserved better. Better

than how I was treating her. Fight or flight? I was sick of doing both, but the fight I had to face was somewhere else, so I took the second option.

"I need to go," I said, hoping I was putting her out of her misery.

"Yeah," she mumbled like it was nothing, and turned and walked over to the girls, not giving me a second glance. As I headed to the doorway and looked back, calling out that I was leaving, they all looked back at me puzzled, all except Effy. She didn't look at me at all. Why would she when I'd just ripped both of our hearts out.

CHAPTER

EFFY

I could feel the burn of tears threatening to break loose as he walked out of the door. And the shame. Shame that he couldn't even be in a room with me for longer than a few minutes without running. I thought we'd made progress the other night when he kissed me. But no. He had to run again. What chance did I have to ever make that okay? To be something to him when we were always one step forward and two steps back. More like two hundred steps to be honest, and I was exhausted. We papered over cracks that would never mend and I wasn't even sure if he wanted to mend them in the first place. I needed to face facts; we were never meant to be together.

"Eff, are you okay?" Emily's gentle tone set me off.

"I'm fine. I just need a minute. Is the bathroom this way?" I kept my voice in check even though my cheeks were wet with silent tears, and I shielded my face so they couldn't see how pathetic I was.

I headed down the hallway, trying to find whatever room

I could to hide in, on the pretext that I was going to the bathroom. But I didn't care where I ended up, as long as they didn't see me cry. I hated that I was this weak fucking mess, and it had to stop. I needed to get a grip.

Pushing open the first door I came to, I was met with a sea of greens, purples and pinks. This was obviously the girls' nursery, and I slumped into the nursing chair set up in the corner and threw my head back, closing my eyes and giving myself a mental pep talk. It wasn't long before Emily and Harper found me. Feeling overwhelmed and embarrassed, I covered my face with my hands, trying to get my emotions in check, but I was too far gone. I couldn't hide this from them.

"Oh, Eff. I'm so sorry. What did he say to you?" Emily asked in that caring tone of hers.

"It's not what he said, it's just... ugh... I can't do this anymore. I'm not strong enough." I gripped the arms of the chair tightly as I tried to calm down, and the gentle sway of it rocking me to and fro helped somewhat.

"Now, listen here. You are strong. Don't ever tell yourself you're not. Whatever happened back there, you cannot let it break you." Emily spoke with determination. She knew what it felt like to fight for what you wanted. But I wasn't Emily. I didn't have her eternal optimism.

"It already has broken me."

I let Emily hug me as Harper knelt down with us and stroked my arm in comfort. I didn't know what I'd do without my friends.

"Men can be jerks," Harper said, shaking my knee to make sure I was listening. "We all know that. Finn is complicated and as frustrating as hell, but he loves you, Effy. I know he does. We can all see it."

"Does he?" If she'd asked me last night, I might have agreed, but today was a different matter.

"Maybe that's what's scaring him most of all? That he loves you so much he doesn't know how to handle it."

So much he can't bear to see this through and bails every chance he gets?

"That's a bullshit excuse and you know it." I sniffed back my pitiful tears and wiped my face.

"I know." Harper had been there. She knew better than anyone what it was like to love someone against all the odds. But Brandon didn't walk out on her, not once. He fought for her.

Why wouldn't Finn fight for me?

Because maybe, deep down, he doesn't want you as much as you want him?

Or maybe, he doesn't have any fight left in him.

"It doesn't make me feel any better. This whole back and forth thing is wearing me down." I sighed. "I don't think I'll come to the cinema tonight. I'm not in the mood and I'm really not great company."

"Okay, just stop right there." Emily leaned back and pointed at me. "You are coming. There's no way we are going without you. And if you don't want to go out, we'll have a girls' night in. End of."

"Yes!" Harper agreed. "I would come too, but these gremlins inside me make me sleepy by six o'clock. Sorry." She rubbed over her bump and the love shone out of her. I felt guilty that it actually made me jealous. I wanted what she had.

"I didn't even wait for you to show me the nursery," I said by way of an apology and to distract myself from my own envy. "I just burst in here like an idiot."

"Oh shut up, you're welcome in any room of ours. Nowhere is off-limits. Do you like it?" She glanced around the room, smiling to herself.

"It's perfect. Did Finn paint all of this?" I asked, but I already knew the answer. No one else could have pulled off something like this.

"Yeah. These were all his ideas." She ran her hand down the wall lovingly. "We both come and sit in here most nights to look at it. He's so talented. He might be rubbish at showing his emotions in real life, but his art says everything about him. He feels too much, too hard."

I looked closer at the magical scenes he'd created with fairies chasing pixies. There were gnomes in various poses; fishing, playing games and falling head first into the water. Elves hid behind doorways in the tree trunks and looked ready to play tricks on anyone who crossed their path. The colours were so vibrant and unlike anything he'd ever done before. And then I saw, camouflaged on a tree branch, the words 'You are loved' and I teared up all over again.

"Eff, you have to do what's right for you," Emily whispered, sensing my shift in mood. "If that means you walk away, walk away. But for what it's worth, I don't think he'd want that. You need to follow your heart."

I choked back a sob as I replied, "Follow my heart? Which part? Because right now, it's shattered into a million pieces." I slumped forward and hung my head in shame. "I don't want to be a doormat."

"You're not a doormat. And fuck anybody who says you are. They're dicks. They know fuck all," Harper stated firmly.

"Are you bitching about Brandon again?" Ryan appeared at the doorway, smirking at us.

"What are you on about now?" Emily teased him.

"You said they know fuck all. I thought you were talking about this knobhead here." Ryan thumbed behind him and Brandon appeared, but from the kindness behind the fake glare he threw at Ryan, I could tell he knew exactly what'd happened in here and what we were talking about.

"I know what I need to know and that's that you're the only dickhead in here, mate." Brandon puffed his chest out, like he needed any more help to look menacing. "Now fuck off, you've outstayed your welcome."

Ryan laughed back at him. "You coming out with us later?"

Brandon shook his head. "Not this time. Me and the missus have a date with Netflix, a tub of Ben and Jerry's, and our bed for tonight."

"Rock and roll." Ryan smirked.

"Wouldn't have it any other way."

I stood up at the same time Emily did.

"We'll give you a lift home and then I'll be picking you up at seven, no arguments."

I went to reply to her, but Brandon butted in.

"We'll take Effy home."

Emily frowned and Brandon turned to Ryan and said, "Don't you have that thing? You know… the thing." He nodded and widened his eyes as if he was trying to jog Ryan's memory on something they'd never even talked about.

"Ah! Right. The thing." Ryan nodded back and then turned to Em. "Come on, we need to go. You'll be alright with this clown taking you home, won't you?" he asked me.

I felt like a kid being passed from one unwilling parent to the other.

"I can make my own way home. It's no big deal."

"Nonsense. We'll drive you," Harper said, waving my argument away with a flip of her hand.

"Has Zak gone all ready?" Emily asked as she walked over to Ryan and wrapped her arm around his.

"Yeah. I think he went after Finn. I'll talk to you in the car." He winked, and I knew that my love-life––or lack of it––would be the hot topic on their way home. But then thinking about what he was insinuating, that he had something to tell her, made my stomach turn over with fear, followed by dread. Was there something they were hiding from me?

We made our way to the front door, said our goodbyes, and then I followed Harper and Brandon back into the living room. Once it was just the three of us, I started to feel awkward.

"Effy, is it okay if we take a detour before we drop you off home?" Brandon asked. "Only, there's something I'd like to show you."

"What the hell are you up to, Mathers?" Harper crossed her arms over her chest and threw accusatory daggers his way.

"Trust me, angel. I think you'll enjoy seeing this too."

She smiled to herself and then reached for her coat from the stand.

"Well, what are we waiting for? Let's go."

—

Brandon pulled the car into the car park of the local park, and when he turned the engine off, we both looked at him and frowned.

"What the hell are we doing here, babe? It's freezing out there. Not really park weather."

He turned to face Harper and then looked back at me sitting in the back seat.

"We aren't here for the park. There's something I want to show you." He pointed towards the far side where there was an underpass leading to nowhere. Everyone who lived around here knew it was the prime spot for the homeless and druggies of Sandland. My mouth went dry. Was he going to show me that Finn was on something or sleeping rough?

Brandon seemed determined though, and despite both mine and Harper's reluctance, we got out of the car and followed him across the grass. A few families were out with their kids, but it wasn't busy. The chill in the air kept the park relatively empty, and as we ventured further in, the green and slightly muddy grass became dirt, broken bottles and litter. There was a slight incline to walk down as we got nearer to the underpass, and Brandon put his arm around Harper to help her so she didn't lose her footing. Once he knew she was safe, he turned around and offered his other hand to me, but I shook my head, letting him know I was okay.

I kept my eyes on the floor to make sure I didn't stumble over a rogue bottle or slip on a can... or worse. When I sensed they'd both stopped in front of me, I stopped too, and when I looked up, I had to reach out to Brandon to stop myself from falling over. There, on the wall amongst the dirt and filth, was a huge painting of my face. It was so big it took up the whole wall. I felt like the rest of the world faded into darkness, muted to black and white as I stared up at myself. The way he'd used flecks of colour in my eyes to make it seem as though I was staring right into my own soul was mesmerising. My hair, layered with so many different browns and gentle highlights, was stunning. I was speechless and I didn't know how to process what I was seeing or feeling.

"Oh my God," Harper gasped. "This is beautiful." She looked up at Brandon with tears in her eyes and then turned to me with a sad smile.

"Did I make a mistake bringing you here?" Brandon asked me as he put his arm around Harper and pulled her closer.

"No. I don't know what to say though." I stood frozen to the spot, but I couldn't take my eyes off the image before me.

"He's my best friend, Effy. I would do anything for him. I want him to be happy, and you… you make him happy. He can't tell you how he feels. He struggles to show you, but this…" He gestured to the wall and sighed. "This says it all. He loves you, Effy. I heard what you said back at our apartment, and I know he isn't the easiest guy to love. I know all about that. But please don't give up on him. If he lost you, I don't think he'd ever come back from that."

I bit my lip, trying desperately to think of something to say.

"I don't mean to emotionally blackmail you," he continued. "Or force you into doing something you don't think is right. But I figured if I showed you this, you'd know that the way you feel, it isn't one-sided."

I nodded and concentrated on not free-falling into a total meltdown in the middle of the park.

"He'll probably kick my ass for showing you, but I think this is the right time." Brandon reached out and touched my arm, squeezing gently as if he were trying to rouse me out of my vegetative state. "Are you okay?"

"It's a lot to take in," I answered as honestly as I could. "I mean, pictures on paper are one thing, but this? This is… everything."

"He'll come round. When he's ready, he'll open up to you. I know because I did. It just takes time. Time and love. You have that last part, just give him the first, yeah?"

"I'll give him forever," I said and a tear fell free.

I knew Finn had been through something bad. I also realised that I needed to listen to the other sounds he made, not just his voice. I had to listen to the meaning behind his actions, his expressions, his body language, and his art. All of it was his way of communicating, and as tough as that was sometimes, it was the only way forward for us, if we were ever going to make it. I had to hear the silence. Accept the unspoken. And live for what I believed… That there wasn't anyone else in this whole world that made me feel the way that he did, and that was worth fighting for.

FINN

One positive about doing the street art in Brinton Manor at this time of the night was that no one was around to see me. I had my lights set up and my equipment ready, but in this part of town, people stayed away. I was thankful for small mercies. At least no one would know it was me. There wasn't a chance in hell I was adding my tag to this piece. This would forever stay anonymous.

I'd avoided looking at my phone for the rest of the day. The guilt I felt over Effy, and the fact that every one of my friends had probably text to say what an arsehole I was stopped me from checking my inbox. That, and the fear of getting another message from the soldiers. I'd bet Adam Noble, Colton King, and the rest of them were having a right laugh at my expense. Revelling in my misery. I glanced around, wondering if they were watching me now, then realised that hiding in the shadows wasn't their thing. If they wanted to watch me, they'd stand right next to me, breathing down my neck. They'd enjoy the intimidation and feed off my fear.

I hadn't planned on putting any thought into this art, but I couldn't switch off my creativity. At first, I figured I'd just improve the words, make them stand out and look more professional, but as usual, my imagination ran away with me.

There were five soldiers, and so I added five skulls underneath their infamous saying. Skulls were a speciality of mine. I'd been drawing them since I could hold a pencil.

I gave each skull its own unique touch to represent its fucked-up member. To the far left was Tyler Evans' skull. A thief, who went from pick-pocketing to grand theft auto in a matter of months, amongst other things that I'm sure were on his rap sheet. I put a black mask over his skull eyes to make him look like the robber he was. Menacing and ready to fuck over anyone who got in his way.

Next to him was Will Stokes, notorious player and all-round fuck boy. I stuck a cigarette in his skull's mouth and made it look like he was winking. A nod to the fact that he looked friendly but would stab you in the back and do it with a smile on his face. Like all the others, he couldn't be trusted.

To the far right was Devon Brady, also known as The Reaper. His skull design didn't need much thought, a black hood and the shadow of a scythe finished him off perfectly. He was death personified.

I put Colton King next. The Joker wore his jester hat like a crown. The king of all jokers. But I saved the middle space for the most fucked-up one of them all.

Adam Noble.

The Psycho.

For him, I made the skull eyes slant to a menacing stare and gave it a tongue that hung out of its mouth, making it look like the crazy psychotic character that he was. I placed a skeleton hand directly underneath, giving the finger to anyone that looked up. I'd taken their shitty spray-painted saying and turned it into a monumental 'fuck you' to anyone who entered Brinton Manor from the Sandland side of the town.

Even though I was proud of what I'd done, I was still pissed off. They were using me as a puppet, holding the fate of my uncle and what he'd done over my head and dangling redemption like an irresistible carrot wrapped up in their evil. So I added one last touch of my own. It wasn't visible from the ground, and if by any chance they saw what I'd done, they'd still think it was cool. I wrote the words 'fuck you' into each eye socket. My message to each one of them. They may have the upper-hand now, but I would beat them at their own game. If there was one thing that spurred me on more than anything, it was seeing a twisted justice served to Tony, and who better to do that than the masters of macabre. The Soldiers of Anarchy.

The whole wall now carried a hellish vibe, and I knew there wasn't a chance that I'd failed in their task. I kept my lights in place and took a few photos to capture every part of the wall. Then I sent them off to the phone number they gave me. No message, just the images. I had hours to go until sunrise, but I was done here. Brinton could kiss my ass.

I packed my equipment back up into the van I'd borrowed for the night from Ryan. I fucking loved that he never asked me what I needed it for, just handed over the keys and even helped me load up my shit. He tried giving me grief over Effy, but one look was all it took to shut him up.

I closed the back door of the van and held my phone in my hand, debating whether to send Effy a text to apologise. But when my phone buzzed and I saw who the message was from, I went cold and headed straight for the driver's door so I could see their response in the privacy of the van.

Once inside, I tapped to unlock my screen and read the one line text they'd sent me.

You did good. We'll be in touch.

What the fuck?

That was it?

Hours of my fucking night creating their bullshit town sign, and for what? A few words that told me fuck all. What were they going to do next? Did they even plan on doing anything or was this some sick fucking joke meant to rile me up?

I threw my phone to the side, turned the keys over in the ignition and started the engine. Then I punched the steering wheel in frustration. Their message wasn't good enough. I needed more. So I grabbed my phone off the passenger seat and typed back.

Is that it?

It didn't take long for them to respond.

Like I said, we'll be in touch.

I threw my phone back down and roared off, clipping the kerb as I went. I was over their bullshit. I wouldn't do anything else for them until they showed me that they could live up to their promises.

-

I felt like I was drowning. The cold, bony claws of my fate were threading themselves around my neck like twisted ivy and I couldn't breathe. In all of the noise, I needed to find my quiet. I needed to see her. So, I swung the van in the direction of the town, heading for the cinema where I knew they'd all be tonight. I didn't know if I'd have the guts to get out of the van and actually talk to her, but I knew just seeing her face would be enough. It always was.

I parked up opposite the entrance, just as streams of people started to come out. I had no idea what film they'd gone to see, but when I spotted Ryan and Emily strolling out with their arms around each other, my heart jumped into my throat. She couldn't be far behind.

I leant forward, as if that was going to give me a better view, and when she appeared, standing out in the crowd, I couldn't keep the goofy smile off my face. That was until an arm landed across her shoulders.

I felt sick.

I wanted to throw up.

Kian had his arm around Effy and he was pulling her into him as they both laughed. She was looking into his eyes like he was a fucking rock star, and my bruised and battered heart gave up completely.

What the actual fuck?

I thought that little shit was my friend, but he was all over her like a rash, and she was doing nothing to push him away. Watching them was sending me further and further into the fucked-up abyss that I was desperately trying to claw my way out of.

I couldn't look at them any longer, I was shaking so badly. And suddenly, I felt stupid for being there watching, like I was some kind of creeper.

I started the van back up and sped out of the car park, not even looking in my rear-view mirror in case I saw something I really didn't want to see. I thought my night couldn't get any worse, but karma wasn't done with me yet.

I drove way too fast back to Sandland and parked the van outside Zak's place. When I shut the engine off, I noticed another message had come through. Sighing, feeling totally exhausted by this whole night, I grabbed my phone and opened it. Another message from the soldiers, only this one was a video link.

Fuck.

It started much the same as the last one, only this time, I had a closer view of my uncle strapped to the chair. A ring side seat to witness his misery, if you like. He looked bloody and beaten and had a rag in his mouth that he moaned and wailed through. A fist flew through the air and landed an almighty punch on his face, causing his head to rear back. It didn't knock him out though. They'd need to hit a lot harder than that to put Tony out.

There was no talking on this video, no voice giving me instructions. This was my reward for a job well done, and that didn't need commentary.

I watched frozen in a fear-induced daze as the camera shook a little then focused on Tony's hands. The bolt cutters came into shot and I tensed and felt bile rise up in my throat as whoever was holding those cutters slid them over Tony's fingers and then clamped down hard. The sound of crunching and screaming followed by men's laughter filled the air around me, and they didn't let up. They opened the cutters again and clamped back down. Once they'd finished with the left hand, they moved to the right, and I felt my head swim with nausea at having to watch this. But I couldn't look away, and my sickness stemmed only from a basic human reaction. I felt no sympathy for my uncle. He deserved this and so much more.

"Won't have much chance to fiddle with kiddies anymore, will you, now you've got no fucking fingers," Adam Noble's distinctive deep voice hissed.

"He won't even be able to wank himself off," Colton King said, cackling.

Meanwhile, my uncle thrashed in the chair as the stubs

of his hands bled onto the floor. Then there was a clatter of metal, probably the bolt cutters hitting the concrete, and the video cut off.

I was shaking so badly I could barely hold my phone. I ran my hand over my face and tried to makes sense of it all. Was this really happening?

My phone buzzed one last time.

Level one completed. Congratulations.

Welcome to level two.

CHAPTER

FINN

I figured there were two things I could do to deal with the black hole my head was currently stuck in. Stay at Zak's and wallow in self-pity and self-loathing, listen to him lecture me about how to successfully pull women and try to block out the horror of that video that I couldn't seem to shake from my memory. Or I could head out, talk to Effy, and sort out the mess that was my life. If anyone could chase away the dark clouds that the video had brought over me, it was her.

I hadn't contacted her at all after seeing her leaving the cinema with Kian that night. And even though I checked my phone way too much for any sane person, she hadn't contacted me either. My phone was officially dead, along with my sorry excuse for a heart. I supposed I should see the lack of contact as a positive, seeing as the messages I got these days usually brought bad news, but it only added to my anxiety. I wanted to see her. I needed to know if it was really over.

After a few more minutes of procrastinating, I gave in and headed out. Life wasn't going to come knocking at my door anytime soon. Not the life I wanted for myself, anyway.

When I arrived in her street, I had an attack of nerves. Should I have rung her first? Maybe she wouldn't want to see me after the last time? Would Kian be there? Was I walking straight into a rejection of my own making?

I tried to ignore the self-doubt plaguing my brain and focus on putting one foot in front of the other, until I was standing outside her door and there was nowhere else to go. I'd ignored my subconscious and let my body take control. The joys of switching to automatic pilot. But now, I was back in control and shaking like a leaf.

I pushed the doorbell and couldn't help smiling despite my nerves when I heard her dog bark in response. Effy opened the door, crouching down slightly and holding her dog back by her collar to stop her escaping and darting for the road. Her mouth dropped open when she saw it was me, and she didn't speak for a few seconds, making me swallow nervously, not sure what to say. But then her face lit up, her eyes shone and she came to stand on the porch with me, locking her dog behind her in the house.

"Hey. How are you?" She pushed her hands into the back pockets of her jeans. "You look well. Did you get everything sorted the other night? You know, the business? I'm sorry if I was a bit off with you at Harper and Brandon's. I was just..." She was rambling. A clear sign she was nervous too.

"It's fine. It's okay. Yes, I got it sorted, and yes, I'm okay. You look well too." I took a few breaths, wondering if the next words out of my mouth would be my biggest regret ever. "I came to the cinema. It was late and you were leaving, but I came. I saw you."

"I didn't see you there." She wrinkled her nose up and stared at the ground like she was trying to remember. "Why didn't you come over to us?"

"You looked busy. With Kian." That was all I could say. My whole mouth had dried up and I kept my hands hidden behind my back so she couldn't see me shaking.

"Kian?" She laughed and then her face turned deadly serious. "Oh my God, did you think something was going on? Seriously? You thought I went there with Kian?"

"He had his arm around you." I spoke quietly. I didn't want to sound like a jealous boyfriend, but my emotions were all over the place and I was losing my grip on reality.

"He had his arm around Ryan most of the night, and Emily too, until Ryan told him to fuck off. Did you really think I was with him?" She screwed her face up in disgust. "I don't like Kian like that. I'd never do that to you."

And just like that the weight pressing down on my chest––making it difficult to breathe––suddenly lifted.

I believed her.

I swallowed, feeling embarrassed that I'd had those thoughts in the first place. If I was truly honest with myself, the thought of Kian and Effy as a thing was ridiculous. Maybe the soldiers were messing with my head more than I realised? Them, and my uncle. My whole grasp on what was real was becoming distorted.

"I'm sorry. I just saw him and you... and I thought..."

"You put two and two together and came up with fifty three thousand. Finn, if you ever doubt me again, you need to let me know. Talk to me. I know you're not a talker, but shit like that needs sorting out, instead of leaving it to fester. If I saw you with another girl, I'd lose my mind, but I'd talk to you about it. That's what normal people do."

Normal. That wasn't a label I'd ever use for my life.

She sighed and I gave her a shy smile, cocking my head to the side to try and look cute.

"Like I said, I'm sorry. I'm an idiot." I shrugged, hoping we could move on from this because embarrassment was as familiar to me as another limb, but I still despised it.

She nodded in agreement and smiled back.

"What have you got behind your back?" She narrowed her eyes at me in playful accusation.

I didn't want to show up empty-handed, but I wasn't the kind of guy that bought flowers and chocolates or stuff like that. The gifts I gave her were always unique.

"It's a rose. But not just any rose."

I'd made the flower myself, saw the idea online and thought it looked cool. It held much more meaning, and at the time, I thought it'd trump any shitty gift Kian might've given her.

"Is that pages from a book?" she asked as she reached out to take it from me and turned it over in her hands like it was delicate treasure.

"Yeah. I swiped pages out of Zak's copy of Harry Potter to make it. I'm hoping he doesn't read it again anytime soon and find out."

She laughed now; a proper, genuine laugh.

"I love Harry Potter, and this is so thoughtful, but I'm not entirely sure how I feel about you massacring a book."

I hadn't seen it like that and I could feel the sweat start to trickle down my back as my cheeks flamed red.

"Just promise you'll stay away from my bookshelf." She chuckled, bumping me playfully with her shoulder. "I'm kidding, Finn. It's beautiful. Thank you. It's way better than a normal rose that'd die in a few days."

"That's what I thought too." See, great minds thought alike. She got me. Even if she did question the safety of literature when I was around.

"I can keep this in my memory box."

"You have a memory box?" I asked. The way she blushed was so cute that I had to press further. "Are you getting forgetful in your old age? It all goes downhill after eighteen," I joked, shaking my head regretfully.

"It's my Finn box," she replied, and then her eyes went wide, and her cheeks flushed brighter. "Oh my God. I really shouldn't have told you that. I'm so embarrassed." She grimaced to herself, but I wasn't going to let her suffer.

"Don't be embarrassed, I think it's sweet. What else is in the box?" I really did want to know.

"Well, there's pictures that you've drawn for me. There may or may not be napkins in there too that you've doodled on."

"Doodled?" I laughed. "I like that word. What else?"

"Why don't you come inside and see?"

And this was why I loved her. Five minutes in her presence and all I cared about was her and how she made me feel. Nothing else mattered.

I had to admit, my stomach flipped at the thought of stepping into her house. I really wanted to go to her room and get a true insight into what made her tick, but at the same time, my nerves were out of control.

"I'm not sure. Are your parents home?"

"Yes, but they won't mind. They'd like to meet you."

I highly doubted that. In my experience, parents didn't take too kindly to guys like me rocking up to see their daughters.

"I wouldn't be so sure."

"Oh, come on. They're cool."

I debated saying no to her again. Emily's parents hated Ryan, although that was a mutual feeling. And Harper's parents still disliked Brandon, even though they were about to have the twins. Why would Effy's parents be any different? I wouldn't want my daughter around a guy like me.

But as much as I wanted to turn around and walk away, avoiding any awkward parental interrogation, I couldn't. Just this once, I wanted to say yes to her and surprise her.

"Fine. But I can't stay long and don't expect me to make conversation. I'm——"

"A quick hello will be fine," she added to put me at ease. "Then you can come to my room and I'll show you my memories."

I smirked. I couldn't help it. The deviant part of me was hoping she'd show me more than just memories.

Cautiously, I stepped into her hallway and her dog rushed towards me, jumping up as I tried to stroke her.

"Luna, get down," Effy scolded. "I'm sorry, she's a husky. They can get a bit hyper when they're excited. She always has way too much energy. She likes you though."

"She's beautiful," I said, petting her and crouching to her level to give her more fuss.

I didn't mind pets. I loved dogs. In fact, I preferred animals to humans half the time. Stroking Luna gave me something to do, distracting me from my racing thoughts.

"It's through here." Effy walked down the hallway and called out for me to follow her. As I walked, Luna came too, trailing me like a trusty shadow, my new found protector.

Effy's house was the complete opposite of mine. The cream carpets were so soft your feet sunk into them. Ours was threadbare and filthy. Walking down her hallway, you could feel the warmth coming from the radiators. Ours were old and never on long enough to make a difference to the overall temperature of the house. This was a family home, full of light and love. Ours was a building to house people who didn't give a fuck about anyone other than themselves.

"Mum, Dad, this is Finn."

I stopped at the doorway to the living room and glanced nervously inside. Effy's mum was sitting on the sofa with her legs up, resting them on the dad's lap, and he was massaging her feet as they watched some documentary on Netflix. When he heard Effy introduce me, he paused the show and turned to look at me, but he didn't scowl like I'd expected. He beamed and then his smile grew wider as he looked to his wife before glancing back at me and saying, "Hey there, Finn. I'm Steve." He slid her feet to the side and got up off the sofa, extending his arm out to shake my hand. "It's nice to meet you."

I shook it, worried that my grip wasn't firm enough and he'd think I wasn't good enough for his daughter.

Effy's mum jumped up next and came over to shake my hand too.

"I'm Jenny, Jen. It's so nice to meet you, Finn. We've heard a lot about you. You're the artist, right? Effy has shown us a few of your drawings. You're very talented. Did you make that rose there?" She pointed at the paper rose still clutched in Effy's hand.

I nodded, but Effy replied.

"He did. Isn't it amazing? He used the pages of a Harry Potter book."

Her mum took the rose off her to get a better look as her dad raised his brows at me as if to say, 'Nice touch.'

"You could make a whole bouquet of these," her mum

said. "My friends would go crazy to buy them. What a fantastic idea."

I stuttered over my words. I didn't want her to think I was some genius, taking credit where it wasn't due.

"That wasn't my idea. I saw it online. I'm not that clever."

"You made it, so it's yours. Don't put yourself down," her mum added. "I've seen your work, remember? I know all about your originality. You're a skilled and talented artist. Own it." Her mum narrowed her eyes at me, but not in an offensive way. More to encourage me not to argue with her. She liked it and that was all there was to it. "Can I get you a drink?" she asked, smiling and instantly lightening the mood.

"No, its fine. I'm okay." I didn't trust myself with a glass. I'd probably end up spilling it all over their pristine cream carpets. But then looking at how excited they seemed to be to meet me, I doubted that they'd care. Not like my mum would've.

"I wanted to show Finn some of the stuff I've collected up in my room. Is that okay?" I stiffened as she spoke. I couldn't believe Effy would go there. I'd expected her to bring it down to the living room. In all honesty, I'd thought she was joking when she suggested I go to her room when we were outside. Her parents were not going to like that, and they sure as hell wouldn't like me anymore if they thought I was trying to get a free pass into their daughter's bedroom. But I was knocked for six when her dad grinned back and then shrugged to his wife.

"Sure. I don't see why not." He patted me on the arm and

sat back down. "It's nice seeing you, Finn. You're welcome here any time."

"Thank you." I bowed my head like I was addressing royalty.

They actually liked me. Probably more so than my own parents. A five minute meeting and I'd found out they knew more about what I stood for than my own parents ever did. There were no threats, no salty looks, and I hadn't been chased out with the family shotgun pointed at my ass. Even the dog, Luna, was licking my hand. I had not expected this.

I followed Effy out of the living room, back down the hallway and up the wide staircase with its highly polished mahogany handrails. I gripped it extra hard to give me the support I needed to carry my shaking legs upstairs.

When we got to her room, I was surprised to find it wasn't all pink and girlie. Maybe that was unfair of me. Effy never really was a girlie girl. She had some kind of fairy lights strung up around the top of her bed, but her carpets and curtains were grey and the walls left white, with just a few framed pictures dotted around. When I looked closer, I realised those pictures were ones I'd drawn, only on a larger scale.

"My dad blew them up on his computer at work. I hope it doesn't freak you out," she said, gesturing to the drawing I'd done of Luna that hung over her bed.

"Not at all. They actually look really cool like that." I glanced around, not really sure what to do with myself. There was one of those swinging, hanging chair things in the corner, but I didn't fancy my chances trying to navigate that, so I sat on the edge of her bed and threaded my fingers together, resting my hands in-between my legs. Effy moved some of the fluffy cushions from off the bed and threw them on the floor, then reached into a cupboard nearby and pulled out a grey velvet box.

"Promise you won't freak out or hate me forever," she said, pretending to tease but looking deadly serious as she held the box in her lap. "I swear I'm not a crazy, weirdo stalker. I just like keeping things." She shrugged and the honesty in her eyes made my heart skip a beat.

"I promise." I swivelled to the side to face her. "Come on, show me what you've got."

She laughed and placed the box down in-between us, and when she lifted the lid, I fell a little more in love with her. She had every picture I'd ever drawn placed inside a plastic pocket to protect it. There were napkins that'd been smoothed out with my random scribbles on them. Printed messages from when we advertised our events online. I saw a few leaflets and other things from our school days, and then I saw a book. I picked it up and frowned at her as I read the title.

"Lord of the Rings? Why do you have this? I don't think I've even read this book."

She shuffled where she sat and then bit her lip, smiling.

"That book reminds me of the first time I saw you."

I was still none the wiser.

"I think you're gonna need to spell this one out for me."

"Okay." She took a deep breath. "I was in the library, at school. It was lunchtime, I was revising for a French test, and all of a sudden, I heard the librarian roaring across the room, and when I looked up, you were sat on the other side of the library looking at her like she'd gone crazy. She was bawling you out for defacing school property, throwing her arms around and everything, and you just sat there and didn't react, didn't even argue back. I watched her grab this book off you and all you did was stand up and walk out without looking back. I couldn't work you out, and I realised that day that I wanted to, more than anything. You drew me in. See what I did there? Drew me in." She laughed at her own joke, and even though it wasn't funny, I laughed too.

When I opened the book all the memories came flooding back. Inside the front cover, I'd sketched out a plan for a piece of graffiti art I'd been working on back then. Some cartoon guy smoking a joint that I thought looked cool and edgy at the time. Now, it was dated and amateurish.

"She put the book on the desk," Effy continued. "And then she stormed off. So I went over and took it."

"You stole it." I gave her an evil grin.

"I guess I did, but I knew she'd throw it away and I didn't want her to do that. Your art should never be hidden, and neither should you."

I held her eyes with mine and my breath started to come in short sharp gasps as my heart beat an unsteady rhythm against my chest. I glanced back down at the box to hide my nervousness and pointed to a stack of envelopes tied together with grey silk ribbon. It was an avoidance technique but it worked.

"What are those?"

"Oh fuck." She sighed as she took them out and clasped them close to her chest. "I forgot those were in there."

"You can't not tell me now," I urged, giving her my wide-eyed stare.

"But it's embarrassing." She could barely look me in the eye, but this time, I found it cute.

"Can't be any more embarrassing than this," I said, holding up the book with my God-awful cartoon stoner drawn in it.

"Fine. These are Valentine's cards."

"From who?" The way my stomach twisted made me grit my teeth to prepare myself for the worst. I didn't like the thought of her keeping cards from other guys.

"From me." She frowned. "I didn't have the courage to send them, but every year, I bought you a Valentine's card and put it in here."

Fuck.

I was gone.

"There's quite a lot of cards tied up there."

"I've liked you for a long time."

My heart was about to burst for her. My head was gone. And I didn't care that her parents were sitting downstairs.

Without saying a word, I took the cards out of her hand. She looked scared, like she didn't want me to read them, but that wasn't my intention. Maybe another day––when she felt comfortable about it––I'd open them, but for now, I had to get as close to her as I possibly could.

I placed the bundle of envelopes back into the box and moved it onto the floor. Then I shuffled closer to her and held her face in my hands, stroking my thumbs along the softness of her cheeks. If I didn't know it before, I did now. This girl fucking owned me.

She went to speak, but I put my lips over hers and kissed her. I kissed her to show her that I loved her. I loved everything about her. I always had. The way she treasured every little thing about me. The way she made me feel like I was worth something. The way she only ever saw the good.

I tilted my head and kissed away any doubts she might've had in the past. My lips stroked against hers to tell her that she was my everything. I slid my tongue forward to taste her and lose myself in her. The way her tongue teased with mine made the blood rush to my head, and I felt myself stiffen in my jeans. I was so turned on and I wanted her so badly, but I couldn't do anything about it today. With her parents right below us, I had to rein it in. But it was tough.

I pushed her back, so that she lay on her bed, and I crawled over her, kissing her lips and then moving to her neck. The sounds she made, gasping and moaning, spurred me on, and I couldn't stop myself from grinding my hips into her, showing her what she did to me.

We lay together, kissing and holding each other. My hands desperately wanted to explore, to touch her in a way she'd never been touched before, and I could tell she felt the same. Her hands threaded through my hair, caressed my cheek and then she moved to snake them around my waist and down to my ass. I smiled as I felt her pulling me towards her, grabbing my ass and lifting her leg so she could feel me where she needed me. My hands drifted down her body, gently lifting the bottom of her T-shirt and touching the velvet softness of her stomach. I was just about to pull the button of her jeans open when there was a knock at the door and we both shot apart.

Effy tried to wipe any evidence of our kiss from her face and started to frantically straighten out her clothing as she stood up from the bed. I sat forward and adjusted myself in my jeans. She took a quick look back at me, making sure I looked decent, before she flung the door open.

"What's up?" she said, sounding breathless and way too guilty.

"I was just about to start dinner. I wanted to know if Finn was stopping? There's plenty to go round." Her mum grinned and glanced over Effy's shoulder at me. From the sparkle in her eyes, I guessed she knew what we were up to, but if she did, she didn't say anything.

"Do you want to stay for dinner?" Effy turned and asked me.

"I would normally say yes, and it's really kind of you to offer, Mrs Spencer,"

"It's Jen. Mrs Spencer is Effy's Grandma." She laughed. "It's homemade lasagne tonight. What do you say?"

Right on cue, my stomach growled, but I couldn't stay. We'd made headway, but I felt like I'd taken enough steps forward. Now, I just wanted to go back to Zak's and think about what came next. To be honest, I wanted to be with Effy, without her parents being there, but some alone time would have to do.

"I can't. I have to get going." Effy didn't look as disappointed as she usually did when I told her I was leaving. I was proud of myself for taking that apprehension away from her.

I stood up to go, now that I'd calmed down and wouldn't embarrass myself, and Effy's mum walked ahead and down the stairs.

"Maybe another time then?" She looked back over her shoulder and smiled at us.

"Yeah, definitely."

I walked down the stairs next to Effy, and when we got to the front door, her mum disappeared off down the hallway. I lifted Effy's chin with my thumb and forefinger and kissed her again. I didn't care if her mum and dad came back out and saw us. I wanted them to know I loved her.

"I'll see you tomorrow," I said with a cocky grin.

"I'll look forward to it," she replied, lifting up on her

tiptoes to give me one last kiss.

I would say I walked away from Effy's house and back down the street, but I'd be lying. I fucking floated out of there, riding a bigger high than any art had ever given me. This feeling was better than any drug. Sweeter than any taste I'd ever known. I was high on Effy Spencer.

I felt my phone buzz in my pocket and I smirked to myself. I really hoped it was a cute message, or better yet, a photograph.

But today was not my day. Once again, fate slapped me around the face and reminded me to wake the fuck up. Real life wasn't all hearts and flowers.

Welcome to level two of the game of consequences.

Your next challenge is to organise an event in Brinton Manor with the rest of your little crew.

Send us a copy of the invite and we'll send you a reward. Fail, and you'll never want to show your face in Sandland ever again.

Time is ticking. You have until midnight on Saturday.

This was fucking bullshit. As far as I knew, they might not even have my uncle anymore. He could've escaped. He had the luck of the devil in him, so nothing would surprise me there. Not to mention, I was getting really fucked off with them thinking they had me at their beck and call. There was no way I could talk the others into an event in Brinton Manor, they wouldn't even throw a tennis ball there, let alone a party. What made these soldiers think I held any power over what we did?

I thought about firing off a quick message to let them know that I wasn't a total loser, but what would I say? No, I won't play your stupid games? Let my uncle go and I'll dole out my own justice? They didn't have a heart. They'd take him out and then drag me down too, just so they could revel in my torment, and I wouldn't ever let that happen. They knew everything, and that was their ace card. I was holding a fist full of jokers with no way out. I couldn't take the risk. I had to at least try and make this happen.

FINN

"I was glad when you called us all to ask us what we were up to today, Finn." Ryan sat opposite me in Zak's living room and glanced at each one of us as he spoke. "There's something I've been meaning to talk to you all about."

Brandon was sprawled in his armchair of choice, sipping his tea and scrolling through his phone.

"You're getting a hair transplant and you want our opinion," Brandon joked without looking up. "I say go for it. Time isn't on your side and the shine from that forehead of yours is making it difficult for me to see my screen." He shook his phone and then threw his head back, laughing at himself.

"Fuck you," Ryan threw back, but he smirked. He loved the banter. "No, I've been thinking about asking Emily to marry me. Thought I'd let you guys know first."

"What, you don't have her father to ask permission, so you're coming to us? That's sweet, dude. We love you too," Brandon teased.

"Like I'd need permission. She's mine, I just want to

make it official."

Brandon finally stopped scrolling and put his phone down. Then he leant forward with a serious expression on his face, like he was about to argue the pros and cons.

"I've been thinking the same thing, but Harper wants to wait until after the babies are born."

"I don't think it works that way," Zak huffed on a laugh, sounding like he was taking the piss out of Brandon's comment.

"What would you know?" Brandon frowned back at him. "You're the expert at sealing the deal in the bedroom, not the fucking church." Brandon was seriously irritated and he wasn't afraid to hide it.

"You'd have a church wedding?" I asked, trying to diffuse the sudden tension in the room, but still shocked that he'd want a traditional ceremony. I knew him better than anyone, and I'd always had him down as a 'run off and get married with the minimum number of witnesses so he could fast forward to the honeymoon' kind of guy. He smirked back at me, knowing exactly what I was thinking.

"That's what Harper wants. And what she wants, she gets."

"Yeah, and she's a chick. Chicks like to be surprised. Don't wait until after the babies come. Surprise her now. That's what she really wants." Zak did have a point.

Brandon rubbed his chin in thought and nodded to himself.

"Maybe you're right…"

"Of course he's right," Ryan shot back, rolling his eyes. "Now, can we get back to me? I'm the one with the engagement ring in my pocket."

"Well, show us it then," Zak demanded.

Ryan reached into his jeans and pulled out a little black velvet box. When he opened it, we all gathered round to look at the diamond ring inside. It looked pretty impressive, but I was no expert.

"She'll love that, Ry," I said.

"Just think of all the car parts you could've bought for the price of that thing," Zak joked.

"Since when did we turn into a bunch of pussies who talk about weddings and look at rings?" Brandon stated, ever the realist.

Ryan snapped the box closed and smiled to himself.

"You'll be the same when you get Harper's ring."

"I've already got it," he replied in a deadpan manner.

"Can we see?" Zak was really getting into the spirit of this conversation, considering he was a sworn bachelor for life.

"No. It's in my bedside drawer at home."

"No, it's not." Zak chuckled. "She's probably trying it on right now and sending photos of it to her mates."

"Fuck off." Brandon grimaced and sat back in his chair, then a panicked expression came over his face, and I could tell he believed what Zak had said.

"So, where are you going to propose?" I asked Ryan, to

take Brandon's mind off the fact that his secret hiding place probably wasn't so secret.

"The asylum chapel. Which brings me to my next point. I saw an ad yesterday. The asylum is going up for auction at the end of the month."

"And?" Brandon asked, gritting his teeth and looking slightly pissed off.

"And I thought, maybe, if we got some financial backing, we could buy it. Together. No more scouting for events. It could be ours. Permanently." Ryan shrugged. "Party central."

"Where are we supposed to get the money to buy a place like that?" Brandon was going to take a lot more convincing.

"You could hit up Daddy Lockwood for it?" Zak was pushing his luck with that comment and he knew it.

"Yeah right. You know, if I had a gun with two bullets and I was stuck in a room with Hitler, Bin Laden, and him, I'd shoot him twice." Brandon huffed, folding his arms over his chest, and then he went back to scrolling through his phone.

"Emily has money from her dad," Ryan carried on, ignoring the obstacles being thrown his way. "She's already offered to go in. Would Harper be interested? Or her parents?"

"I wouldn't ask them for an opinion, let alone a loan," Brandon shot back without sparing a single glance at any one of us.

"Harper would though, especially if it meant we could expand the business." Ryan turned to face me. "What about Effy? Her parents aren't short of a few bob." He was starting to sound desperate.

"I would never ask her. If you want the Spencers to invest, that's your call, not mine. Couldn't we put on a few extra events to make money ourselves for the deposit?" I decided to steer the conversation my way for once.

"That's a good idea." Brandon's attention was caught again. "I'm not fighting though. I've got bookings for my workshops for the next few months. Anyway, it'd stress Harper out and I wouldn't want to put her through that at the moment."

"You don't have to fight. We could put on *a* fight but it wouldn't have to be you. We have enough contacts to make it happen. That's a good idea, Finn. Let's do it." Ryan was buzzing, I could tell.

"I have an idea for a venue too." Now I'd reached my next hurdle, and it was a hell of a lot bigger than the last one.

"Oh yeah? Where?" Brandon leant forward in anticipation.

"The old Clarkson's Plastics factory." I held my breath, waiting for the penny to drop.

"Wait, what? The one over in Brinton? Why the fuck would we want to use that? It's a shithole and the soldiers would bomb the place with us still in it if we stepped on their manor." Ryan had made up his mind, but Zak stayed quiet and Brandon stared at me, trying to suss me out.

"Why do you want us to go to Brinton, mate?" Brandon could tell there was more to this than I was letting on.

"Alice lives there now. And I figured there were buildings there that we hadn't really looked at before. Maybe it's a goldmine we've over-looked?" I shrugged like it was no big deal.

"Alice barely leaves the house. She's never attended one of our parties and we've been doing them for years. What's the deal here?" Brandon was like a dog with a bone when he thought he was onto something.

"No deal. I just thought it'd be cool." I couldn't look him in the eye though. He'd call bullshit within seconds if I did.

"Cool? Bloody suicide more like." He scowled back at me as Zak and Ryan watched us like they were at the Wimbledon final.

I stayed quiet and Brandon huffed out his annoyance.

"Come on then. Talk us round. You're supposed to argue with me, not give in the first chance you get." Brandon was always trying to push me out of my comfort zone, and this was no different.

"All right, fine. You never listen to me. You always make all the decisions and expect me to go along with it. I'm stuck on the outside most of the time, and just this once, I want to have a say."

"That's more like it." He spurred me on. "What else? Don't hold back on us."

"I think we need to think bigger than Sandland. If you want to make this a viable business, then we have to expand our network." Ryan nodded when I said that. He always saw the bigger picture.

"And the soldiers?" Brandon piped up.

"They won't be a problem."

For you, anyway.

"And you know this how?" He wasn't giving up.

"Because I've spoken to them. They're cool." Brandon flinched like I'd slapped him around the face.

"What the fuck are you talking about? They aren't cool. They are as far from cool as humanly possible." He was offended by what I'd said. He didn't like that I'd spoken to them and he didn't know about it.

"When did you see them? What's going on Finn?" Ryan spoke calmly. He knew one angry interrogator was enough for today.

"I went to visit Alice and I saw them in the street." All the truth, now to thread in the lies that I was so awful at telling. "They said they'd heard about our events and asked why we'd never put one on in Brinton."

"Because even Satan himself would give that place a wide berth," Zak snapped.

Brandon held his hand up to shut Zak up. He was still stuck on the fact that I'd spoken to them and he needed more information.

"So, you're on friendly terms with them now? Since when? And why don't I know about this?"

"Because I don't run everything past you." Before all the shit with my uncle leaving prison, I would have, but things had changed. He was a family man now, and I had to take responsibility for my own shit.

"Oh, I know that," he said, sounding pissed. "Seen any long lost family members lately?" I blushed and instantly he dropped his gaze to the floor. He regretted what he'd just said. "Sorry, man. I didn't mean that."

"It's fine. And no, I haven't. He's gone."

Brandon raised his eyebrows and I could tell he didn't believe me.

"It's true. All sorted. So... are you going to let me check out Brinton? Take a few photos and maybe even get you down there to see it for yourself?"

"Finn, we trust you. If you think that'd be a good idea, go for it," Ryan said.

Brandon glared over at him, then back at me. He didn't know what to think, but he wasn't about to go against Ryan's judgement.

"Looks like we're gonna be honorary soldiers for the night then, doesn't it?" he said, his voice dripping with sarcasm, but when the tension in my shoulders eased up, he smiled.

Ryan joined Zak where he sat with his laptop and the two of them became engrossed in watching some YouTube video. Obviously, this conversation had ended, and luckily for me, it had gone just how I wanted it to.

I watched as Brandon got up and came to sit next to me on the sofa.

"Something's going on with you," he said on a whisper. "You know you can talk to me, right? If you're being forced to do this. If the soldiers are threatening you, you would tell me, wouldn't you? You know I've got your back."

"I'm fine," I whispered back so the other two wouldn't hear. "Alice is safe. He's gone. And I just want to make a contribution is all."

"You know I don't believe you, but okay. I'll let it go. But I swear, if those fuckers do anything, if they put one foot wrong, I will kill them. I don't care how fucking psycho they are. When it comes to my friends, I get just as fucking crazy. And you are my best friend."

Brandon could smell bullshit a mile off, but he also knew what I was like and he didn't want to push me. I appreciated it, because with everything going on, I needed to focus on what was important, and worrying about the reaction Brandon would have to the blackmail was not something I wanted to face.

"I've got your back. Always," he repeated and stood up, patting my back as he did. "More importantly," he stated in a louder tone. "Where's the biscuits? How do you expect me to drink my tea without a fucking biscuit to dunk? The service in this place is fucking shite."

CHAPTER Sixteen

FINN

It didn't take much more convincing to bring them all on-board. I paid a visit to the old factory, took photographs and sent them to the lads. Within a few days, they'd all agreed and the messages were sent out to our 'We've got you covered' group to let them know when and where the next event would be held.

Clarkson's Plastics factory in Brinton Manor.

I sent the evidence to the soldiers and as per their M.O, they replied that I'd done a good job and that they'd be in touch. I wasn't in a hurry to see what video they'd send next, or to hear from them at all. Alice was still up north and safe. My uncle was being taken care of, I hoped. And I wanted to focus on something far more important. Tony had dictated the way my life had gone for so long, it was my turn now, my future.

I'd stood at the end of her road and waited for her parents to leave. When I saw a car backing out of the driveway with both of them inside, I stayed in place by the hedge I was using to camouflage myself, keeping my head down and my hood up. They sped off down the road and I made my move, heading over to her house.

I wasn't as nervous this time, coming to see her. Sure, I still had butterflies, but they were the good kind. The kind that meant I was excited about how this would play out. She opened the door and grinned wide when she saw it was me. She looked stunning in a little tight crop top and joggers.

"You look amazing," I said, feeling myself getting tongue-tied.

She looked down at what she was wearing and replied, "These are my comfies. I'd have made an effort if I'd known you were coming."

"That's all the effort I need," I replied, then blushed, realising I was staring at her tits, but it was really hard not to when she wasn't wearing a bra and her nipples were poking through the sheer material. Fuck, I'd turned into one of those creeps.

"You look good too." She laughed, thankfully not taking offense at my ogling. "Smiling suits you."

"I have a lot to smile about these days."

I had one thing to smile about, but she didn't need to know about the rest of the bullshit going on.

"Are you coming in? I'm alone. Are you gonna be okay with that?" She waggled her eyebrows and I fought the urge to pick her up, throw her over my shoulder and run straight to her room.

"I think I'll survive," I answered, stepping into her hallway and shutting the door behind me.

She went to walk towards her living room, but I stopped her by grabbing her arm and asked, "Can we go to your room? Only, there's something I want to give to you, and I don't want to run the risk of your parents coming home and seeing."

She frowned playfully, and then walked back towards me.

"Okay. Should I be worried? Are you going to show me your etchings?" She giggled to herself.

"Something like that."

She started to walk up the stairs and I jumped up after her, like a lovesick puppy. I'd spent all night on this gift, and I really didn't want to fuck it up.

When we got to her room, she locked the door behind us and I sat down in the same spot on the bed that I'd sat in last time.

"So..." She plonked herself down into the space next to me. "What's up?"

"I have something else for your memory box."

Instantly, she lit up like a kid at Christmas with her eyes going wide and sparkling. "I love that! What have you got?" Her body swivelled round to face mine, and she clapped her hands excitedly.

"After I saw your cards, the Valentine's ones, I kind of felt bad. So, I made you these."

I pulled out the stack of cards I had hidden in the front

pocket of my hoody and passed them to her.

"What is this?" she asked, turning the pile over in her hands.

"You need to open them in order." I grabbed the pile and turned them back around. "They're my Valentine's cards to you. Eighteen of them."

"Eighteen?"

"Yes. One for each year you've been alive."

She sighed when I said that, and I knew I was onto a winner.

"Where did you find eighteen different Valentine's cards to buy in November?"

"I didn't. I made them myself."

"Of course you did." She shook her head and laughed.

I watched as she placed them in her lap and started to open the first one. Then she stopped, and with an apprehensive look on her face, she said, "Is it okay for me to open them now? In front of you, I mean?"

"That's why I brought them. If I didn't want to watch, I'd have posted them through the door and done a runner." She knew what I was saying was the truth.

"I'm glad you didn't," she replied, and a small contented smile spread across her face and warmed her eyes.

I was glad too. Being here and seeing how this affected her was better than any high. My body was tingling with the anticipation and my head was fuzzy with a feeling I couldn't quite describe. Was this what love felt like?

She opened the first envelope and her brow furrowed when she saw the drawing of an apple and a chocolate bar. She narrowed her gaze as she looked to the side at me.

"I know everything you do has a special meaning, but I have no idea what this one is." She held the card up as she spoke and I just shrugged.

"Read it." I knew it'd all become clear to her the moment she did.

So she opened the card and read aloud.

"You thought nobody saw you put that apple and chocolate bar into Elliot Small's pocket when Brandon tripped him over in the school cafeteria. But I did. I notice everything about you. And now, I want to tell you all the things that make you special." Her voice cracked slightly, but she carried on reading. "Reason number one, you do kind things for others, even when they don't know it was done by you. You're the most selfless person I know, and I love that about you."

She gasped and put her hand over her mouth. I could see the shine in her eyes. She wanted to cry, but she didn't. Not yet. She took a deep breath, closed the card, and then without looking at me, she said, "That's so sweet, Finn."

"Keep going," I urged, eager for her to open the rest of them. "There's seventeen more there that I worked on last night."

She beamed and placed the first card down on the bed next to her then moved to card number two. I'd drawn a gift-wrapped heart on the front, and when she opened and read this one, she started to choke up.

"To everyone who knows you, you are a gift. The day Danny died, you put everything aside to be there for your best friend, Emily. At the funeral, I was watching you from the back and I saw you change seats to sit by Em and hold her hand, even though her dad asked you not to sit at the front. You didn't care about breaking protocol, you wanted to support her. You always put others before yourself. You're everyone's rock, and I love that about you. But I hope, that one day, I can be that rock for you." She sniffed and glanced over at me. "You give me strength even though you don't realise it, Finn. You always have."

I shrugged my shoulders and huffed flippantly like it meant nothing, but hearing her say that made my heart swell and my throat close up. I don't know what strength she thought I'd given her, but I'd take it.

"I think I'm gonna be a wreck by the time I get to number eighteen," she joked and placed card two with the first.

The third one she opened had her smiling face beaming back at her, but I'd given it an Andy Warhol twist. There were about twelve grinning Effys staring at her from that card.

"Don't panic," I told her. "This one's a happy one."

She took deep breaths to calm herself, bit her lip nervously and then opened it to read aloud.

"You have so many different smiles, and each one gives me butterflies. The gentle smile, when you think no one is watching and you're smiling for yourself. But I see it. The sweet smile that makes your eyes sparkle. It makes my stomach flip over too. The laughing smile, when your whole face lights up. It sets my soul on fire. The genuine smile that you give to all your friends. I love that nothing about you is fake. But my favourite smile of all is the one I see when you see me. That's my smile."

I fiddled nervously with my fingernails and started to second guess myself. Had I used the word love too many times? Were my words too soppy? Was I being a total loser?

"I love your smiles too. I'm glad I get to see more of them these days." She took a deep breath and moved onto card number four, clearly struggling with her emotions after opening and reading the first three.

This one had a picture of her playing with Luna in the park on the front.

"I love the way you draw her. You always capture her playful side," she said as she touched the picture like it was the most precious thing she owned.

"And yours too," I said, nudging her, and she gave a happy sigh in response.

"One of my favourite memories," she read. "Was when I saw you in the park one day, playing with your dog. You didn't see me and I was glad because I was enjoying watching you be so carefree. I loved the cute voice you used whenever she jumped up and the way you scrunched your nose up when she rolled around in the mud then shook herself and drenched you with it. You didn't get angry. You never do. You have a patience and grace that makes everyone around you feel safe and loved. You have a way about you that makes everyone want to be near you, just so they can experience your light, even if it's just for a moment. I've had more than my fair share of your light, and I pray that it never ends."

"It never will." She sniffed, not even trying to hold back her tears now.

I sat and watched her open card after card that told her all the reasons that I loved her. From the way she wrinkled her face up when she was thinking about something, to the compassion in her eyes when she was listening to others. The fact that she'd drop everything if someone needed her, and the way she stayed focused on her goals and never gave up. She'd never given up on me, and for that I would always be eternally grateful.

When she eventually came to the last card, I felt emotionally drained, and yet, this was the most important one of them all. On this one, I'd drawn the White Rabbit from Alice in Wonderland. Having a sister called Alice meant the story was as familiar to me as anything. We'd had several versions of the book in our house growing up and it'd always fascinated me. For this picture, I'd drawn the White Rabbit holding his pocket watch, checking the time.

"I love this, Finn. I love all of it." She was shaking and I wanted to put my arms around her, but I also needed her to read this last message. "Okay, here goes nothing. I'm a nervous wreck now anyway, but something tells me you're gonna slay me with this last card."

I smirked to myself. One of us was getting slayed. I really hoped it wasn't me. Then, I held my breath as she opened it up and began reading.

"I've wasted so many years. Thrown away such precious time. Today that all comes to an end." She frowned and looked up at me. "It doesn't say anything else. I don't get it."

"Look on the back," I said, twisting my finger in the air as a sign for her to turn it around.

"Okay. Today it all comes to an end..." She turned it round. "Effy Spencer, the sweetest, kindest girl I know... Will you be my girlfriend?" She stared at the words on the paper, blinking and breathing slow and steady. "Is this real? Do you really mean this?"

I grabbed her face in my hands, forcing her to look at me.

"Of course I mean it. Will you? Be my girlfriend, that is? I know we haven't really properly dated, but––"

I didn't get to finish. She smashed her lips hard against mine to shut me up, and when she pulled away, we were both grinning like a couple of idiots.

"Yes." She nodded frantically.

"Yes?"

"Always yes. I'll always say yes to you, Finn. I'd do anything for you."

I loved this girl more than anything in my pitiful little life, and I thanked God every day that she'd stuck around and waited for me. And now that I had her in my arms, I couldn't hold back anymore.

Softly, I placed my hand on her cheek and used my other arm to pull her closer to me. And while I stroked and caressed her cheekbone with my thumb, I kissed her. Gentle at first, but then, when I slipped my tongue inside her mouth to taste her, it was as if a switch was flicked on for both of us and our kiss turned more frantic and needy. Our tongues were greedy; massaging, tasting, loving. The way they entwined so perfectly together showed that we were made for each other. This just felt right. She felt right.

We kissed as our breathing turned into panting, and then Effy wrapped her arms around my neck and swung her leg across my lap to straddle me. I grabbed her ass to pull her up closer, so she was sitting directly over my rock-hard dick, and she moaned and rubbed herself against me.

Her hands were in my hair, tugging at the ends. Her lips moulded against mine. And her body; her perfect, beautiful body was pressed against me as we sat up on her bed, taking what we'd longed for all this time. The way she rocked against me made me want to come right there, I was so turned on.

I shifted on the bed, holding her tightly in my arms, and laid her down on her back. Then I crawled over her and held myself up with my arms. I stared into her eyes as she looked back at me with so much want I could feel it tugging at my heart, making it difficult to breathe. Her lips were swollen from where I'd kissed her like my life depended on it. We were both panting, trying to get our breathing under control but not wanting to break this spell.

"I want you so fucking much, Eff. But I'm not going to rush you into anything." I moved a stray wisp of hair from her forehead and placed a gentle kiss there.

"I want you too," she whispered back to me. "And I'm done waiting."

She grabbed the bottom of my hoody to pull it up and off. It wasn't easy for her to do, so I pushed myself up to sit on the bed and helped her. Then, when I'd thrown it onto the ground, I turned back to face her, feeling like a wild animal; ravenous and ready to devour its prey. I wanted to savour every damn minute of this. Moments like these didn't happen for me, but today it was all going my way. Every dream was coming true.

She slid the crop top she was wearing up and then pulled it off over her head. I took a deep breath when I saw her for the first time, laying there in only her joggers. She was the most beautiful girl I'd ever seen. She took my breath away. She was bright, light, every colour there ever was, and the rest of the world was dull and grey compared to her.

I was caught in a daze, but she pulled me out of it when she reached forward and ran her hand down my chest, sighing. I needed to be close to her and feel her warmth, so I leant back over her and kissed her slowly, moving my hips against hers and running my hands from her waist up to her breast. She arched her body, pushing herself further into me, and I touched her, memorising every inch of her skin as the priceless art that it was. The feel of her breasts against my chest as she wrapped her arms around me made me hungry for more. I needed to know this was what she wanted, because God knows I was desperate for her.

"Are you sure about this?" I whispered into her ear and then kissed her neck, nuzzling into her as she replied.

"I've never wanted anything more in my whole life."

I moved to look her deep in the eyes and ran my nose slowly against hers, loving the closeness and feeling of intimacy we had going on right now, but at the same time, I needed so much more.

"I'll stop at any time. Just say the word and I will."

"I don't ever want you to stop." She reached down and pulled the button of my jeans free, and I couldn't stop a quiet moan from escaping. This was really happening.

She used both of her hands and began to push my jeans down, so I got up from the bed and stood in front of her. My heart was jack-hammering out of my chest and I couldn't stop shaking, but I wanted this too. I wanted it so fucking much. I pulled my jeans––along with my boxers––down and then kicked them off. I stood stark naked in front of her, my dick was painfully hard and pointed right at her, and yet, I didn't feel embarrassed or ashamed like I thought I would. I just felt a desperate, overwhelming urge to be near her, inside her, as close I could possibly get. I wanted it all.

She lay there looking at me, her chest rising and falling at a rapid pace and her eyes full of lust and love. I swallowed to try and wet my dry throat and crawled back onto the bed.

"Is this okay?" I asked as I pulled the waistband of her joggers over her ass and down her legs. She nodded but didn't say a word. The intensity of this moment was too much for her too.

I threw the joggers on the floor next to my clothes and then sighed at the sight of her in her little black lace knickers. Suddenly, I noticed her expression change. She was nervous.

"What's wrong?" I asked in a low voice. I didn't want her to be scared. "Do you want me to stop?"

"No. It's not that, it's just…"

I climbed back over her, pulled her into my arms and buried my face into her hair as I hugged her.

"What's wrong, Eff? Talk to me."

"I haven't done this before. This is my first time and I'm scared. I don't know what I'm doing."

She sounded so insecure and it broke my heart.

"And you think I do? This is my first time too."

She pulled back and looked me dead in the eyes.

"It is?"

"Of course it is. Do you really think there'd ever be anyone else for me? It's always been you. I'd have waited forever for you, Eff."

I could see the tears in her eyes and I pulled her back into me to hug away her fears.

"You don't know how much it means to me to hear you say that, Finn. All this time, I've always wondered… What with the whole Renaissance Men reputation… I thought…"

"You thought I was like them. That reputation, it's a shitty one, started by Zak, exacerbated by Brandon and totally and utterly despised by Ryan and me. That's not what I'm about."

"I know that. I do. But sometimes, I'd doubt myself."

"Don't. Don't doubt yourself. This, us, it's real. I love you, Effy. I always have. And if that means we stop this now, I'll still be the luckiest guy in the world, walking away knowing Effy Spencer is my girlfriend. She could have anyone but she wants to be with me."

"I love you too," she replied, her voice all breathy and sexy, sending a jolt straight down to my dick. "God, Finn, I want this so much. I want you so much."

I breathed her in and held her in my arms. My whole world. I hated that she'd doubted that she was the one for me, but then I hadn't given her an easy time and I vowed to myself that I'd never do that again. Everything was for her. I had a lot of issues and bullshit going on, but she'd always been the one constant in my life. I wanted to show her what she meant to me.

"I don't want you to stop." She gasped so quietly I almost didn't hear her.

"Are you sure?"

"Yes. Just… bear with me. Be gentle with me."

I stroked her face and placed a soft kiss on her lips.

"I don't know how to be any other way."

EFFY

I'd never been so nervous, excited, scared, and aroused at the same time in my whole life. I'd always dreamed that when the day came, and I lost my 'V' card, it'd be with Finn. But here we were, about to jump over the edge, and I couldn't quite believe it.

When he showed me the Valentine's cards he'd made for me, I knew everything would change. But this was a step into a whole new existence, and as I lay there, watching him watching me, I knew I couldn't wait a second longer to take that leap and make him mine.

Without saying another word, he lifted himself up and then put his thumbs into the sides of my knickers and slowly, teasingly, he pulled them down my legs and off, throwing them onto the floor. I could barely breathe and my whole body was shaking, but when he moved my legs open, I let him. I wanted him to see all of me.

He moved to sit in-between my legs and I felt myself blush as he stared and panted out his own breaths. I was so wet for him, and my core gave an involuntary clench as he grabbed his dick in his hand and gave it a few slow pumps, never taking his eyes off me, lying on my back, fully exposed to him.

"My shy girl isn't so shy anymore." He smiled a wicked smile and I grinned back.

"Neither is my shy boy."

And then I froze as he pushed my legs open wider and lay back down with his head right there.

His tongue licked a slow, painfully seductive trail from my pussy right up to my clit, and then he sucked softly. His eyes met mine as I gasped out and he pulled away––only slightly––and asked me, "Is this okay?"

"More than okay," I replied, breathlessly.

"Am I doing it right?"

"So right."

He licked again, a long steady stroke of his tongue, and when I cried out at the contact with my clit, he whispered, "You like it there?"

I nodded, because the feel of his breath on me and the anticipation of his next lick was too much. I wanted to focus everything on this feeling. Words weren't needed.

He swirled his tongue around my clit and then licked and rubbed over it before sucking it into his mouth. Sometimes he was gentle, sometimes a little harder, but every time it was perfect, and I started to rock my hips into his face to keep the waves of ecstasy going. I went from grabbing my pillow and writhing under him, to reaching for his hair and threading my fingers through the silky strands to guide him. And all the time, he held my legs in place and used his tongue to paint a masterpiece on me.

Just as I was about to cry out for more, he sensed what I needed, and his fingers stroked me as his tongue worked its magic. I moaned and bit my lip as he inserted a finger and curled it perfectly inside. Watching him, with his eyes closed, licking and stroking me into oblivion as he gently rocked himself into the mattress to get the friction he needed was the hottest thing I'd ever experienced in my life. And then he opened his eyes and looked up at me and groaned. The feel of his tongue and the vibrations sent me over the edge and I tensed up, which in turn made him jolt up and ask, "Are you okay?"

"Don't fucking stop," I cried, grabbing his head and pushing it back down. "I'm coming."

He went back to work, literally burying his head in-between my legs like it was his life's mission to make me come. My thighs clamped tightly around his ears and I started to convulse, pulsing with the strongest orgasm I'd ever had. My legs were shaking and I couldn't stop myself from crying out in ecstasy as the walls of my pussy clamped down hard. He groaned when he felt it, and wrung every last drop of my orgasm from my body, never stopping until he sensed that I'd started to relax back into myself again. Coming on Finn Knowles' tongue truly was an out of body experience, and now

I was in a blissful, hazy state of euphoria.

"That was the hottest thing I've ever seen," he said in a husky voice as he crawled up my body, the evidence of my orgasm still coating his face. I smiled and wiped it off then kissed him, grabbing the back of his neck so I could deepen the kiss.

"That was the hottest thing I've ever felt."

He lay over me, his body gently pressing me into the mattress and his dick grazing the inside of my thigh. I looked up at him, looking down on me. Our breaths were panted but shallow, our eyes searching each other's for something neither of us could put into words. What we'd just done was amazing, but I wanted more. He did too.

I reached down between our bodies and took his dick in my hand, giving it slow gentle strokes like I'd seen him do earlier. He held my gaze and rocked gently into me, but when I started to use his dick to rub through my folds, he pulled away and said, "We need to do this right."

He reached down to where his jeans were on the floor and stuck his hand into the pocket. I noticed him blush as he pulled the condom out.

"Are you one hundred percent sure about this?" he asked, holding the packet up apprehensively.

"Yes, now stop asking me and just do it," I snapped, but thankfully, he laughed.

I was fascinated watching him rip the foil and then roll it onto himself. He was long and thick, and even though I was slightly intimidated, I knew I'd definitely be doing that for him next time. He lay back over me and lined himself up. We kissed and I could feel him trying to push into me, but every time he did, I flinched, and sensing my wariness he didn't force it. He let me set the pace.

Every moment that we lay there I became needier, more desperate for him. Always close but never close enough.

"I don't want to hurt you," he whispered into my ear.

"I think you're gonna have to," I said and lifted my knees up so he had better access.

This time, when he pushed himself forward, it was easier. He sank further and further into me and we held each other's gaze, lost in the sensation of us, together. I knew he wasn't fully inside me and I could tell he was holding back, so I grabbed his ass to spur him on. It worked, and he thrust forward, making me cry out as he filled me.

He was panting, holding himself over me and staying still as I got used to the sensation of being stretched by him. That initial thrust had hurt, but now, as I felt myself gripping tightly around him, it didn't hurt as much. It felt new, different, and if I was being honest, totally fucking amazing.

"You can move," I whispered and kissed his shoulder.

He buried his head into my neck and started to swivel his hips slowly.

"Eff, you feel... amazing. I'm not sure I'm gonna last very long."

I didn't care how long he lasted. This was about so much

more than his performance. It was about a connection. Mine and his. After today, every tear and every moment of heartache would be worth it, because he was finally mine.

He pulled out and then pushed back inside me, and I moaned, loving the way it felt to be stretched and massaged in this way. He went slow at first, circling his hips and grinding into me. And all the time, he wrapped me in his arms like I was the most precious thing he'd ever held. On each thrust, he groaned, and it was the sexiest sound I'd ever heard. I wanted to make Finn groan every day. I could come from hearing his voice alone.

I lifted my knees up higher and then wrapped my legs around his waist, moving my hips in time with his and letting him sink deeper into me. I held onto him, running my fingers down his back, and when I touched his ass and felt him clenching as he pushed inside me, I moaned and grabbed harder. It was the sexiest thing ever, feeling him like that.

"Fuck, Eff, I'm so close." He lifted himself up so his weight was balanced on one arm and then looked down to where we were joined; thrusting himself harder and groaning.

"Touch yourself," he moaned. "I need you to come too."

I reached down and started to rub over my clit, but I was so turned on it didn't take long before my second orgasm took hold and my walls clenched, squeezing him and driving him crazy. He placed his hands either side of my head and drove hard into me as I cried out. And then he was there too, thickening and pulsing on cries of 'Oh fuck. Oh yes.' He kept thrusting until he couldn't take it anymore and he collapsed his whole body over mine.

We lay in each other's arms for a few minutes, getting our breath back. Our bodies were slick with sweat, but we didn't care. And the most amazing thing of all was he was still inside me. I never wanted him to leave.

Eventually, he slowly pulled out, but he didn't let me go or roll away. He held me in his arms and kissed me.

"I love you," he said in a sleepy, dreamy voice.

"I love you too." I laughed as his eyes started to drift closed. "You'd better take care of the condom before you fall asleep though."

He grunted and looked down at himself, then sighed.

"I supposed I'd better, but I don't want to leave you."

"I'm not going anywhere. I'll be right here. My bathroom is only there." I pointed to the door opposite my bed.

"You have your own bathroom?" He frowned and I felt embarrassed, realising that ensuite bathrooms probably weren't a thing for him. Emily, Liv, and I, had grown up taking a lot for granted, obviously. "I've got the best girlfriend ever." He laughed.

He went to get up off the bed but I held on for one last hug, pulling him back into me.

"Thank you," I said, holding his face in my hands.

"What for?"

"For making me the happiest girl ever. I never thought we'd get here. But now that we have, I can't stop smiling."

"You should always be smiling. I'm sorry I ever made you frown."

I went to say that he'd made me do a lot more than frown, but I thought better of it. The past was in the past. All that mattered was the future, and I was so excited for mine. Ours.

"I take it this means you've got everything sorted? You're ready to leave those demons of yours behind?" I really hoped he'd say yes, even though I still had a nagging doubt in my mind that something was going to come along to burst our bubble.

Sure enough, my instincts weren't wrong, and he hung his head and sat up, moving away from me.

"Hey, talk to me." I grabbed his arm to stop him making his escape to the bathroom. Those years of avoidance were over. We were a couple now. If something needed facing, we'd do it together.

"It's still not great, but I'm getting there," he admitted.

"And you'll get there a damn sight quicker if you share it with me."

Because I'm not letting you face this alone.

"One day, I will. I promise. But for now, just trust me when I say it's all in hand. I'm not there yet, but I will be. Soon."

This was the story of our lives and I was so over it.

"Don't pull away from me, Finn. Not now. Not after everything. Don't shut me out," I said, but to be honest, he didn't have a choice in the matter. I was here to stay.

He turned and placed his hand over my cheek.

"I'll never shut you out. I'm protecting you from the darkness."

"Your darkness doesn't scare me."

Never had. Never would.

"It scares me. It scares me that it might drag you down too."

"Then join me in the light. God, that sounded cheesy. I'm sorry." I put my hand over my face to hide my embarrassment at how whiney I sounded.

"Don't apologise. It's not cheesy, it's true. You are the light." He took a deep breath and then gave me a quick kiss on the lips. When he pulled away he said, "I'm the best I've ever been. That's all you need to know. And every day is only going to get better. It's our turn now, Eff. Our turn to shine." He pressed his forehead against mine and smiled. "It's all about you."

I laughed.

"That's good enough for me."

And it was. All my life––well, all my teenage life––I'd wanted Finn to notice me. And now, he was making my dreams come true.

I was all he noticed.

Me.

And knowing that made everything else fade into oblivion.

Finn Knowles was and always would be my happily ever

after.

CHAPTER Eighteen
FINN

Never in my wildest dreams did I think I'd turn into one of those guys. The kind that clings to his girlfriend and wishes the rest of the world would fuck off forever. But I *was* that guy now, and when my phone buzzed with a call from Ryan, I didn't want to answer it. I let it go to voicemail and stayed under the covers, holding Effy in my arms as we talked about our plans for the future.

The future.

I couldn't believe I actually might have one of those.

My phone buzzed again a few more times and she insisted that I pick it up, but when I grabbed it off the floor, I saw it wasn't only Ryan trying to get in contact with me, the soldiers were after me as well.

Theirs wasn't a message I wanted to open up in her house. I didn't want any of their filth infecting this part of my life. Looked like I was going to have to check back into reality pretty fucking quickly, and what a shitty reality it was too.

Reluctantly, I got up and started to get myself dressed,

stopping every few seconds to lie back down on the bed she was still lying on and kiss her. I didn't want to leave, but I explained that I needed to see Ryan about our latest party. She'd had the invite, so she knew all about it, and being the perfect girlfriend that she was, she didn't argue. We made plans to go out the next night, and when she walked me to the door, I wrapped my arms around her and hugged her so tightly she gave a little squeak. There was another reason that I loved her; the cute noises she made. The thought of spending the rest of my life with this girl, and finding more and more reasons to love her made me smile. For once, luck was on my side.

I started to walk back towards Zak's place. I hadn't spoken to my parents in weeks, but I really didn't care. They had my number and they hadn't rung me either. Pretty sure if I won the lottery they'd have been kissing my ass though. They only wanted me when I was useful to them, and I wasn't paying rent anymore, so I was officially surplus to requirements.

The roads were quiet, but my mind was not, so I took a detour through the park and headed to the underpass where I'd painted my Effy masterpiece all those months ago. I ducked through the bushes that were growing wild and made my way to the secluded spot, away from prying eyes and listening ears. Leaning against the wall opposite, I grinned to myself when I looked at her. It was a pretty good likeness even if I did say so myself. And then, I ducked my head down and took my phone out of my pocket. From heaven to hell in a matter of seconds.

I opened their text and clicked the video link. It was the same as before, grainy footage taken in the warehouse. The lighting was dimmer this time, but I could still see my uncle slouched forward on the chair he was tied to. His fingers, or rather, the place where his fingers used to be, were a bloody gruesome mess, and he sounded like a wounded animal, crying and groaning in pain.

I turned the volume up, hoping to hear something from the soldiers or some clue as to where they were keeping him, but I couldn't make anything out. The camera panned across his face, his body and then moved back to show the full view of him sitting down again. I heard banging next, which made me flinch slightly with how loud the volume on my phone was turned up. A soldier came into view holding a steel baseball bat. This guy had a black and white bandana tied across his face. It wasn't Adam Noble or Colton King, that much I could tell, but I had no idea who this one was.

He started to laugh like a freak and just stood there, to the side of Tony, looking down at him like this was the funniest thing he'd ever seen. Then he put both hands on his bat and lifted it up, swung it back down and *bang*, he smashed it into Tony's legs. Tony cried out and threw his head back in agony. But this guy didn't let up, he kept going, lifting his bat up and swinging it back down on his knees with so much force I thought the bat would break in two. Tony's legs jolted at first on every impact, but eventually that stopped, and he sat there limp and pathetic as the soldier smashed his kneecaps into dust.

When the guy had had enough, he threw his bat onto the floor and grabbed a fistful of Tony's hair, yanking his head forward to face the camera.

"No more running from the police for you," the guy said in a sing-song voice, toying with my uncle. "You'll never be able to run away from the filth that you are ever again." He pushed my uncle's head back and then wiped his hands on his jeans with a hint of disgust. I held my breath as he walked with a confident swagger towards the camera, staring right into the screen like a psycho, then gave me the peace sign.

And then it cut out.

This wasn't over yet.

My uncle was still alive, still breathing air into his rancid, vile body.

I needed it to be over. For me. I didn't give a shit what they did to him, but I was tired of this. Tired of the constant panic that he might escape. Or that they'd kill him and still spread his vicious legacy wherever they could. Would I ever be free of this nightmare that he'd dragged me into all those years ago?

My skin prickled with revulsion and I felt vulnerable and exposed, even though I was hiding under this underpass. I had to get away. Having her looking down on me while I thought about what he'd done made me want to throw up. So I ran out, sprinting my way back through the park, and when my phone rang again, and I saw it was Ryan, I answered.

"Dude, why are you ghosting me?" He sounded pissed off, but I didn't give a shit.

"I wasn't. I was with Effy." I panted, breathlessly. Not that I felt the need to justify myself. I was tense, antsy, and I had to take it out on someone, right?

"Cool. I'll let you off this time. Em told me you and Eff are official now." News certainly travelled fast. To be honest, I was glad he was chilled out and hadn't picked up on my anxiety. "Are you free to come with us to scope out this factory then or what? It was your idea."

I froze, not really loving the idea of crossing over into Brinton Manor after everything I'd just seen, but I didn't want to raise any suspicions. Not now. There was too much at stake.

"I'm ready when you are."

"Be at Zak's in ten minutes or we're leaving without you." Ryan was back to his matter-of-fact, curt responses.

I heard some sort of commotion down the phone, like he'd dropped it, but then Brandon's voice came through and I knew he'd grabbed it off Ryan to say his piece.

"Get here when you can. We aren't going there without you. Ignore the grumpy fucker. I think Emily's on her period or something. He's in a foul mood."

I laughed at Brandon's remark. He always had this uncanny knack of pulling me out of my slump.

"Fuck you," Ryan said in the background just as the

phone cut off.

I sighed and stuffed my phone into my back pocket. Being a part of so many different worlds was getting exhausting, but my fate was already sealed. I'd played their game, and as it stated in the title, there were consequences. Mine being that I would forever be plagued by Brinton Manor and the devils that inhabited it until the day I took my final challenge. Whatever and whenever that would be.

—

Thirty minutes later, I was in the back of Ryan's car with Zak. Brandon sat in the front, and despite the chatter about football and cars, there was still a sense of tension in the atmosphere.

Or maybe that was just me?

I was finding it hard to separate all the factors of my life. Juggling so many balls and spinning plates was becoming difficult to maintain. I'd spent my whole life compartmentalising everything and putting on a show for the appropriate audience, so they wouldn't see the cracks beneath the surface. But those cracks were widening, and I had no control over it. The only constant and positive thing I had right now was Effy and my friends. I didn't want to fuck any of that up.

"It's looking good for the auction coming up," Ryan announced.

"What auction?" Brandon shot back.

"The one to buy Sandland Asylum. It's being held in a few weeks' time, dumbass." I saw Ryan giving Brandon the side eye. "Emily has a lot of collateral to put forward, and her Gran has offered up some of the money too. I think she feels guilty for being a useless piece of shit after all the crap that went down with Em's parents."

"I'm happy for you." I don't think Brandon could've sounded more unenthusiastic even if he tried, and the way he stared blankly out of the window only highlighted the fact that he had absolutely no interest whatsoever. "We'll all come and visit once you start up your new business."

"Our business," Ryan bit back. "I don't care who invests what; money, time, it's all the same to me. We work together or we don't work at all. I'm doing this for us."

Brandon turned to look at him, furrowing his brow in confusion. "You want us all to be equal partners, even if we don't contribute the same amount of cash?"

"Yes. Partners being the operative word. Me and Emily, you and Harper, Finn and Effy, and Zak and whatever flavour of the month he wants to bring to the table."

Zak folded his arms over his chest and laughed. Brandon nodded his head in affirmation and went back to staring out the window. And I took a long, deep breath. The fact that he'd acknowledged that there was an Effy and me made me tingle with pride. It felt good to be part of our team.

"You're a good man, Hardy. Shit taste in music though," Brandon joked, flicking the radio from Taylor Swift to fill the car with a bit of Shinedown and bobbing his head in time to the beat.

I held the arm of the car door as Ryan took a corner a little too fast and we entered the main street into Brinton Manor. My recent graffiti with the five skulls stood out like a beacon as we drove down that road, and I saw Ryan slap the side of Brandon's leg and nod over to it. Neither one of them said a word, but Brandon turned in his seat to look at me. He knew that was my work, and judging by the way he narrowed his eyes, he knew there was more to this party and the location of it than I'd let on. I swallowed nervously and braced myself to answer his questions, but he didn't speak, just turned back around and folded his arms. He'd got the disappointed father act down to a tee already and I hung my head, suddenly feeling ashamed.

We raced through the empty streets, all looking out the windows at the derelict buildings and dirty pavements of a broken town.

"Do you think people are actually gonna come here, to this party? This place is a right crap hole." Zak screwed his nose up in disgust and sat back in his seat.

"They'll show up anywhere if we tell them to. It's gonna be fucking awesome," Brandon replied, keeping his eyes on the road ahead of us.

The car started to bump us around as Ryan pulled off the road and into the uneven car park of the plastics factory. He parked up right by the entrance and shut the engine off, peering up and out of the front windscreen at the building ahead.

"It's certainly big enough," he said, then turned to face me. "Are we gonna have trouble filling this thing?"

"No. It looks big, but once you get inside, you'll see how perfect it is. There's a main entrance where we can set up all the security checks. That leads onto a larger hall where Zak can do his stuff. The rest of the rooms can be opened or cordoned off depending on how much of it we want to use. It's pretty safe in there too. No dodgy flooring or anything like that."

I had done my homework. This was the best that Brinton had to offer. There'd be a lot less work setting up this place than we'd done in previous venues.

"Let's take a look then," Brandon announced, opening his door and stepping out.

We all followed him, slamming our car doors shut and picking our way across the rubble. The front gate leading into the factory was held closed by a chain and a broken padlock. It'd been like that when I'd first come here myself, and I guessed that the iffy security was the work of the soldiers. They probably used it as a base for whatever the fuck it was they did when they weren't screwing with me or torturing my uncle. It had crossed my mind that they might have been keeping him here, but I searched all over and they weren't. This place was clean. Well, as clean as a forgotten rundown factory could be in this area.

Ryan entered the building first, and when he pushed the doors open, the birds that'd taken up residence inside started to flap around wildly. It wasn't as damp in here as the waterworks we'd used previously, but there was still a musty, earthy smell about the place that made us cover our noses until we grew accustomed to it. The walls were sturdy enough and the opportunity to create my art here was one of the positives. I'd found another blank canvas, a new gallery to showcase my work. Every cloud and all that.

The lads nodded their approval and we wandered around checking windows were boarded up securely and that any fixtures weren't a hazard. Then, when we entered the main hall, I heard them gasp and whistle.

"This is fucking amazing, Finn. You did good." Ryan glanced up at the high glass ceiling that was surprisingly still intact and he spun in a circle, clearly in awe of the place.

"There's an anti-hall just to the left there, but I'm not sure whether we'll use it because of the staircases and landings around it. It kind of looks like a Victorian prison to be honest."

There were about three levels to that hall, and each one had a walkway running the perimeter of the room, with wrought iron railings painted white, making it look like Broadmoor. But when we walked in to have a look, Brandon's eyes grew wide in wonder.

"This is perfect for the fight." He pointed to the different levels. "The crowd stand up there and everyone gets a ringside seat. The further up you go, the better view you get. I'm having this," he stated, crossing his arms over his chest proudly. "My fighters are gonna love it."

"Are Callum and Joe still up for it?" Ryan asked, referring to the boxers Brandon had lined up for the night.

"Yep. Got a few other lads that want in too. I'm thinking it'll be a few matches that night. It's gonna be a top night."

Everything was coming together. The boys were happy. The venue was perfect. And I'd passed my second challenge with flying colours and come out the other side smelling of roses growing amongst all the shit.

Or so I thought.

The other three wandered off to check out the rest of the factory, but when my phone started to buzz and I saw why, I stayed back. The nerves kicked in again and my stomach turned over as I opened the message.

Challenge time, Mr Knowles. Are you ready?

A close friend of ours, Joe Hazel, is signed up to fight at your little party. Your next challenge, should you choose to accept it, is to get your man, Brandon, to fight against him.

No Brandon.

No deal.

And your little secret goes viral.

Now, you may be asking yourself, why not bite the bullet? Call our bluff and see if we have the guts to go through with it? I suggest you don't do that. I'm sending you a little video that might help to persuade you on this. If we get confirmation of Brandon fighting by midnight on Friday then you're safe. Nothing, and we will fucking destroy your life.

I was shaking so badly it was difficult to tap my screen and see what they'd sent. When I clicked it open, I almost lost it completely. I felt the bottom fall out of my world.

There was video footage of me that I knew had been taken today because I was wearing the exact same clothes. That, and I was coming out of Effy's front door. I gripped my mobile in my sweaty hand as I watched her close the front door, and saw myself walk away down the street. But whoever was recording didn't walk away, they started walking forwards, down her driveway, up the side of her house, and then they were videoing her through the window. I watched them watching her making herself a cup of coffee. After a few seconds of watching and feeling like I was dying inside, I saw the camera pan down to the door handle leading into her kitchen, and a gloved hand pushed it down and the door opened. The video stopped, and so did my fucking heart. They'd got to Effy, and whoever was videoing her had broken into her fucking house.

I didn't bother to read their next message. Frantically, I scrolled to her number and felt every beat of my heart thumping against my chest as the dial tone sounded in my ear.

"Hey, Finn. Are you missing me already?" She sounded so playful, but it did nothing to calm my raging mind. There would be no relief, not until I knew she was safe.

"Where are you?" I snapped a little too harshly.

"I'm at home. Why? What's happened?" Instantly, her playfulness had gone and in its place was suspicion.

"Is there anyone with you?"

Please tell me you're safe. I don't know what I'd do if anything happened to you.

"Mum and Dad just came home with a Chinese takeaway. What the hell is going on?"

"So you're safe? Your dad's there?"

"Yes, but now I'm worried sick about you. Are you okay?" I wasn't. I was a nervous, erratic mess and I couldn't even think straight let alone form words that made sense.

"I'm fine," I lied. "Listen, I need you to go to your back door. The one opposite the island in your kitchen and lock the bloody thing." It was on the tip of my tongue to have a go at her over that fact that it was ever open in the first place.

"Okay. Wait. How do you know where my back door is? You've never been in my kitchen. And how do you know it's open?"

"Jesus, Effy. I don't have time for this. Just do it. Please."

I heard her breathing down the line as she walked from wherever she was to the kitchen and then she said, "Done. I've locked it."

"Do you always leave the back door open?" My resolve to not accuse her of shit had broken pretty fucking quickly. I knew she lived in a nicer part of Sandland, but who the fuck leaves their doors unlocked in this day and age?

"I leave it open when Luna needs to go outside to the

garden. What the hell is this, Finn? You're freaking me out."

I was freaking myself out.

"Are you sure no one got in? Are you absolutely sure you're safe?"

"Yes. If anyone had got in the CCTV would have picked it up."

Bingo.

"You have CCTV?"

"Yes. Dad had it installed ages ago when all the stuff with the Lockwood's cars getting trashed happened."

"Where?"

"Where what?"

"Where are the cameras?" My instincts told me that if they were outside, the soldiers probably would've disabled them somehow. But I could always pray for a miracle. Maybe they weren't as clever as they thought they were.

"One on the front door, one over the garage doors and one in the back garden," she answered.

"Does it cover your kitchen door?"

"Well, no. It covers the patio doors, but Dad had internal cameras put in too. Only downstairs though, you don't need to worry. Is that what this about? You coming over earlier? Are you worried Mum and Dad will have seen you?" Her naivety was endearing but it worried me to death. She wasn't street-smart enough to deal with the kind of problems I had going on in my life.

"No. It's me checking you're safe."

"Finn, if anyone tried to break in we'd know about it. The kitchen sensor picks up any movement. I'm fine. Stop worrying."

Something wasn't adding up.

"And the sensors didn't pick anything up after I left you?"

"Well, no. They weren't switched on."

"You're fucking joking me? What about the CCTV outside?"

"I switched that off too."

Un-fucking-believable. I threw my head back and let out a frustrated growl.

"Jesus Christ, Eff. What's the point in having security if you don't use it?"

"I switched it off because I was at home and it's daytime. What the hell do you think is going to happen?" She was getting pissed off, I could tell by the way her tone of voice was getting higher and higher, but I was pissed off too. I couldn't understand why she saw the issue of her own safety as such a hassle. An inconvenience. I'd thought everybody lived on high alert, forever on guard in case the worst should happen. Evil didn't always wait until it was dark to strike.

I ran my hand over my face and sighed. This wasn't her fault, I knew that. She lived a different life to the one I was used to. If I wasn't careful this was going to turn into an argument, and I really didn't want that on day one of us being together.

"I'm sorry. I fell asleep and had a bad dream. When I

woke up I panicked and needed to make sure you were okay. Don't hate me. It's only 'cos I love you."

She sighed right back at me.

"I'm okay. I wish I was there to hug you though and make you feel better. You sounded crazy when I answered the phone."

"I was." Crazy was putting it mildly. I was about to self-combust. "Eff, I have to go. I think Zak's ordered a pizza and the delivery guy is at the door." I was surprised how easily the lies were rolling off my tongue today. "I'll speak to you later, yeah?"

"Okay. I love you." Her voice was back to its playful sweet tone, and even though my heart was still splintered into a million pieces, piercing my lungs and making it difficult to breathe, some of the fog in my brain began to clear.

"I love you too," I whispered down the phone to her. Then, I hung up and reluctantly I clicked onto their text message.

Do we have a deal?

Before I could type a response, I heard movement coming from behind me.

"I knew it," Brandon hissed. "I knew there was more to this than just a convenient venue and some bullshit about them being your friends. They're threatening you, aren't they? The Brinton crew have something over you. Or is it your uncle who's behind all this?"

Brandon stood in the doorway but he didn't look mad, he

looked concerned.

"How much did you hear?" I really hoped I could formulate a plan and talk myself out of this.

"All of it. You thought someone had broken into Effy's house. Are they threatening her too? I swear to God, I will cause a fucking shit-storm if they are. I'll fuck them up so badly they'll wish they'd never met you. He'll wish he'd never touched——"

I cut him off. "I can handle this."

"Can you? Because from where I'm standing you're not. You're doing a really shitty job of keeping it together. You're shaking, sweating, losing your shit, and I'm not about to stand by and watch that happen... Not again."

I took a few deep breaths. There was no time like the present to ask him if he'd consider fighting. It wasn't like things could get any worse for me.

"Brandon. I need a favour."

"You need a favour? Or are they forcing you to ask me for a favour?"

"Does it matter?"

He didn't answer and so I carried on.

"I need you to fight. At the party. I need you to fight Joe Hazel."

Brandon bit his lip, smiling an ironic smile and shook his head.

"Un-fucking-believable. You know I can't do that. Harper was put on bed rest earlier today. Her blood pressure is through the roof. Doctors are worried about her. I can't do that to her."

Fuck.

I darted my eyes left and right trying to think of another solution.

"What if we just advertised that you were fighting but changed it at the last minute?" I was starting to sound desperate. Hell, I was desperate.

"Mate, you're not making any sense. Why would I do that?"

"Because if I can't prove that you're gonna fight on that night then I'm a fucking dead man." Nothing like being brutally honest to get what you want.

"No one is going near you. I'd never let anyone hurt you."

"You can't be there all the time, though, can you?" I grabbed a fistful of my hair and groaned. "Ugh. I didn't mean literally dead. I meant figuratively. My life won't be worth living if you're not fighting."

I slumped down onto the floor, sitting against the wall and burying my head in my hands. This was useless. I didn't want Brandon to fight either, and I'd never put Harper or the babies at risk. I was cornered by the wolves, and there was no way out.

"It's fine," I stated like I believed it. "I'll think of something else. Forget I even said anything. Harper and the babies come first. You're not fighting."

"You're desperate. I've never seen you like this. I'm

gonna go and pay these fucking soldiers a visit. Let them know--"

"Please don't," I begged, cutting him off. "I know you want to help but that'll only make it worse. Plus, you need to think about Harper and the babies. Would she want you stirring up shit with the Brinton lot?"

"No, but I don't like feeling fucking useless." He gritted his teeth and cracked his knuckles, giving a glare that told me he was on his last nerve. Holding back wasn't Brandon's strong point.

"I don't know what to say." My fight had turned into flight. My best option looked like leaving Sandland forever, just like Alice had told me to, but thinking about that made my heart hurt. I could never walk away from Effy.

"I'll do it." I snapped my head back to look at Brandon as he spoke, feeling like I'd just been smacked in the face. "Well, maybe not the whole fight, but you can use my name if it'll help to get you out of whatever hole you're in. Personally, I'd rather leave here and tear down Brinton looking for those fuckers, then rip their throats out for ever talking to you, but I guess that'll be bad for Harper's stress levels too." He huffed out a laugh but neither one of us found this situation funny.

"I wouldn't want that either," I said, looking up at him from my place on the floor. I knew it went against every fibre of Brandon's being to give in to blackmail and play their game, but the rules changed when you were a family man, and he had other priorities now.

"Give me a few hours to talk to Harper, then I'll announce it myself on social media and you can send the screenshots to whoever needs to see it. Is that okay? Will that be enough?"

I nodded and he walked over to me, putting his arm out to help me stand up.

"Looks like we have a winner, lads," Ryan shouted, coming back into the hall and bristling with excitement.

"Certainly does." Brandon glanced to the side and gave me a wink. "Think I might even come out of retirement to fight here myself. It'll kill me to sit on the side-lines and watch."

Ryan's eyes went wide and he shook his head disapprovingly.

"You're a glutton for punishment," Zak said, appearing from behind Ryan and smirking. "Harper will never forgive you."

Ryan narrowed his gaze at Brandon but didn't question him. My guess was Ryan knew something wasn't right too, but like Brandon, he wasn't ready to tackle us about it.

"She loves me," Brandon replied, giving his signature grin. "Besides, I'll tell her it's my final curtain call before the babies come." I had to admit, he was putting on a very convincing performance.

"Yeah, she's gonna love you having two black eyes in the delivery ward. Or better yet, lying in a bed next to her as she gives birth," Ryan snapped.

"Two for one." Zak laughed.

"We don't do things by halves." Brandon smiled and rubbed his hands together like he was relishing the thought.

"Mathers, you're gonna be the death of me," Ryan chastised him as he headed towards us. "I'd better warn Em. She likes watching you fight about as much as Harper does."

"Better get that ring on her finger then. She can spend the night looking at that instead." Brandon bumped his shoulder into Ryan's as he walked past and made his way back into the main hall.

"Already in hand, my friend. Just watch this space."

CHAPTER Nineteen

FINN

Ryan dropped us all back home, and within the hour, Brandon had posted online that he was fighting at the next event. Sure enough, his socials blew up, everyone believed it. He sent me a text to let me know that he'd told Harper everything. They didn't keep secrets and he needed her to understand that it was all fake. I messaged back asking him how we were going to get out of this once the date for the fight drew closer, but he told me we'd cross that bridge when we came to it. I had to hand it to him. He'd always come through for me. Always.

-

That night, I turned up at Effy's door wearing my smartest jeans and white shirt under my leather jacket. It was our first official date and I felt slightly guilty about that. She'd agreed to be my girlfriend, given herself to me, and I hadn't even bought her a drink. It was official; I was a sucky boyfriend.

The door opened and I braced myself, wearing my cheeky grin to start this date off on the right foot. When I saw her dad standing on the other side, my face grew hot, and I knew I was blushing and probably looked like a grade A loser.

He stuck his hand out to shake mine and I took it, shaking it back with a tight grip. I had to redeem my credibility in some way.

"It's good to see you, Finn. Come on in." He held the door open and stepped back to let me past. "Effy's still upstairs getting ready but we're just having a glass of wine. Come and join us."

I stuttered over my words as I walked into the foyer and glanced around, begging Effy to suddenly emerge and save me from my awkwardness.

"I don't drink wine," I said by way of an answer.

Her dad laughed. "You don't have to drink wine, we have beer too."

"I don't really drink beer either." He raised his eyebrows at me. "Okay, maybe I do drink beer, but I'm taking your daughter out tonight. I should really keep a clear head."

He slapped me on the back, still laughing.

"That's exactly the reason you should have a drink. Are you driving?"

"No."

"Then have one. It might help you lighten up. You seem nervous."

I was always nervous. That was nothing new for me.

He led me into their living room, where Effy's mum was sat on the sofa reading her kindle. She looked up when she saw me and grinned, putting her kindle down to give me her full attention.

"Finn! Sit down." She patted the seat next to her. Jesus, I was going to need that drink after all. "Where are you off to tonight?"

I got tongue-tied answering, telling her I was taking Effy to the cinema and maybe for something to eat afterwards. Luna, the dog, must've smelt my fear because she came bounding in, tried to jump up on my lap, and then after a bit of fuss she settled for lying right over my feet, like she was guarding me. I reached down to give her head a scratch and then told Effy's mum that I'd have Effy home before her curfew. I didn't want them getting their pitchforks out for me quite yet.

"She doesn't have a curfew," her dad, Steve, announced as he came back into the room holding a bottle of beer out for me. "She's almost nineteen years old. We're just relieved she tells us where she's going and who with. We're her parents not her keepers."

I didn't know what to say to that. Parents, keepers, it was all the same thing in my book. Not that mine had ever been either for Alice or me. Promises, memories, trust, they didn't *keep* any of it.

I must've been silent and staring at the floor for too long because Steve sighed and sat down next to me, and Jen, Effy's mum, put her hand over mine and patted it before sitting back onto the sofa to let her husband do the talking.

"Finn, we like you, we trust you and you make Effy happy. That's all we care about. When you come into our home we want you to feel welcome. There's no hidden agenda here. I'm not about to go all psycho, over-protective father on you. Don't get me wrong, if you hurt her, I will hunt you down. But I don't think you're that kind of boy, are you? Not from what I've seen and heard. I… *we*… think you're one of the good guys, and we're very good judges of character."

"Yes, we are," Jen piped up.

I took a swig of my beer and then placed it down on the coffee table in front of me, making sure I used a coaster.

"I wouldn't ever hurt her," I said, honestly. "I love her."

"We know," Jen replied. "A blind man can see how much you two love each other. We think it's sweet."

"I'm guessing you haven't heard a lot of positive things about yourself over the years," Steve continued. "But we brought our daughter up right. Being with her should give you all the confidence you need. Be proud of yourself. I know she's proud of you."

Right on cue, Effy walked into the room, looking like every dream I'd ever wished for. She was wearing a burgundy floaty dress that skimmed her ass, and boots that went right up to her thighs. My mouth was literally hanging open when I said, "You look stunning." Then I turned to Steve to see if he was going to tear me a new one and send her back upstairs to get changed.

"You do," was how he responded, and I felt stunned into silence. I couldn't believe there were parents out there like this. I mean, Ryan's dad, Sean, he was the best, but if Ryan had a sister, you can bet your ass she wouldn't get that reaction.

Effy's parents were actually cool. They liked me, and they loved their daughter unconditionally. My shoulders eased up slightly, and I had to admit, I was beginning to feel comfortable sitting here. Maybe family wasn't so bad after all?

"Thanks." She smiled and then pointed right at me. "Sitting on the sofa in-between my parents and drinking beer? Where's Finn and what have you done to him?"

I chuckled and threw back the last of the beer before I stood up.

"It's called family bonding." Steve smirked. "You kids have a good time now. We won't wait up."

—

I let Effy choose the film we watched. I say watched, but I spent most of it cuddling up to her, kissing her, and watching her face as she laughed at the screen. I found her far more entertaining than the movie, I could watch her all day. When she rested her head on my shoulder halfway through, I pulled her into me and enjoyed the feeling of being at peace.

When the movie credits started to roll, we followed the rest of the people out into the foyer. Effy needed to use the ladies, so I took the opportunity to head to the men's room. That was my first mistake of the night.

I pushed the doors open and strolled in, surprised to find it empty, but when the doors behind me banged against the wall and I turned around to see why, I instantly regretted my decision to come in here. Adam Noble, Colton King and Devon Brady stood in front of the exit, blocking any possible escape I could make. The Soldiers of Anarchy were channelling their horsemen of the apocalypse vibe. I was glad there was only three of them and not four, not that either odds were in my favour, but I figured the others were keeping watch over Tony.

"What do you want?" I hissed, keeping my voice level and my stance strong. As Brandon had taught me all those years ago, you can never show weakness. These vultures would smell it a mile off.

Adam smirked, putting the hood from his black jacket down. Even without their masks, bandanas, or balaclavas, they all still looked like evil motherfuckers. But tonight they'd attempted to blend in with the standard teenage crowd. It wasn't working. They still looked like three psychos on a day trip from the detention centre.

"Having a nice night?" he asked me, knowing he was being ironic but enjoying fucking with me all the same.

"I was until you showed up. Isn't your online bullying enough? Gotta taunt me out here too?"

"I'd be careful how you speak to us, Knowles. You're not in a position of power, and you'd do well to remember that."

His grin turned to a scowl and he looked at me like he was trying to burn holes through my soul.

"Story of my life." I shrugged like it meant nothing. "Do you actually think I give a fuck anymore?"

At that moment, the door behind them swung open and some guy strolled in. Adam glanced over his shoulder and using his cold, psycho persona he said, "We're closed. Fuck off."

The guy's eyes grew wide when he saw what was going on and he spun round and left as quickly as he'd entered. From the recognition behind his stare, I guessed he wasn't off to get help. Typical coward.

"You give a fuck, of course you do, otherwise you wouldn't be jumping every time we tell you to." Adam snapped right back to business. "How is Alice, by the way? Still avoiding Brinton? That's a shame really. We were looking forward to getting to know her."

Hearing him say Alice's name instantly made my back go up.

"Stay away from my sister." I clenched my fists and braced myself. If they'd come in here for a fight, I'd give them one. I might not have Brandon's strength, but he'd taught me a few moves that'd help. I wouldn't make it easy for them.

"Guess we'll have to settle for that little brunette you've been pawing over all night. Can't say I blame you. Tight little ass and pert tits. I'll look forward to meeting her soon myself."

Anger meet uncontrollable fucking fury.

"Stay the fuck away from her! You can do all the fucked up shit you want to me, but I swear to God, if you go anywhere near her, I will kill you." I'd die for her. Nobody was getting near her. Not again.

"Those are big threats for a little man. I think you should stay in your lane, Knowles. You can't run with the big boys. You're not in our league. Now Mathers, that's a different story. Nice touch getting him to announce the fight on his socials by the way. But you know…" Adam took a step forward to try and intimidate me, and the two stood beside him followed suit. "I'm starting to think something isn't right." He tilted his head as he spoke, making him look more demonic and psychotic than he usually did. "I've got a good feeling for things like that you see, it's like a sixth sense. So, I figured it was time I paid you a visit. Reminded you what's at stake here. You see… if you try and pull a fast one, get Mathers to back out at the eleventh hour, you and Alice won't be the only ones with a tale to tell about old Uncle Tony. I wander what would happen if we left that little brunette you're with tonight in a room alone with him? He might have no fingers and busted up knees, but his dick is still intact."

Forget red rags to a bull, he was throwing gasoline onto the fire that was my rage.

"You're fucking sick, mate. Sick in the head," I said, hitting my temple with my finger.

"Yep." He shrugged matter-of-fact. "To be fair, it'd be a waste sending her to him. Might keep her for ourselves. Do you reckon she can take five men at once? She might prefer it, after bouncing up and down on your needle dick and getting nothing in return."

Hearing his sick remark, I charged forward, but Devon and Colton grabbed me, each one holding me by the arms to keep me in place.

"No need to get all defensive." Adam stood square in front of me, pushing his face right into mine so our noses were almost touching. And then he did that insane twist of his head again, tilting it to the side like his brain was as imbalanced as his morals. "Because it's not going to happen, is it? You're going to be a good boy and do as you're told. That way, everyone gets what they want. Except Uncle Tony that is. He gets fucked up, but does anyone really care?" He patted my cheek, smiling, and took a step back. "You can let him go now. I think he's got the message."

Devon and Colton loosened their grip and I shrugged them away roughly then rubbed over my biceps where they'd squeezed too tightly and probably left a mark.

"Check your inbox, Knowles... And you're welcome. We'll be in touch with the next task." He turned to walk out and then spun back round to face me. "You're so close to the end, I can almost taste it," he teased and stuck his tongue out like the freak he was. And then they were gone, and I was left standing there, wondering when I'd become such a pushover.

Time to start fighting back, Knowles.

That war you wanted to win might've changed course

and it might involve a whole new strategy, but you've lost focus.

That stops now.

You can still play their games and come out the winner. All you've got to do is keep your eyes on the prize. After everything you've been through, you've proven time and time again that you are unbreakable.

He might've stolen your past, but he sure as hell won't rob you of your future.

I leant against the wall and let my head fall back. Then, when I was done putting it off, I pulled my phone out and opened up their video. This time there was a soldier stood behind Tony as he sat slumped forward, moaning and bleeding. I was pretty sure it was Colton, I recognised the tattoos on his hand as he held up a knife. He had his hood up and a black bandana over his face, but in his eyes I could see pure excitement. He loved the thrill of it all.

He grabbed a fistful of Tony's hair and pulled his head up, then I felt my stomach roll over as I watched him take the blade to Tony's face and slice again and again. Tony's muffled screams pierced the air as he tensed with every cut. Eventually, all I could see was blood soaking through where his face had been. Chunks of flesh falling away and Colton laughing.

Then a voice closer to the camera said, "You're as ugly on the outside as you are on the inside, aren't you? Dirty, filthy, paedo scum. We should let you choke on your own blood, but we haven't finished with you yet."

Colton nodded and lifted Tony's head back up, then held the knife under his chin, ready to make that fatal cut. And then darkness. The video cut off.

I couldn't stop shaking. I went over to the sink to splash cold water on my face and then stared at myself in the mirror.

"You're so close to the end, I can almost taste it."

That's what they'd said, and I believed them. They were going to slit his throat, but they needed one more favour from me. One more task and this would all be over.

The door behind me opened and a guy walked in and asked, "Are you Finn?"

I eyed him suspiciously.

"Yeah, why?"

"Because there's a girl outside who asked me to come in here and check that you're okay," he said, thumbing behind him.

Fuck.

Effy.

I pocketed my phone and pushed my way past him. When I made it back into the now-deserted foyer she was frowning with worry.

"Are you okay? You were in there for ages. Do you feel sick?"

I did feel sick, but not in the way she assumed. I was sick because of what I'd watched, sick of being fucked by life and sick of getting back up to fight every damn day. It was exhausting.

"I'm fine," I stated a little too abruptly. "We need to leave." I stormed ahead, taking purposeful strides towards the exit, but when I noticed she wasn't following me, I stopped and spun back around. "What?" I held my arms up, questioning why she was still standing in the same spot with her arms folded and her face like thunder. That's when I realised I'd made my second mistake of the night. I'd pissed my girlfriend off.

"No." She unfolded her arms to point at me like she was a teacher scolding a kid. "You don't get to do that. Not anymore."

"Do what?" My innocent act was shit. I knew I was behaving like an ass, but I had to roll with it. Stubbornness was another one of my traits that I couldn't seem to shake, and so I owned it. "What is it I've done wrong, huh?"

"Walk away from me as if nothing happened. You were fine when you went in there and now you're out here and back to being an arsehole. But tough shit, Finn. I'm your girlfriend now and I get to call you out on it. Cut the bullshit or at least tell me what's wrong."

I threw my head back and sighed then ran both of my hands through my hair, tugging on the ends in frustration.

"I'm fine."

"Again. Bullshit. If you were really fine then why are you acting like a prick?"

I couldn't help but smile. I actually liked that she was

calling me out on my shit. It showed she really cared.

"I'm just stressed out. I got a message when I was in there and now I'm pissed." I figured I'd give her the P.G. version of events.

"What message?" She narrowed her eyes at me. She wasn't about to give it up anytime soon.

"A message from the boys." I wasn't lying. I just hadn't specified which boys. "This party we're doing, it's all getting out of hand." Again, no lie there. It was out of hand. Every day it drew closer was another day I lived with the dread of what would happen. I had a bad feeling about it and I knew the soldiers had something planned. Something which was aimed at destroying me.

"If you need help, I can help you. You only need to ask. Even if it's just to sound off. But let's get one thing very, *very* clear, Finn Knowles." She started to walk slowly towards me, still pointing and still looking pissed off. "You don't walk away from me again. Not ever. You've done it enough, and I won't stand for it anymore. Understood?" She stopped right in front of me and cocked her head, only this was cute and playful and made me grin like an idiot.

"Understood." I gave her a cheeky captain's salute which made her laugh. Then I knew she'd forgiven me when she wrapped her arms around my waist.

"Good. We're a team, remember? That's the deal." She gave me a cheeky wink and it broke my sour mood completely. This girl was the sparkle and sunshine to my grey clouds.

Being with her made me want to shake off the masks I'd always worn that had held me back from knowing what true love felt like. I kissed her forehead and returned the hug, wanting to absorb everything about her into my whole being.

"Are you gonna be okay?" she asked, peering up at me with her gorgeous brown eyes full of concern.

"I am now I've got you in my arms." I groaned. "Jeez, that sounded cheesy even for me."

"It's a good job I happen to like cheese." She grinned back, and I was relieved that the storm brewing between us only moments ago was fading into the distance. Smiling, I leant down to plant a kiss on her lips.

"Let's get out of here."

"Do you want to go and get something to eat?" she asked, threading her arm around my waist as we started to walk towards the exit.

"I'm not hungry. I mean, I will if you want to, but right now, I just want to be alone in the car with you."

"Me too." She squeezed my side and I vowed to put all the bullshit to the back of my mind for a few more hours. She deserved that much.

-

We drove around for a while, chatting about anything and everything. Eventually, she pulled into the empty car park at the back of the waterworks where we'd held one of our last parties. She left the engine running so the heaters stayed warm, but when she turned to me there was a mischievous glint in her eyes.

"Let's get in the back," she said, breathing a little deeper and then biting her lip.

I didn't need to be asked twice. I reached across the middle console, and with the palm of my hand I stroked across her cheek and then pulled her towards me for a kiss. I threaded my fingers through the hair at the back of her neck as we lost ourselves in each other.

The kiss started off slow and tender, but soon the intensity of our feelings took over and it became deeper, more desperate. She pulled away first, placing her hand on my chest and panting out her breaths as she said, "Back seat. Now."

The way she spoke, staring at me from under her eyelashes in such a needy way was the sexiest thing ever, and I nodded, climbing over and then sitting back with my legs open and my arms resting over the top of the back seats. When she climbed over after me, I reached out to pull her across safely and then she straddled me and I gripped her waist, wanting to have her as close as I could.

"I need you," she whispered into my ear and ground down onto my rock-hard dick.

I tilted my head and started to kiss her again. This time there was no slow, only greedy. We couldn't get enough of tasting each other, swirling our tongues together and moaning with how turned on we were. I put my hands flat on her thighs and ran them higher and higher up her legs until I was underneath the soft fabric of her dress. I groaned, realising she was wearing a thong, and palmed her ass hard as she lifted herself up to give me better access.

She whimpered as I smoothed my hands over her ass and then squeezed.

"Do you like that?" I asked, kissing down her neck and biting into her soft skin.

"I love everything you do to me," she replied, all breathy and sexy. "Touch me here." She reached back to take my hand and guided it between her legs.

I used my fingers to rub her through the lace. She was wet and feeling it made my dick strain hard in my pants.

"More," she whispered, and I lifted the fabric to the side and started to run my fingers through her folds.

"Like this?"

She buried her face into my neck as her hips rocked on my hand and she grabbed the back of my neck as she moaned, "Right there, but I need you inside me too."

I knew what she needed, but I wasn't done playing yet. I could feel the hard nub of her clit and I smoothed my thumb up and down, then around. With my fingers, I stroked her and then pushed inside of her.

"Oh God, Finn. Just like that." She held my neck tighter and fucked my hand, gasping into my ear and growing wetter as I curled my fingers inside her and stroked her walls.

"So good," she said, angling her hips, and then she reached down and put her hand over mine, setting the pace, directing where she needed me to touch and rubbing herself hard into my palm. I watched her face as she closed her eyes, and then she threw her head back and I felt her pulsing as she came for me.

"So beautiful," I whispered, watching her come down from her high. When she opened her eyes I saw so much love and lust I couldn't wait any longer.

"I really need to fuck you."

She didn't answer, just nodded and pulled her thong down. I undid the button of my jeans with her still on top of me, and pushed them down to my ankles. I did the same with my boxers, but she helped me this time. Then, I held my breath as she ran her hand in-between my thighs and then cupped my balls, massaging and stroking them. Watching her hands on me, touching me, was everything. She moved to hold my dick and started to give me slow spine-tingling pumps and I threw my head back, savouring every single sensation.

"Do you still want to fuck me?" she asked, as if that was even a valid question at this point.

"More than I want to breathe."

I opened my eyes to find her staring straight at me.

"How do you want me?" she asked.

"On top. I want you riding my dick." I put my hand over hers and gave my dick a squeeze, then reached down and pulled a condom out of the pocket of my jeans. I lifted the packet to my mouth and her eyes shone as I ripped the foil with my teeth.

"Can I put it on?" she asked, biting that damn lip of hers, and it crossed my mind that a blow job would be really fucking awesome. The thought of having her lips wrapped around my cock made me want to come then and there. But I shelved that thought--for now--and smirked as I handed her the condom.

"Be my guest." I wriggled my hips forward and settled back.

She placed the condom onto my tip and rolled it slowly down over my cock using a firm grip, and I groaned. It certainly felt better than putting it on myself. And now, all I could think about was being inside her, feeling her walls around me, gripping me and squeezing. I was addicted to her and I fucking loved it.

Her legs were open and she was hovering right over me, still holding my dick. I lifted the skirt of her dress so I could watch her as she rubbed me through her folds and then dipped me teasingly into her pussy and back out again. Just a gentle agonising tease, pushing herself over my tip and then pulling out again and rubbing my cock over her clit.

"I love you, Effy," I said, grabbing her by the back of the neck. "And I love how fucking dirty you're being right now."

I yanked her forward and stuck my tongue down her throat, grabbing her around the waist with my other arm and thrusting up into her tight little pussy. Her cries were drowned out by my mouth on hers, and that spurred me on even more.

I carried on kissing her as I held her hips and pulled her

down hard onto my cock, slamming into her over and over again. She pressed her forehead against mine as we panted together, our lips so close we were breathing each other's breath and our moans filled the air along with the sound of our bodies grinding, slapping, riding each other. She held the back of the seat and rotated her hips, but when I reached down and started to rub over her clit, she grabbed me around the shoulders and pulled me into her.

"Fuck, Finn. I'm gonna come."

It was music to my ears, and I kept the pace; rubbing, thrusting, holding her so fucking tight I swear I'd leave bruises. But I couldn't stop. She was a drug and I was as high as a fucking kite.

I felt her walls clamp down hard on my cock, pulsating as she whimpered and moaned, and it took everything in me to hold onto my own orgasm and not shoot my load early like a teenage boy. She started to slow down, but I hadn't finished with her yet. So, I moved to lay her on the back seat and then lifted her legs at the knees. Her pussy was glistening, swollen, and I couldn't wait to push inside her again and feel her come at the same time that I did.

I climbed over her and held my dick, guiding myself back into her and she groaned as I pushed inside, stretching her open. I held onto anything I could grab in the back of that car to keep myself steady, so I could thrust into her hard. She lay back, her eyes hooded and boring into mine as I slammed into her. She lifted her knees up higher, wedging them into place, and I sank deeper, groaning at how fucking amazing she felt on my cock.

With each thrust, I could feel my balls tighten and then I reached the point of no return. I couldn't hold it back any longer. I gritted my teeth, closing my eyes to try and ride the sensation out for longer, hold back my orgasm until I'd made her come again.

"Look at me." She gasped and so I did.

When I saw her hand reach down and her fingers stroke through her folds and over her clit, I lost it. I came hard, and so did she. The pulse of my own orgasm was heightened with every squeeze I felt from hers. I kept thrusting and grinding as I felt hot cum spurting into the end of the condom. Every inch of my body was consumed by how fucking amazing it felt. I never wanted it to end.

Gasping for breath and still hovering somewhere between complete and total fucking ecstasy and nirvana, I slumped over her. My dick was still inside her and I couldn't stop my hips from moving, gently thrusting so that I could squeeze every last drop of this feeling from her. She wrapped her legs around me and held me close. And for that moment, there was nothing else in this world other than us. Nothing else mattered. She was everything to me, and this feeling was one I wanted to experience every day until the day I died.

CHAPTER Twenty

EFFY

We lay together in the back of my car, panting to get our breath back and holding each other like it was the last time we'd ever see each other. My heart was so full of love for him, and I knew from the way he buried his face in my neck and stroked my hair that he felt exactly the same.

I always knew he was my soulmate, I just had to wait until his soul was ready to meet mine. It was all about timing. I used to scoff at Emily when she told me, 'If it's meant to be, it will happen,' but she was right. This was meant to be. There was never any awkwardness between us, conversations weren't forced, and everything felt right; magical even. After what had happened back at the cinema, I needed him to know that his happiness was intrinsically linked to mine. There was no him and me anymore, only us. We had to work together, stay in balance with each other. When one was hurting, the other felt it just as bad if not worse.

I know I did for him.

I suppose it was like having a twin, only he was my soul

twin. The other half of me. I once googled what a soulmate was and it told me, 'A soulmate is a reflection of yourself. Someone that will hold your hand and walk with you through the darkness.' Finn lived in the darkness but I didn't care. I'd always hold his hand.

Liv didn't get it. She thought I acted like a freak over Finn. But she'd never understood the whole unconditional, all-consuming love like Emily and I did, maybe because she'd never found it herself. That, and she didn't read the same kind of romance novels that we did. I couldn't be mad at her for it though. One day, she'd find it too. And when she did, it'd knock her for six.

I sighed as Finn lifted his head and then kissed my cheek.

"I don't want to leave you tonight. I know I've got to, but I don't ever want to let you go." His words warmed my heart even more.

"Why do you have to leave me? We could go to yours, well, Zak's, and I could stay the night."

He lifted himself up to look at me and asked, "Really? You'd do that? But what about your parents?"

It was sweet that he was being respectful and thinking about them.

"I could text and tell them I'm stopping with Ryan and Emily. Say that we drank way too much and it's easier to crash there."

"Won't they check?"

"No. To be honest, if I told them I was stopping at yours, they'd be fine with it. They like to think they're cool parents. But I know it would freak you out if I told them the truth. Plus, I'd probably never get you over to my house ever again because you'd feel too embarrassed." He smirked because he knew I was right. "So, I figured a little white-lie would benefit everyone."

"Go for it." He smiled and we both reluctantly parted and started to sort ourselves out.

I sent a quick message to my parents on our family group chat and instantly they responded with, "It's fine. Hope it was a great night. See you tomorrow."

"All sorted." I shook my phone at Finn to confirm it.

"I really do have the best girlfriend ever."

"Yes. Yes you do." I nodded smugly.

-

When we got to Zak's, he was still awake and playing on his X-Box in the living room in nothing but his boxers. When he looked over his shoulder at us, he smirked.

"Hey, Eff. Are you stopping the night?"

I smiled and nodded as Finn stalked around the room picking up empty cans and dirty plates. Then he threw a blanket from the sofa at Zak and told him to put some clothes on. Zak just laughed and pushed it off. He didn't care.

"It's like living with my mother all over again," he joked, watching Finn through the door that led to the kitchen, seeing him load the plates into the dishwasher.

Finn didn't respond, but the noise from the crockery crashing about was answer enough. He was pissed, probably because he felt embarrassed about living here, and the fact that Zak was sitting in ridiculously tight boxers that left nothing to the imagination. Not that I was looking.

"I think I might head off to bed anyway." Zak lifted his arms up and gave an over-exaggerated yawn. "And just so you know, I wear earplugs, so you needn't worry about the noise." He winked and I flinched as the door of the dishwasher was banged shut.

"Night." I gave Zak a sheepish smile as he got up and walked past me and out of the living room.

"I should've text beforehand, let him know to get dressed." Finn shook his head then put his hand out to take mine.

"Stop worrying." I threaded my fingers through his and he led me to his room.

When we walked in, he clicked on a lamp next to the airbed that he slept on and then tutted to himself.

"It's not a lot but it's a damn sight better than my parents place," he said, fussing over the bed linen and smoothing it down.

"I'd have spent the night in the car with you if it meant we could be together." And I would've.

I knew he was nervous but I wasn't the kind of girl who was bothered about material things. I didn't care that he was stopping in Zak's spare room. He kept it clean and he was obviously respectful about staying here.

When he was satisfied that the bed was as tidy as he could make it, I laughed and said, "You do realise we're getting in that thing now?"

"Yeah." He grinned and blushed. "Sorry. I don't know why I'm nervous. It's only you. I mean... not *only* you. What I meant was, I'm never nervous around you... not anymore, anyway..."

I'd never heard Finn waffle before and it was beyond endearing.

"Shut up and get naked." I laughed to try and calm him down and it worked. He smirked then shrugged his jacket off, placing it carefully on the back of a chair. He watched me through hooded eyes as he unbuttoned his shirt and then peeled that off next, laying it over the jacket. He lifted one leg after the other, popping his trainers off and pulling his socks off last. And then he stood up tall and proud, yanking the buttons of his jeans open, pushing both his jeans and boxers to the floor before kicking them off. When he was standing in front of me naked, he smirked and held his arms out to the sides.

"Now your turn," he said, gesturing to where I stood.

He sat down on the mattress then climbed under the covers, getting himself comfortable to watch me.

I lifted my dress over my head and then smiled hearing him groan at me pulling my boots down and off my legs.

"Fucking love those boots. Might have to ask you to put those back on again later." He winked and I threw them to the side of the bed, giving him a sexy smirk as I did. If he wanted that I'd do it. I'd do anything for him.

I stood in front of him in my black lace bra and knickers. I figured he'd want the panties to come off last, so I reached behind to unhook my bra and then let it fall to the floor. The way his eyes darkened as he looked at me made my insides tingle.

"Can I take those off?" he asked, nodding at my lacy G-string.

"I'd love you to." I knelt on the mattress and he opened the covers so I could slide in next to him. He pulled me to him and kissed me, his tongue slowly circling mine and making me wetter and hungrier for him. I could feel his hard dick pressing against my thigh and I reached down to take it in my hand and stroke him. He moved his hips slowly into me and then, when he couldn't hold back any longer, he lifted himself up and sat on his knees between my open legs.

I lay back as he hooked his fingers into my knickers, and slowly, he pulled them down my thighs. I lifted my butt to help him and then moved my legs so he could take them off completely. He threw them on the floor and then looked at me.

"You are so beautiful, Eff. But lying here, wet and ready for me, it's the hottest fucking thing ever."

He started to fist his cock as he stared at my pussy. So I gave him a show I knew he'd love. I ran my fingers through the wetness and rubbed over and around my clit, and he moaned.

"That's so sexy," he said, still pumping himself and never taking his eyes off my fingers. Then, when I pushed a finger inside myself, he let out the loudest moan. "Fuck. I want inside of you so badly. Keep doing that. Don't stop."

I carried on using my fingers to pleasure us both and he licked his lips as he watched. I was so close that I arched my back and used every trick I could to hold off my orgasm so it'd be better, stronger, when I did finally come.

"I need to taste you," Finn said in a low gruff voice and leant down, moving my fingers away and pushing his tongue into my pussy. I whimpered as he licked right up to my clit and circled, then sucked it into his mouth over and over again. Words couldn't ever describe how good it felt. I had no words, only sounds and feelings. Fucking amazing feelings.

"I'm gonna come," I cried out, and then I grabbed the bed sheets in my fists as I came hard with Finn's tongue buried as deep inside me as he could get. Wave after wave of intense pleasure that was magnified by a million because having him there; lapping, sucking, teasing me, it made everything so much better, more sensitive.

I felt him kiss me over my pussy and then my clit, a gentle peck that made my heart swell. Then he crawled up my body and held himself over me. His face glistened with the evidence of what he'd just done and a soppy grin on his face.

"I love it when you come," he said, and I gave a low laugh,

wiping his mouth and kissing him; tasting myself on his tongue.

"I love it when you make me come. It's better than the orgasms I give myself," I whispered into his ear and he pulled back and frowned at me.

"Have you done that recently? Given yourself an orgasm?"

I chuckled. He almost looked jealous. Or worried?

"No. Not since I drafted you in for that job."

"Good." He nestled back down into my neck, kissing me and nibbling. "I'm forever at your service."

"That's good to know." My eyes rolled into the back of my head as he kept on sucking and nibbling my neck. "Now hurry up and fuck me."

I felt his shoulders jiggle as he held in his laugh.

"I never knew you'd be such a dirty talker," he said and bit into my shoulder.

"You ain't heard nothing yet," I hissed, secretly loving the wilder side of him.

We lay kissing, touching and loving each other, and when he finally pushed inside of me, we both gave a satisfied moan at how good it felt to be joined this way. I loved the feeling of him stretching me, there was nothing like it. I lifted my knees and wrapped my legs around him as he gave me slow long thrusts. This time we didn't fuck, we made love. There was no rushing, just savouring, taking what we both needed but letting our bodies enjoy each other. We had all night, and as I felt the crest of my orgasm building, I knew we wouldn't be getting much sleep. Tonight was about cementing our love, drowning in it. And I was more than okay with that. Sleep could wait, but the way he made me feel, that couldn't.

CHAPTER Twenty One

FINN

I loved having her in my bed, being able to take my time. It was everything I'd always dreamed of and more. I never realised it would be possible to feel this way about another person. I'd always loved Effy, but now it was so powerful and strong I felt like I'd cease to exist if I ever lost her.

The whole night had been perfect, apart from the glitch in the middle that I didn't want to think about, but right now was my favourite part of all. She had her head resting on my chest, her arms and legs wrapped around me, and I could feel the tickle of her breath as she slept. My arm had gone dead hours ago but I didn't care. I never wanted to move. This was what heaven felt like.

She started to flinch slightly, rousing from her sleep, and I hugged her tighter to me and kissed the top of her head.

"Morning," I whispered into her hair. "Are you feeling okay?"

She lifted up to look at me then nuzzled back down and yawned.

"I'm perfect." She reached up to smooth her hair down. "Why is my hair so matted? I mean, I know we were... active last night, but it's all knotted."

"Sorry. That might be my fault. I was stroking your hair while you were asleep." I hoped she didn't hate me for it, but I couldn't help it. She looked too damn cute.

"Oh my God, that's the sweetest thing I've ever heard." She squeezed me tightly around my waist and I hugged her back. It was so warm in this bed, I doubted either one of us would ever want to leave.

"Are you working today?" she asked me, and reality hit like a bolt of lightning. I'd promised the others I'd be at the factory today to help prep things ready for the party.

"Shit. I've got to meet the lads to sort out Friday night."

I grabbed my phone from the floor to check the time and groaned. I had about twenty minutes before I was supposed to be there. There wasn't a chance in hell that I was going to make it, so I fired a text off to let them know I was running late.

"I have to be in uni later, anyway. Don't worry." She patted my chest and we both sighed at the prospect of leaving this room and facing the rest of the world.

We put if off as long as we could, but eventually we dragged ourselves out of bed, got ready and headed out into the living room to find Zak grinning at us with a plate of croissants in his hand.

"Just in time, lovebirds. Get them while they're still

warm." He thrust the plate forward and Effy took one. I couldn't stomach food yet though. I still had the nagging dread of what would happen later when Brandon cancelled his fight.

"You running late too?" I asked him, surprised he was still here.

"We're running late. I saw your message on the group chat, so I figured I'd wait for you and we could go together. I'll drive. Eff, we can drop you off home too."

"No need." She smiled, looking between us. "I have my car outside. You boys have fun today, though." She patted my chest as she made her way to the door.

I followed her, feeling like I didn't want to say goodbye. Not yet.

Effy had borrowed one of my hoodies to put over her dress from last night. And I knew she wanted to go home, get properly showered and changed before she headed into uni. But seeing her in my clothes did something to me, and I really wished she'd keep it on, just so every guy there would know to stay the fuck away from her. She was mine.

I found it hard to say goodbye to her, especially with Zak hovering and watching us from the doorway, but knowing I'd see her later helped. There were no more endings for us, only a see you later, and I liked that. I'd never had it, I'd always wanted it, and now... I'd got it. My own happiness.

–

When we arrived at the factory an hour later, I headed

straight to where Brandon was camped out in the boxing area, setting up his hay bales that he still insisted on using. In typical Brandon style, he had a cigarette hanging out of his mouth as he lugged a bale across the room.

"I thought you quit?" I knew he'd cut them out ever since Harper fell pregnant and I was surprised to see him back to his old ways.

"I did, but it's been a tense few days and I needed one. I'll quit again once I get back home," he said with the cigarette still hanging out of his mouth.

"Is Harper okay?"

He stopped what he was doing, dropped the bale to the floor and sat on it, then he took a long drag on his ciggie before blowing out the smoke.

"She's uncomfortable and I'm worried sick... about both of you." He flicked his cigarette to the floor and stared back up at me. "I spoke to Harper last night about the fight. We both agreed that I can't back out. But let's be honest here, was that ever gonna happen? I'm not a quitter. If I said I'll fight, I'll fucking fight. I wouldn't let people down like that. If they're paying money to see me, I'll give them what they want. Harper agrees. She doesn't like it, but she trusts me." He stood up and started moving bales again as he spoke. "I've always said the bout only stops when someone drops, but it won't be me. I'm still fit and Joe Hazel is a lazy boxer. He'll go down, I'll save face, and you get whatever it is you need from me doing this."

I was stunned.

"I don't know what to say."

"Say you'll tell me what this is all about when it's all over. I fucking hate being left in the dark." He turned to glare at me and I was so fucking thankful to him for what he was doing. I could never find the words to let him know how truly grateful I was.

"I will. I promise," I said, feeling the words stick in my throat.

I grabbed a bale and helped him to stack them up. It was the least I could do. I had plans for artwork, but that could wait. I felt like I needed to do something to show him I wasn't totally blocking him out. Not on purpose, anyway.

"Don't look so worried," Brandon said, looking calmer now as he interrupted my racing stressed-out thoughts. "It'll be fine." He smiled. "We've got you. Did I mention we want you to be godfather when the babies come?"

"No. Mate, that'd be awesome. Thanks so much for choosing me." I went over and gave him a manly hug, patting him on the back. Thinking about those babies helped to get some perspective in all of this. I couldn't wait to meet them.

"Harper wanted to ask you when we were together, and she'll probably give me grief for telling you now, but you looked like you needed a boost today." Brandon nudged me as he spoke, making the clouds that were darkening my mood clear slightly.

"That's quite a boost too." I grinned and pulled my phone out to text Effy and tell her.

"Focus on that. That and Effy. It's what I do when shit gets too much. We're fighters, you and me." He punched my shoulder for effect and I smiled and tripped back a little as he did. "Only, I fight in the ring. You've been fighting every day of your life."

I stopped texting and looked up at him, my expression turning serious.

"Don't think we don't all see how hard you fight, Finn. We do and we're all here for you. Hell, if you asked Ryan or Zak to fight in the ring for you, they would. The girls too probably. I'm respecting your wishes that you don't want to share this, whatever *this* is. But I need you to know, whatever happens this weekend, we are all beside you."

"I know and I appreciate it. I really do."

I might've been dealt a shit hand in the family stakes, but when it came to my friends, I'd hit the jackpot. I just hoped that wouldn't all come crashing down when the weekend finally came.

CHAPTER

FINN

It was the day of the party, and I couldn't stop my mind from serving up a whole host of dreadful, awful scenarios of what might happen. I knew the soldiers would be there. It was a party in their manor. They wouldn't be able to stay away, but I didn't trust them not to say anything or cause trouble. I had to be on high alert tonight, and that included keeping Effy close to me at all times. I usually rocked up to these things on my own, but for this one, I wanted to go with her. I didn't want to spend it alone, lost in my art. I wanted to share it with Effy.

There was still a few hours to go until kick off, but I couldn't stop myself from pacing the room and climbing the walls. I had to do something to take my mind off the main event, I was slowly going insane. I decided to go to Effy's and pick her up earlier than we'd agreed. I made sure I texted her first though, so she had enough time to get ready. I wasn't that clueless about women, despite what it looked like.

As usual, she looked stunning in a little black dress, but when I said I wanted to stop off at the park before sunset, she frowned, looking down at her outfit and said, "I'm not dressed for the park. I'll look silly going there like this."

I shook my head and then looked her up and down, letting her know that I fully approved of what she'd got on. She was as sexy as hell and I didn't care where we were. I wanted to show her off.

"Are you really bothered about what other people think?"

"No, but I don't want people looking at me."

Usually, I loved that she was as shy and reserved as I was, but not in this case. I didn't want her to ever doubt how gorgeous she was.

"Let them look." I smirked, pulling her into my arms. "You're beautiful. Own it." She smiled back, and lucky for me, she didn't argue.

We got into her car to drive the short distance to our local park. I wasn't entirely sure how she was going to react to what I had to show her, but I didn't want to keep it a secret anymore, and the butterflies I had thinking about it were a welcome distraction from the dread that kept trying to drag me down.

I hated how I had to second guess every damn thing. Would she think I was a creeper, or worse yet, some kind of psycho stalker? I tried not to send myself completely insane from overthinking it all. I had enough spiralling emotions and thoughts running through my brain as it was. This was supposed to be a distraction. Something to take my mind off what I was facing tonight and keep me focused on what mattered. Her.

We pulled into the car park and Effy shut off the engine.

"Please don't freak out when I show you this," I said, watching for her reaction, but she didn't seem to be on edge or confused in any way. She looked calm, happy even.

"I won't freak out. I promise." She reached over and grabbed my hand, trying to put me at ease.

We got out of the car and I walked round to her, holding her hand and threading my fingers through hers as we picked our way over the stony path that led to the underpass.

"It's just over here," I told her as I led her down the small embankment towards my hidden masterpiece.

I half expected her to complain about the state of the place or question why I was bringing her here, but she didn't. She just squeezed my hand in encouragement and said, "Is this another memory box moment?"

I really hoped it would be. I couldn't second guess how this was going to go, but I hoped she took it for what it was. Me, showing her how much I had always loved her.

We both stumbled our way to the entrance of the underpass and I led us a few more steps forward until we were standing opposite my graffiti portrait of her face. In the orange glow of the sunset, her painting looked even more magical. The colours of her hair shone and her eyes sparkled back at us as we both stood there open-mouthed. We stayed like that for a few seconds, neither one of us speaking, but when I looked to the side to gauge her reaction, she was looking right at me with tears in her eyes.

"I love this, Finn. And I love that you've brought me here to see it." She was breathless as she spoke, like the wind had truly been knocked out of her at seeing this. "But you know what ... most of all... I love you." A tear fell down her cheek and she sniffed as I reached up to wipe it away. "I feel so... honoured that you'd do this... even more so that you're showing me."

"I couldn't keep it secret anymore. I wanted to show you. I did it months ago, back when stolen glances were all I had to live off. When I felt like life got too much, I used to come down here to be with you."

Her breath hitched as I spoke.

"Could you be any more perfect?"

"I'm not perfect, Eff. Far from it. There's a lot about me that you don't know. Things that I worry will scare you away."

And every day I live with the fear that you'll find out and I'll never see you again.

"Nothing could scare me away, and you *are* perfect. Perfect for me."

She wrapped her arms around me and I held her close as we both looked at her picture. My wall for Effy.

"I don't know how you're gonna get this one in the memory box." I laughed. She shook her head as if to say, 'Watch me,' and pulled out her mobile phone.

Using both hands to keep her phone steady, she held it up, ready to take a photo, but then she stopped, like she'd forgotten something.

"Wait, I want to do something," she said, walking over to stand closer to the wall. Then she bent down and picked up a spray can that I must've left behind.

"Shit. I didn't know that was there. I'm usually good at tidying up after myself." I blushed, feeling embarrassed.

"Maybe it's fate?" She smiled and shook the can to see if there was anything left inside. "Do you mind if I add my own touch?" She peered over her shoulder at me and I put my arms out to let her know she could have at it.

"Be my guest."

She stepped back and looked at the portrait then moved to the side so she didn't spoil it. When she started spraying, I couldn't help but laugh at the way she scrunched her nose up and held the can like it was a loaded gun. I would've given her some pointers, maybe helped her, but I was too mesmerised, frozen in place, watching her spell out the words.

Effy loves Finn.

She drew a heart too before the can gave out, and when she dropped it back on the floor, I went to stand behind her and wrapped my arms around her, burying my head into the crook of her neck.

"Now it's perfect," she said, twisting in my grasp and kissing me. "Thank you."

"Thank you for what?" I asked.

"Thank you for being you. Thank you for loving me."

I leant down and rubbed my nose against hers, feeling

like my heart was about to explode.

"Thank you for not giving up on me," I replied.

"Like that was ever going to happen."

We held each other's stare, lost in the moment.

"I need to take a photo before the sun sets." Effy sighed and then turned around. Taking a few steps back, she lifted her phone to get the shot she wanted.

"One day, you need to take your art from the streets to the galleries." She turned and gave me a serious smile.

"The streets are my gallery. I make art for the people." I didn't want to sound like a pompous arse, so I added, "I like brightening things up. Some people live awful lives, stuck in the darkness. If my work can touch just one person and bring colour to their world, then that makes it all worthwhile to me." I stared at the ground and shuffled my feet. Opening up like this was always tricky for me. Easier with her, but still tricky.

"And it does... bring colour, that is. Every time I see something you created, it... does something to me. I can't even put it into words. You're special, Finn."

I shook my head, finding it difficult to take so many compliments on board.

"I know you find it hard to hear stuff like this, but just know that I am going to spend every day reminding you how fucking awesome you are. Okay?"

"Whatever." I dipped my eyes, giving her a sexy stare from under my hair and she chuckled.

"Good. Now let's go and get this party started."

I decided I wanted to capture the moment too and pulled my phone out to take my own photograph, but when I tapped to unlock the screen, I saw a message waiting for me.

We'll be seeing you tonight. You're gonna kill it.

I went cold.

Was that some kind of hidden message? Did they expect me to kill someone in exchange for them taking Tony's life? What the hell had my life turned into?

"Are you okay?" Effy came to stand next to me and put her hand on my arm to pull me out of my daze.

"Yeah. I'm fine." My obligatory response for everything.

"I felt like I lost you for a minute there."

I snapped a quick photo of the wall and pocketed my phone.

"You'll never lose me," I said, putting my arm around her and leading her out of the underpass. "Let's go and do this thing. The sooner we get there, the sooner it'll be over."

―

When we arrived at the factory, the queues outside were already streaming around the building, and it wasn't even opening time yet. Girls wearing next-to-nothing shivered in groups. Some held onto their boyfriends for warmth, others swigged out of bottles, hoping the alcohol would numb them to the winter chill. Those bottles would be confiscated at the door, so I couldn't blame them for necking them. Plus, it was freeze-your-balls-off weather out here. I didn't feel it though.

I was numb with fear. The cold didn't affect me.

The thump of the bass from Zak's set boomed loud as we got nearer, and I noticed a few people nudge their friends and point at me. Granted, I was the lesser known Renaissance man, but I was still one of them, so I guessed I was somewhat of a celebrity to some of them here.

"His graffiti is fucking awesome," I heard one guy say as I pulled Effy through the crowd that'd gathered around the door.

"Fucking genius, mate," his friend replied.

If they knew the real me, they wouldn't say that. I was the biggest fraud of them all.

"Good to see you," Paul, one of our door security, said as he let us through and shut the door behind us, keeping the paying customers out for a little longer. "You've upped your game tonight. Should be a top night." He smiled and waited for me to respond. He obviously didn't know me very well, because I just stared back at him and stopped myself from answering in a way that'd cut him off and probably cut him down.

"It's so exciting," Effy answered for me, and I huffed, walking away from the foyer and into the main hall.

Usually, I didn't even come in here. I spent my time utilising the space, getting into the zone, feeling and creating my art. But not tonight. I had Effy to think about, and she wouldn't want to miss out on the drinks, the dancing, and the fun. Tonight, I had to suck it up and stay here with her. If the soldiers were going to show up, I wasn't about to hide. I might be a coward, but not when it came to her.

"Relax," she said with kindness radiating from her eyes. "Try to enjoy it. You've all worked hard to put this together." She squeezed my hand as we both stood and looked around us.

I hadn't worked hard, but the others had, and this place looked amazing. Zak's strobe lights lit up the area and the rush job I'd done to brighten up the walls and boarded-up windows glowed down on us, adding a nineties retro feel to the room. I'd sprayed phrases like 'Knowledge is power' and 'Fuck the police' in neon paint alongside old school boom box stereos, gold chains, yellow smiley faces and other iconic images from back then. Not that I'd ever experienced the nineties myself, but it was a cool era and I hoped I'd done it justice.

"This is amazing." Effy gasped, looking around her. "I don't know how you do it, but you nail it every time."

I gave another shrug. My heart hadn't been in this project. I'd faked every minute of my enthusiasm when the others were around. Funny that of all our events, this was the one people were freaking out over.

"Should we go over and say hi to Zak and Kian?" Effy pointed to where they both stood behind the decks, programming stuff and doing whatever the fuck it was they did up there.

"No. They're busy. We can talk to them later," I replied and took her hand, leading her through the area, past a few more bodies that had been let in early under the premise that they'd help test out the sounds and other shit.

Walking from the main hall into the anti-hall, where Brandon's boxing ring was set up, I felt myself grow tense from the nervous energy building up inside. The area wasn't as dark as the party zone, but it was dimly lit, and there was an aura of destruction and doom, a grim intensity about the place. It was perfect for Brandon. He loved creating that sense of danger for all his fights. But for me, tonight, it felt all too real.

There were a few spotlights set up on the walls around the side of the room, pointing right at the ring and providing the only light source in here. On every level, where the people could stand and watch the fight below, were flags, football banners and slogans like, 'Beat 'em to the punch,' 'Show your killer instinct,' and 'Time to throw in the towel.' Brandon had really gone to town this time. It looked like a proper British boxing arena, Mathers' style.

"I'm not sure I'll be able to stand in here and watch." Effy grimaced and glanced up at the currently empty balconies that looked down on us. "Brandon's fights scare me to death."

"I don't like watching him fight either. I will if I have to, but I prefer to wait until it's over and slap him on the back for knocking them out."

Brandon had been doing this for years and he'd never lost a single bout. It was his proudest achievement, being an undefeated boxer. His reputation in Sandland was legendary, and the feedback he'd gotten from announcing he was going to return to the ring tonight had created a massive buzz. The soldiers had their wish. Getting Brandon out of retirement was putting him, the party, and Brinton back on the map.

We walked through into the corridor that led to the rooms assigned to the fighters. Brandon was leaning up against the wall with his arms folded over his chest, talking to some dude who had more tattoos than he did. When he saw us coming, he didn't bother to stop and introduce us, just walked over and ushered us into what must've been his room. His set-up always remained the same; bottles of water, a few old plastic chairs, and a table with a packet of cigarettes and a lighter on it. I think if Brandon had made it big, he'd still have kept to his shitty rider. No champagne and bowls of blue M&Ms for him. That just wasn't his style. He was proud of the fact that he came from the streets.

"How you feeling?" I asked, biting my nails despite the fact I'd stopped doing that years ago. "Are you ready for tonight? Is there anything I can do?"

"You can stop acting nervous for a start," he said, stalking around the room with a swagger he always saved for fight nights. "You know I've got this. Even Harper's more chilled out than you are tonight."

"Is she here?" I asked, peering over his shoulder, expecting to see her.

"Of course not. She's on bed rest. I told you that. I'm under strict orders to ring her straight after though. And I'll bet she has Em on the line later, giving running commentary during the fight." He picked up the packet of cigarettes and took one out.

"Should you be doing that?" Smoking wasn't the best pre-match routine, but I did feel guilty calling him out on it, seeing as he was only fighting because of me.

"I've just seen Joe Hazel and the dude looks like he's snorted so much coke he can't even see straight. It's pure fucking suicide, mate. On his part, that is. I don't think one ciggie is gonna make much difference. His fate is sealed."

Brandon lit his cigarette just as my phone started to vibrate with a new message.

I pulled it out of my back pocket, and my stomach dropped when I saw it was from them.

The soldiers.

Every inch of my skin turned cold with goosebumps and I started to shake, hovering my finger over the screen to open it. I guess it was too much to hope they'd leave me be tonight. I was the mouse caught in their trap, and they were having way too much fun swatting me with their paws and teasing me as hope of my escape dwindled with every passing second.

"Is that Ryan? He mentioned he was running late. Something about Emily and a message from her half-sister. I didn't pay much attention." Brandon shrugged and sat down, taking another drag of his cigarette, totally oblivious to the shit-storm that was about to rain down on me.

I didn't respond. I couldn't. Effy sat in one of the other

plastic seats and I stayed standing where I was in the middle of the room and opened up the message.

Congratulations, Knowles.

You've reached the final stage of your game of consequences.

One more challenge and it's all over. Complete this, and we'll send you confirmation that dear old Uncle Tony is no more. Fail, and everyone will know your secret. Every dark, dirty detail. The choice is yours.

To complete your game you have one more task to carry out.

Get Mathers to throw the fight.

If he goes down and Hazel wins, then so do you. If Mathers wins, then you'll regret it until the day you die, which may be sooner than you think.

Tick tock, Knowles.

Time to make your choice.

"What's up? You look like you're about to throw up?" Brandon stubbed his cigarette out on the foil ashtray on the table and glared at me.

I shook my head, feeling beads of sweat start to trickle down the side of my face, and I clutched my phone like it was a grenade that I was about to detonate.

What the hell was I supposed to say to him?

Every one of my nightmares was coming true. My whole life unravelling in front of my eyes. Brandon fighting was one thing. But losing? How the hell was I supposed to do that to my best friend?

Brandon stayed calm, quiet, and studied me for a few seconds. Then his jaw clenched with irritation.

"That's them, isn't it?" He nodded to my phone. "What are they saying to you? What have they got on you to make you react like this? Talk to me, goddamn it." He smashed his fist down on the cheap plastic table and made Effy and me flinch. His eyes burned with fury and my shame made it difficult to look him in the eye. "What the fuck is going on, Finn?"

"You've gotta throw the fight," I blurted out, not stopping to think how best to word it. What was the point?

"What?" His face screwed up as if he couldn't believe what he was hearing. His expression was a picture of disbelief laced with fury, and he crossed his arms over his chest as if he was trying to stop himself from lashing out.

"They said you've got to throw the fight." I stared at the floor, wishing the words coming out of my mouth could've been different. Anything but this. "They want you to go down and let Hazel win. If you don't––"

"If I don't what happens?" Brandon shot up, standing tall as if to show me how powerful and in control he was. "Are they gonna throw their weight around? Act like the big men they think they are? I'd like to see them try. I'll fucking knock the shit out of every one of them."

Typical Brandon, thinking his fists could solve everything. But that wasn't the case this time.

"It's not that simple." I sighed.

"Isn't it? They're bullying you, Finn, because they think they're hard. But guess what, they haven't met me yet. Send them to me. I'll show them what a real hard man looks like." I knew he meant it too, but even Brandon couldn't compete against five psychos like the soldiers.

"They play dirty. This isn't about fighting and––"

"Well, what is it about then?" Brandon snapped, stepping forward and willing me to spill my guts.

"They have stuff. Stuff they're gonna tell––"

"They don't have shit on you, mate."

"They do. They've got Tony."

Hearing me say that name, Brandon's back went up.

"And?" He furrowed his brow, not really getting what the soldiers having my uncle meant for me. What effects it could have on my life.

"And if I don't get you to throw the fight, they're gonna tell everyone what he did. They'll make it go viral. I can't let that happen."

That was my truth, and I thought it'd help to explain things, but the water was still as clear as mud to Brandon.

"It doesn't matter what they say. No one will listen," he shouted, his face growing redder and angrier by the second. "If anything, they'll support Alice. It wasn't her fault."

"I can't do that to her..." I shook my head furiously. "I won't let her down again."

"You've never let her down and she wouldn't want you going through this." He pointed right at me, willing me to hear what he was saying, but he didn't know what he was talking about.

"I have to do this. I have to see it through," I stated firmly, even though I knew that by me seeing this through it meant him losing everything he'd worked so hard for. I was stuck in a catch twenty-two and there wasn't a thing I could do about it.

"Why do you have to see it through? So that five bellends with a devil complex don't tell the world your sister was abused by your uncle?" I heard Effy gasp from behind me at Brandon's admission, but I didn't look her way. I couldn't.

"Because I owe her that much," I replied, swallowing the rest of my answer back down.

"You don't owe anyone anything, Finn." Brandon took another step closer to me, still pointing his finger as Effy stood up and watched us, speechless.

"I let it happen," I said, feeling so weak that I barely had the energy to stand up.

"You were a kid yourself. What the fuck could you have done?"

"I didn't fight."

"You fight every fucking day."

"It's all my fault."

"It's not your fucking fault."

"I'm so ashamed––"

"What are you ashamed about? TELL ME!"

"I'm ashamed... because he raped me too."

Silence.

The three of us stood in total silence.

All I could hear was my panting breaths and the buzzing in my ears. My secret was out and there was no going back.

Brandon was the first to break the blisteringly painful silence.

"I'm so sorry. I'm just so so sorry." He hung his head in shame, wincing as if he was in physical pain and whispered, "I know I shouldn't say this, but I've always suspected something might've happened to you too. I didn't want to push you on it, but I had a feeling." He sighed and took a few deep breaths as I stood frozen and numb. I was shocked at myself for finally saying it out loud. "It's not your fault, Finn. None of this is your fault."

"It is." My voice cracked as I spoke. "I should have fought back. I let it happen." I hung my own head, feeling too ashamed to look either one of them in the eye. The secret that had eaten away at me over the years had finally destroyed my life. Nothing would be the same after this. I had lost everything.

"You were a kid. A teenager. Mate, I feel guilty myself. I should've knocked him the fuck out or at least tried to tell someone for you." Brandon was trying to reach out to me, give me hope, but it was too little too late.

"I didn't do enough." He clucked his tongue as I said that, but I knew I spoke the truth. "And even if you had told someone or tried to help, it wouldn't have made any difference. It had already happened. The damage was done." Brandon breathed heavily through his nose and shook his head in disagreement. "I feel disgusted with myself. I'm disgusting. What kind of guy lets that happen to him?" I wrapped my arms around myself and backed up into the corner.

"Don't say that," Effy cried, coming over to me and bending down as I sank low against the wall to sit on the floor.

"Don't touch me." I flinched, pulling away from her kind embrace that I didn't deserve. Like the coward I was, I buried my head in my hands to hide the tears I didn't want her to see.

"No. Don't do that, Finn. Don't push me away." She put her arms around me despite what I'd said, and then when she realised I wasn't going to move, she pulled at my arms, trying to get me to uncover my face.

Eventually, I looked up at her with a wet, pitiful expression and I said, "Do you really want to be with someone who's let that happen to them? Someone weak like me?"

"You're not weak and you didn't let it happen." The empathy and understanding that shone from her beautiful face made my splintered heart ache even more. "Something terrible, awful, happened to you, but it's not your fault and it doesn't define you. If I told you I'd been raped, would you think I was weak?"

"No, but––"

"It's no different, Finn. And you need to face this. You've buried it and let it fester away and hurt you for too long. Let me help you. I want to help."

It had festered for too long, buried so deeply into my psyche that I wasn't sure I'd ever be free of it. Her optimism did something though, a ripple of hope on a tidal wave of desperation. I wanted to cling to her. Find my way to the light, through her.

"But I'm scared that I'll never be able to deal with it, Eff. I can't bear to think about it," I said, cutting myself open to metaphorically bleed at her feet. I was being as honest as I could be in that moment. As honest as my shattered pride would let me.

She cupped my face in her hands and feeling her warmth, seeing the love in her eyes, it broke me.

"With time and love, we'll work out a way for you to cope. You can get through this. You're stronger than you think. You have me by your side. I'll always be here... and Brandon..."

We both turned to where he'd been stood, but Brandon wasn't there. The fact that he'd left without a word showed he had his own demons to contend with and he needed space away from us to do it. I understood that more than anyone. I'd always faced my demons alone. Sometimes, it was the only way to quiet the voices and dull the pain.

I turned back to look at Effy, my Effy, trying to hide the way her hands were shaking and the unsteady breaths she was struggling to keep under control.

"Do you still want to be with me?" I couldn't help but ask the question that had plagued me since the day I'd laid eyes on her. Would she want to be with a guy who'd been raped? A guy who was abused as a child and still carried scars that were as fresh and painful as the day they were inflicted. A man who felt hollow, broken, not a man at all. Well, not one worthy of love, anyway.

"This changes nothing," she replied defiantly, lifting her chin and giving me a resolute smile. "If anything, it makes me love you even more. You're a fighter. The ultimate warrior. A silent warrior, but I don't want you suffering alone and in silence, Finn. We'll get through this together. There is no you and me anymore, only us."

Her words were the glue I needed to help me begin to mend my broken soul, my fractured mind and my splintered heart. No more hiding in the shadows, I had to heal for her and for me.

"I was the lucky one, really. Alice was abused so many times I lost count. For me, it only happened twice. Once when Alice had to stay overnight in hospital when she had her tonsils out, and the night before he was arrested for armed robbery. I got off lightly."

"No, you didn't. You're a victim just as much as Alice is. Don't undermine what you went through or belittle your ordeal. An adult in a position of trust abused you, took away more than just your security and safety, he stole your innocence, your childhood. It's no wonder you don't like to be around people." She'd hit the nail on the head. In a world of over seven billion people, how did I manage to find the one that truly understood me?

"I like being around you."

I nudged her shoulder with mine, feeling that even though we were opening up, getting somewhere on this road to recovery, tonight... I had done enough. I had admitted what happened to me. And now, I wanted to lose myself in the way she made me feel; like there was hope and light in my future.

"I'm glad you like being around me. I like being with you too, and I'm telling you right now, I'm not going anywhere." I pulled her closer to me and she sighed. "I'm so proud of you." She kissed my cheek and then rested her hand against my jaw, forcing me to face her. "You'll always be my hero."

I didn't understand why she was proud of me. What had I done? Hidden abuse, let myself get blackmailed, and let all my friends down, Brandon the most. But I didn't say anything. I leant over and buried my face into my favourite spot on her neck and breathed her in to help calm the storm raging inside my head.

We stayed on the dirty, dusty floor of Brandon's changing room, holding each other. Both of us shedding tears and gaining comfort from the other. I wasn't ready to talk about everything that'd happened, but I told her a few things, like how I used to screw my eyes shut and wish myself away from that room, transporting myself to far off places every night. The silly dreams that I used to replay in my head over and over again like a movie to block out the bad memories. The art I created to help me deal with the anger building up inside of me. And the loneliness. The feeling that no one else had gone through this and no one would ever understand. Alice did, but that's because we shared a secret we never wanted anyone else to find out about. Not our friends or other kids. Not the teachers at school. We wanted to blend in; be normal. We didn't want to be labelled as those kids. The ones with the issues. The ones no one would want to befriend because they were tainted. Broken.

Effy listened without judgement. When she spoke she said the right things. Things that made me feel like I wasn't a freak. Words that started to slowly break through the mental barriers I'd create over the years that had always told me I was in some way responsible for it all. I'd always believed that because I hadn't helped Alice, it'd happened to me too. I'd brought it all on myself.

I knew I had a long road ahead of me. It wouldn't be easy to find peace after living with a raging black hole of noise in my mind for so long. But that road *was* ahead of me now, and I'd taken a step on the journey. As Alice always told me, 'Take each day as it comes.'

It was all I could do.

"I'm guessing that message you got, the one that told you to get Brandon to throw the fight, was from whoever's been blackmailing you?" she asked, and the reality of my situation suddenly reared its ugly head again, crashing down on me like an anvil.

"Shit. I need to get that sorted." I jumped up from my

spot on the floor.

"Was it your uncle who sent it? Is he behind it all? I heard you talk about the soldiers, but are they working with him?"

Neither one of them knew about the videos. As far as Effy was concerned, my uncle could've been trying to play with me, but I decided to come clean. No more lies.

"The soldiers are evil. They've been holding my uncle at some warehouse and torturing him. They send me videos and then ask me to do stuff. If I do it, they torture him some more."

Her eyes widened in shock and disgust.

"And you've gone through all that on your own? You didn't tell anyone?"

"I didn't want to drag anyone else into my mess."

"Your mess is our mess. That's how this works."

It was hard for me to accept that I had a support network for this after living with it for so long. I guess coming to terms with it would be easier said than done.

"I need to find Brandon," I replied, changing the subject. "He can't lose that fight."

"Of course he will. He'd do anything for you. Didn't you see the look on his face when you told him? He's hurting too."

Effy was right, but I still had to try.

"I can't let him do this."

"I don't think it's your choice anymore."

CHAPTER Twenty Three

FINN

The fight zone was packed out and every platform that ran around the edge of the room was heaving. Wall-to-wall bodies, all here to watch my best friend fight. I'd never seen so many people crowded into one space to watch a match, and the thought that Brandon was about to do something so monumental in front of so many people made me nervous and sick to my stomach. People were chanting his name, shouting and drowning out the bass from the other room.

Effy and I had stalked the whole building, trying to find Brandon and talk him out of whatever he was going to do, but we couldn't find him. When it came closer to the time we knew he was due to fight, we headed to where we stood now, right by the doors to the changing rooms, in the hope we could get to him before he entered that ring. He'd always been unpredictable, and tonight was no different. I honestly had no idea what was about to go down, but if I could stop a disaster from happening, I would.

I spotted Zak, Ryan, and Emily pushing through the

crowds, heading straight for us. Must've been Kian's moment to shine on the decks.

"Where is he?" Ryan asked as he took his place between Zak and me to watch the warm-up fight. "I couldn't find him in his room and he's not answering his phone." He craned his neck to look around, but I knew Brandon wasn't in here. The crowds would soon alert us to his presence if he was.

There were two guys I'd never seen before punching the hell out of each other, but everyone was still chanting Brandon's name, regardless.

"I don't know," I answered truthfully. "But we looked for him too and he's not out there." I thumbed behind me to where the corridor to the changing rooms was.

"I hope everything's okay," Emily added. "I was supposed to video call Harper during the fight so she could see it all, but she sent me a text about a half hour ago to say she couldn't watch it and to text her when it was all over."

I felt a thud of dread dropping through my whole body. She knew he was going to throw the fight and that's why she couldn't bear to watch. He'd rung Harper to tell her and she couldn't face it.

Just as Effy started to chat to Emily about some email and her half-sister, the crowd went wild, the spotlights dimmed, and we all stopped talking to look over at the ring. *Rage Against the Machine, 'Killing in the Name,'* blasted through every speaker, and when the lights flashed up again and Brandon walked into the room from the opposite side to where we stood, the whole place erupted. He was like a fucking film star, except for the tattoo-covered bare chest, grey sweatpants hanging low and his angry scowl.

Joe Hazel walked in after him, but Brandon didn't even spare him a glance. He held his arms up to the crowd, grinning like a motherfucker. Then after he'd strutted around a bit, whipping his fans up into a frenzy, he gestured with his hands for them to lower the noise and listen.

He took his place right in the centre of the ring, leaving the ref and Joe standing to the side like spare ends. This was the Mathers show, and he was in full control.

"Hold onto your hats," Zak joked. "Shit's about to get messy."

When Brandon started to speak, the whole room stopped to listen.

"I'm the fucking comeback kid," Brandon shouted out proudly, and the hush as he spoke ran around the room. He turned towards Joe Hazel and Brandon slapped his own chest as he said, "I'm the one they've come to see. He might look like he's hard." He thumbed towards Joe, laughing. "But there's only one of me."

The roar and chants filled the air again, and Brandon went to stand nose-to-nose with Hazel.

"You should feel lucky we even let you through the door." He pointed right into Hazel's face as he spoke. "Your swagger's fake as fuck. I hope you enjoy face-planting the fucking floor, 'cos you're too stoned to know when to duck."

The crowd laughed and Brandon gave Hazel a dirty look then stalked away back to the centre of the ring.

"I'm the undefeated king." Another slap of the chest and a glare Hazel's way. "But you're welcome to shoot your shot. I apologise in advance for the bruises, but know this... I'm coming at you with everything I've fucking got."

The two of them stalked toward each other like wild stags ready to claim their territory, and the ref got in-between them to break them apart and recite the rules.

"He's gonna do it," Effy whispered low into my ear. "But he needs it to look authentic. Brandon's all about the show. This is no different."

She wrapped her arm around mine but I couldn't move. Every muscle was tensed, every inch of my soul was slowly dying. Would he really throw it all away? He lived for this, for the notoriety and the prestige that fighting gave him. Could he kiss that all goodbye? I felt nauseas at the thought that he would and that it was all my fault.

The ref called them to toe the line and the crowds cheered and shouted encouragement even before the first punch was thrown. Brandon stayed back at first, like he always did, studying his opponent and letting Hazel get a few lucky punches in. They both weaved and ducked, dancing around the ring. But Brandon was the better boxer, it was painfully obvious, and he was outshining Hazel by a mile.

After a few hits to the side of his face and his stomach, punches that didn't even wind him, Brandon smashed his fist into Hazel, sending the kid sprawling to the hay bales. He reined blow after blow on the punk as Hazel held his hands up to protect himself. Then, Brandon powered a right hook into his face and Hazel faltered, grappling to stay upright as blood started to pour from his nose. The ref stepped forward and intervened, asking Hazel if he was okay, and the crowd jeered at the interruption. The ref didn't care and he shooed Brandon away and ignored the crowds. I doubt he'd have given Brandon the same level of care and that made something click in my mind.

"Did we choose the refs?" I leant over to ask Ryan.

"Not this guy. He turned up with the others. Said Ron couldn't make it and he'd come in his place."

Was it paranoia on my part to suspect that this ref might favour Hazel and could be working for the soldiers? I wouldn't put it past them.

The fight carried on and we watched Brandon out-smart the guy at every turn. Pound after pound his fist powered into Hazel, perfect jabs that sent him staggering around the ring like an idiot trying to claw back some dignity. Like he'd said to me back in the changing rooms, this was a done deal. The kid wasn't even in the same league as Brandon and his lack of ability was painful to watch. Maybe this wasn't going to go the way I thought it would after all?

But then it all changed.

Everything turned to slow motion as I watched Brandon drop his arms to his side and look straight at me. He mouthed something, either 'I'm sorry' or 'It's all right' I couldn't make it out, and then Hazel smacked him hard in the face and Brandon stumbled backwards. He didn't drop to the floor, but he did a damn good job of looking punch drunk. So when Hazel went in for the second right hook, Brandon fell back like he'd been knocked out, giving the crowds the perfect performance, and the perfect reason to go absolutely crazy with anger at what they were seeing.

The sheer madness of all the boos and jeers from the room was deafening. They couldn't believe what they were witnessing here tonight, and we moved to stand under the cover of the corridor as things started to be thrown from the platforms above in protest. They shouted for Brandon to get up and called it a fix and a set-up. No one could believe that some scrawny punk with half-assed punches and zero power had knocked their hero out. I even shouted myself for him to get up and keep fighting. But he'd made his decision and he was sticking to it.

Brandon chose friendship over glory.

I would never be able to repay him.

"Shit, this is bad. What the fuck is going on?" Ryan had his hand over his mouth in pure disbelief. When he surged forward to try to get to the ring and to Brandon, Emily held him back.

"This is a fucking joke," Zak shouted, mirroring all our thoughts as he shook his head. He didn't even try to offer up any wise cracks. He was as speechless as the rest of us.

"Thank God I wasn't videoing that for Harper. It'd destroy her," Emily cried, looking as white as a sheet.

Ryan just stared blankly ahead, with Emily holding onto him to stop him making another run for the ring that was becoming over-run with crowds of irate people.

"I've seen him take harder hits than that and come out of it laughing. I have absolutely no fucking clue what's going on. I thought he said he was fit?" Ryan turned to look at me with a questioning frown on his face. "He's been training non-stop since he announced his comeback."

I didn't know what to say. Thinking about Brandon training, being so focused on this fight and winning, made my head swim even more with guilt.

"I need to get to him. We can't leave him out there." Ryan tried once again to push his way through the crowds, but once again Emily pulled him back.

"Please don't go out there," she begged.

Zak patted Ryan on the back and told him, "I'll go. You stay here with Em. It's not safe out there."

Ryan wasn't happy about stepping down and letting Zak take over, but he put his arm around Emily and kissed the top of her head, bowing in defeat. "Fine. Text if you need us," he told Zak, and we all watched Zak disappear into the sea of people crowding around the ring.

"Maybe we should wait for them back in Brandon's room?" Effy suggested.

"What if he gets carted away in an ambulance?" Emily's

eyes were swimming with tears as she spoke.

"There won't be any ambulances," Ryan told her. "Even if he died out there, he'd come back to life just to kick our asses if we put him in one."

Ryan was right of course. It was one of Brandon's golden rules. No police. No ambulances. No fuss. If we could patch him up, then that was good enough for him.

"He might have concussion," Emily argued, looking truly heartbroken.

"And if he does, we'll deal with it. Come on. Let's wait back there before it turns even nastier in here. Let security calm this mob down." Ryan guided Emily away with his arm around her shoulder and we followed.

The four of us made our way to Brandon's room, and seconds after we got there, a group of security guys and Zak carried Brandon in and dumped him into one of the plastic chairs. He wasn't knocked out, but he was acting dazed and confused. The minute the door locked and it was just the six of us, he snapped right out of it, reaching for a cigarette and then eyeing Ryan as he lit it.

"What? Never seen a fixed fight before?"

"You don't fix fights. What the hell is going on?" Ryan stabbed his finger into Brandon's face in fury. He was seriously pissed off.

Brandon sat back and blew out smoke like it was nothing; keeping his cool despite the fact that his world had just crumbled at his feet only moments ago.

"Em, will you ring Harper and tell her it's over and I'm okay?" he asked, turning his attention to Emily who stood stunned in the corner.

"And should I also tell her you just threw a fight, in front of hundreds of people out there?" Emily snapped back, her pale face now a bright shade of red.

"She already knows," Brandon announced drily, shrugging his shoulders.

"It would've been nice if we'd known too. I'm still freaking out here." Emily held up her shaking hand as proof of her shattered nerves. "Brandon Mathers, you'll be the death of me. I swear I don't know how Harper puts up with you." She didn't wait for an answer, not that Brandon was about to give one, she just flounced off to call Harper somewhere quieter and probably give herself some much needed space too.

"Seriously, is someone going to tell me what the fuck is going on?" Ryan spat, but when the door flung open, I figured he didn't need an explanation from us. He was about to get the low-down from the five fuckers that were walking into the room like they owned the place.

Brandon's nostrils flared and he stood up, charging forward to take them all on.

"You're fucking dead men," he snarled, pointing at them from over Ryan's shoulder as he and Zak held Brandon back.

I just stood there frozen to the spot, praying that this whole nightmare would end. I had nothing left in me to fight anymore.

"We knew you'd come through for us." Adam Noble smirked at me and reached into his pocket then pulled out a wad of cash. "Your little stunt earned us a fuck load of money tonight. Thanks for that."

"It wasn't a fucking stunt," Brandon snapped. "You've been blackmailing him and tonight I put a stop to it. Do you hear me? This ends now." Brandon looked ready to rain hellfire down on every one of them, but Adam wasn't fazed at all. In fact, he had the balls to laugh at Brandon's reaction and the other four followed suit, cackling like a pack of hyenas.

"You should've made a few bets yourself. The odds on Hazel winning were ridiculous."

"Is that what all this is about? Money?" Ryan looked between Brandon and Adam Noble, trying to suss out what was going on between them.

"Isn't everything about money?" Adam replied, not taking his eyes off Brandon. "Don't pretend you're different to us. You get blood on your hands and get paid for it. Only difference is, we're smarter. We don't get our heads kicked in for a pay day."

"No, you just do the kicking you fucking psycho freak." Brandon tried to get past Ryan again to show Adam Noble how he really felt, but the wall of Zak and Ryan weren't budging, and Adam cackled out a laugh, taking a step back and folding his arms over his chest.

"I think you'll find we kept our end of the bargain. We are men of our word, after all." Brandon scoffed, but Adam ignored him, turning to face me, and his grin turned to an evil glare. "Check your phone. I think you'll like what you find on there. We might be sadistic fuckers, but we step up when we're needed." He turned back to glare at Brandon. "Unlike some."

"What the fuck is that supposed to mean?" Brandon was like a rabid dog trying to escape his cage. "Your word doesn't mean shit. Do you actually think you have honour when you fucked with my mate's head like that?"

Adam chuckled to himself and shook his head, then walked right over to where Ryan and Zak were holding Brandon back. His eyes were demonic in the way he stared at them all.

"I did what you couldn't. I took out the paedo scum of Sandland. I cleaned up your mess."

They didn't call him psycho for nothing. This guy had balls of steel to stand up against us and talk like that. I moved to stand shoulder-to-shoulder with my brothers, completing our unit. They were always there for me, so I wanted to show the soldiers that despite keeping their game a secret, that hadn't changed. But when Adam saw me, he sneered and side-stepped to stand in front of me.

"You think you're a big man now you've got these three next to you?"

"I'm not scared of you." I held my nerve and looked him dead in the eyes, but nothing fazed him. He pushed his face right into mine, grinning from ear to ear.

"Like I said before," Adam hissed. "You should be. In

fact, you should be thanking me. After what that paedo fucker spilled to us about you when we gutted him like a fish, you should thank your lucky stars we took care of him. Filth like him doesn't belong in Brinton."

"But filth like you do?" Ryan butted in, stepping forward.

"We look after our own," Colton King piped up, moving closer to Ryan to exert his dominance. "If scum like his uncle come onto our manor, we deal with it. You should take notes. You might learn something."

"We don't need to learn shit from you," Ryan spat back, looking Colton up and down like he was dirt.

"Then shut the fuck up and let us finish this," Adam snarled, cutting Ryan off. Then he snapped right back to calm mode like the psycho he was and looked at me with a smile on his face, like he was telling me I'd won the fucking lottery. "We won't say a word. Not about Alice, you, or any of the others."

The rush of adrenaline that shot through me when he mentioned others made me falter where I stood. My ears buzzed with white noise and sparks danced across my eyes, making it difficult to keep my balance. I felt truly sick to my stomach. In my heart, I always knew there might've been more victims, but I'd hoped and prayed there wasn't.

"We feel proud of ourselves," Adam carried on like he hadn't just shattered my soul. "If we hadn't seen you that night in Brinton, lurking around in the shadows, we'd have never known to go looking for the filth that was hiding close by. And just so you know… he was dead before we'd even sent you the first message."

The final stab to my heart.

They were even crueller than I'd realised.

"You fucking bastards." Brandon lurched forward, and this time, it took all three of us to hold him back. Not that I wanted to protect them, but I didn't want Brandon starting something that could end in tragedy.

"They're not worth it, mate," Ryan growled.

"Think of Harper," I added.

"Yeah, Mathers. Pipe down. We did the job you couldn't. Get over it. It's done."

Brandon's nostrils flared like he was ready to breathe fire. Adam stepped back to join his boys, and then with an evil glint in his eyes, he said, "Enjoy watching the video, Knowles. Colton gets a little carried away at the end, but I think that added to the overall effect. Who'd have thought a neck would spurt so much blood like that? I thought the films were exaggerating." He spoke so flippantly. Taking another man's life, despite who that man was, was obviously nothing to him.

"I think you've outstayed your welcome." Ryan folded his arms and we all stood strong, waiting for the five of them to leave, but they didn't. They wouldn't do anything they were told to. They'd leave when they decided and not before.

At that moment, Emily and Liv came bounding into the room. Both girls frowned when they saw the soldiers, but Emily bypassed them, heading straight over to Ryan and calling out to Brandon, "You need to call Harper right this minute. She's having pains. She thinks she might be going into labour."

"Shit," Brandon cursed, and didn't hesitate to grab his phone and head for the door. Before leaving, he spun round and growled, "This ain't over. I'm fucking coming for you," at the soldiers, and then he was gone.

We wanted to follow too, but from the look on the soldiers faces, this wasn't over yet.

Adam Noble leered at Emily, looking her up and down and licking his lips on purpose to wind Ryan up. Ryan pulled her to him protectively, which made Noble cackle out a laugh. But then he spotted Liv, who had gone over to comfort Effy, and his face froze. I guess leggy blondes in tight red dresses was his thing, because when he took a few steps towards her, he stared at her like she was the only person in the room. Instinctively, I moved closer towards them. I didn't want him anywhere near Effy, or Liv for that matter.

"Come outside," Noble barked at Liv, and when she didn't react, he leaned closer to her, running his nose along her hair like he was breathing her in and said in a low, demanding voice, "I said, outside. Now."

Liv jerked away from him in disgust.

"Like I'd go anywhere with you, you freak," she spat back, and I held my breath. I think we all did.

"Liv, don't," Effy hissed quietly.

"Don't what?" Liv laughed out loud. "He's a fucking creep."

"Liv." Adam said her name like he was trying it out on his tongue, seeing how it felt. He wasn't expecting a response from her. No. Instead, he wrinkled his forehead in confusion, like he was debating something in his sick, fucked-up mind and then he laughed to himself.

"You're not fucking funny," Liv snarled. "I don't know why you're laughing."

I watched Noble closely for his reaction, waiting for the impending fireworks to explode. His Adam's apple bobbed as he swallowed and he tilted his head and furrowed his brow like he didn't know exactly how to react, but the fireworks I thought would go off didn't. I guess he'd met his match, or he simply couldn't work out what to do next.

"I don't think you understood me." He spoke calmly and folded his arms across his chest. "It wasn't a question, it was a statement. I want you to come––"

"I heard what you said and the answer's still no." She leant forward, going right into his face. A move that he usually did on others, but now he was on the receiving end. "Do lines like that work on girls in Brinton? Because they don't with me, so jog on. Cunt."

There was a snigger from across the room, and Adam took a step back, keeping his eyes on Liv. Liv was no pushover, and if she didn't want to go anywhere or do anything, she wouldn't. She wasn't scared of men like Noble. Plus, she hadn't been in here to hear what he'd done to my uncle, so she still had her nerve and balls of steel firmly intact.

"You heard her." Zak suddenly found his voice. "She's not interested."

"Who asked you, Atwood?" Adam whipped his head around and then moved like a panther, stalking across the room, ready to rip Zak's throat out for daring to speak to him. "Growing some fucking balls there, huh?"

"Just fuck off out of here," Ryan snapped.

He was reaching the end of his already short fuse, judging from the way he clenched his jaw, but with no Brandon, and only me and Zak for back up, his chances of taking these guys on was slim to none. "You got what you came for, now fuck off."

Adam looked back at Liv and narrowed his eyes at her, like he was calculating his next move.

"What I want just did a one-eighty. But she'll keep." Liv huffed as he said that and he grinned. "I'll be seeing you around... Olivia."

"Oh fuck off," Liv shouted as the five of them walked out with Adam laughing to himself.

Ryan kicked the door shut behind them.

"Who the hell does he think he is?" Liv whined. "*Come outside*. I'd rather eat my own toenail clippings."

"He doesn't care, Liv," Effy replied, wrapping herself around me. "He's disgusting." She buried herself further into me and whispered, "Please don't watch it... the video, I mean."

I knew what she meant. She didn't need to explain.

"I don't know if I can make that promise," I answered

truthfully. Part of me needed to see it to know it was all over, even if it did scar me even more.

"But if you watch it, it'll mess with your head, and I don't want that."

"Neither do I." I sighed and decided to go with a compromise. "What if I watch until I can't? I promise I'll stop if it gets too much."

"I really don't think you should, but I trust you."

Truth was, I didn't even know if I could watch it, but I had to try. I had to put this to rest.

None of us spoke about the shit-storm we'd just weathered. Instead, we all made our way out of the room, leaving the elephant in there behind. I don't think any of us could stomach facing any more drama. Not tonight.

Ryan hugged Emily and Zak tapped away on his phone, moaning about shutting shit down before it went viral. I assumed he meant Brandon's fight. Liv came to the other side of Effy, and where I had my arm around her shoulder, Liv snaked her arm around her waist and said, "This is a party I'll never forget."

Little did we know how true that statement would be by the morning.

CHAPTER Twenty Four

FINN

We entered the fighting arena to see the aftermath of what a Mathers loss looked like. There was rubbish and crap all over the floor. A few people were hanging about arguing and trying to throw down with the security guys. From the look of it, there'd been total carnage going on in here when we were out the back dealing with the soldiers. Some guys who were throwing their weight around suddenly noticed that we'd entered the room and the tension escalated.

"This is fucking bullshit," one of them shouted, marching over to us.

"We want a rematch," another called out, pointing right at us.

"This isn't what we paid for," his mate added. "You've fucking scammed us."

"Leave this to me," Zak stated, pocketing his phone. "Get the girls out of here. I'll deal with them." And he headed over to them with his hands in the air like he was showing his surrender, or trying to placate them.

Ryan spotted Kian lingering in a doorway across the room and he ran over to him, gesturing for him to go and help Zak. In hindsight, we should've all stopped to sort it, but Ryan had Emily and I had Effy and Liv to care for. In that moment, all we wanted to do was get the fuck out of there and find out if Harper and Brandon were okay.

The music in the main hall was still blasting out, and we decided to take a detour down a side corridor to exit via a fire door out the back. We didn't fancy running the gauntlet of the main crowds. They were pissed up, fired up and ready for anything.

Once outside, we made our way to the car park, walking around the perimeter of the building and picking over the mud while we listened to Liv complain about the state her heels were in and how much she'd spent on them.

Ryan and Emily headed to their car with Emily typing away on her phone, trying to get either Harper or Brandon to answer and let her know what was going on. Liv pulled the back door of Effy's car open and climbed in without saying a word, her huffing and puffing said all she needed to say. She'd had enough. And Effy and me stayed outside, leaning against the car.

"Watch it now," Effy said, biting her nails nervously and nodding to my pocket where I kept my phone.

"Why?"

"Because I want to be here when you do. And I want you to get it over with so you can delete every one of their sick messages. Tonight has been... awful. But tomorrow is a fresh start. Get it out of the way and then we can try to move on."

She did have a point. I wasn't about to sleep on it and watch the video over my cornflakes. There'd been a shit load of crap thrown our way tonight. Might as well get it all done with in one go.

"Fine. But I don't want you to see it."

I moved so I was standing opposite her and pulled my phone out. She bit her lip and waited, clutching her little handbag to her chest and taking deep slow breaths.

I tapped my phone screen to life and opened up my messages. Sure enough, there it was, a line of text and a link to a video clip.

Congratulations. You completed the game of consequences. Happy viewing!

There was an emoji of a laughing joker at the bottom of their message and seeing their fucked-up logo made me want to throw my phone to the gravel. But I didn't. I clicked the video and gripped my phone tightly, hoping there were no more surprises in store.

The video started right where they'd left off last time, and after hearing them say he was dead before they'd sent me the first message, I realised this had all been one long video, cut up to form their sick and twisted games.

Colton King stood behind Tony, holding a knife to his neck. The whole thing looked like a cheap horror movie, albeit a real one. I'd muted the sound because I didn't want Effy or any of the others to hear any of the screams, but I could see the way Tony's mouth was contorted in pain. His face a mess of blood and skin. Another soldier walked on, his face covered with a black balaclava and he held a spiked club, swinging it around like he couldn't wait to use it. Colton's eyes lit up as the other guy lifted his club up and then smashed it down into Tony's lap. Then he put his boot onto Tony's leg to steady himself and yanked the club out of him, lifted it again and smashed it right back down into his groin.

I couldn't stop myself from flinching as my own nuts shrivelled in response to what I was watching, and Effy reached forward to place her hand over mine.

"Stop if it's too much," she urged, but I shook my head. He was still alive. I wasn't finished watching yet.

I kept my eyes on the screen and tried not to react as the second guy rained down blow after blow with this club, making the wood turn dark with the blood stains. But Colton grew restless and couldn't wait any longer. He wanted his fun too. So, he yanked Tony's head back, then started hacking with the knife. Blood was pouring everywhere and I could see Tony's body go from twitching furiously to limp. But it didn't stop Colton. He was on a fucking mission to take his head off, and that was something I didn't need to watch. That was the moment I had to tap-out.

I stopped the video and deleted it. I deleted them all as Effy held me tightly and whispered that it was over.

"What the fuck is that?" Liv said, interrupting us as she

hung her head out of the open window of the car.

We all turned to look at her, Ryan and Emily included, and when we saw she was looking at the factory behind us, we spun our heads around, and that's when we saw the smoke billowing into the night air.

"What the fuck?" Ryan darted into action, telling Emily to get into the car, but she wouldn't listen. She was right behind him as he ran across the grass towards the building.

I couldn't believe what was happening. I had just dragged myself out of one nightmare, only to land slap bang into another.

Without a second thought, Effy and I chased after Ryan and Emily, with Liv stumbling behind us. Our hearts were racing as we ran towards the front of the building, watching people staggering out of the factory, coughing and hacking up from the smoke that was spilling out of every door and boarded up window, doubling over in pain as others led them away to safety.

"Oh my God. It's on fire," Emily cried, just as sirens from fire engines in the distance rang out.

"Fuck! Zak! Kian!" Ryan shouted and ran towards the doors.

"No, Ryan! Please!" Emily ran after him, but he was too fast and she lost him in the crowds. Not knowing what to do, she sprinted back to us and started to cry. "I lost him! I couldn't run fast enough and I lost him!"

"I'll find him," I said, prying Effy's hands from me as she

begged me not to go. "I can't let him go in there alone. Please. Stay here with Em and Liv. I'll be fine."

I didn't wait to hear what she said. I charged my way through the crowds that'd started to gather around us, choking on the smoke and dropping to the cold wet grass to recover.

By the time I'd reached the door, the fire engines were blocking most of the entrance and forcing people back. It didn't matter how much I argued, they wouldn't let me past. I moved against the flow of people, trying to get myself into a position where I could make a run for the door, but then I heard, "Mate, I can't get in. I tried."

Ryan was panting and he rested his hands on his knees, bending forward to catch his breath.

"They won't let me through. I feel fucking useless," he cried, screwing his face up in pain.

I put my hand on his shoulder in solidarity and I waited for him to calm himself. When he straightened up, he ran his hands over his face. "We fucked up. I fucked up," he groaned.

"You were right the first time," I admitted sadly. "*We* fucked up. We shouldn't have left them both in there to sort our shit out."

This whole night had taken a grave turn and it looked like I had more than one person's fate left in my hands. It was too much for anyone to bear.

More sirens blasted out, cutting across the screams, shouts and collective noise of the firemen and the fire they were here to fight. Police started to take names and numbers, getting details of what'd happened here. And we stood frozen to the spot, having absolutely no idea whether our friends, our best friends, were safe.

"We should talk to them." I nodded over to where the police were taking their statements.

"Yeah, in a bit," Ryan replied absent-mindedly. I don't think he actually heard what I was saying. He was lost in his own head. As if to prove my point, his head shot up and he glared at me in panic. "Is Emily okay? Is she still out here?"

He darted across the grass, heading to where we'd been standing before.

"She's fine," I shouted out after him, but he didn't hear me and he didn't respond. Or maybe he didn't believe me until he'd seen she was okay with his own eyes. He pushed people out of the way and frantically searched the crowds, calling her name as he did. When he saw her, he grabbed her to him and held her, rocking her in his arms.

"Thank God," he kept saying over and over again.

I held Effy too, and then Liv put her arms around us both. All we could do was stand and watch the flames as they engulfed the building. Listen to the crash of the beams and other internal structures as they broke and collapsed inside from the heat. Watch the fire service as they risked their lives to save the ones still trapped inside. And pray that everyone got out safely.

"What do you think caused this?" Liv asked the question

that was plaguing all of our minds.

We each shrugged, too dumbfounded to formulate an answer. But somewhere in the deep recess of my brain I knew this wasn't an accident. In my gut, I felt like this was a deliberate act.

Arson.

We had our enemies, but it didn't take a genius to guess who could've done this. Five psychopaths without an ounce of empathy between them. Five men who didn't give a fuck who they hurt. They'd have done this just to spite us. It wasn't enough that they messed with me. They had to go out with a bang. A fuck you to the Renaissance men. I thought they wanted the party held in Brinton so they could do something good for their community, put Brinton on the map, but I was wrong. They lured us here like rats to a sinking ship.

And I'd made it happen.

Now, I'd have to live with the fall out.

Forever.

CHAPTER Twenty Five

FINN

After hours standing around waiting for news and watching the emergency services clear the site, we decided to head for the hospital. Nobody could confirm whether Zak or Kian had been brought out, but there'd been a few ambulances leaving the site, and we prayed they were in one of them and not still trapped in the debris of the now-smouldering wreckage.

We abandoned our cars wherever we could and raced towards the hospital entrance. But when we asked at the desk for news on Zak and Kian, we were told we'd have to wait and were directed to the visitors' waiting room. We felt powerless and desperate for news.

I sat on the plastic chairs, holding Effy for support. Ryan paced up and down as Emily tried to offer up words of encouragement.

"They'll be okay. They have to be. We have to stay positive." She nodded, agreeing with her own statements.

Liv stayed quiet, but I could tell what she was thinking.

She was a realist and she was bracing herself for the worst.

When we heard, "What the fuck are you all doing here?" we turned to find Brandon stood at the exit of the hospital shop that was adjacent to the waiting room, holding chocolate, crisps, bottles of water and a whole load of other snacks.

"Is Harper okay?" Liv asked, buying us some time before we had to tell him about what'd happened once he'd left.

"She's in pain and every word that comes out of my mouth seems to make it worse. But apart from that, we're all good." He looked knackered and motioned to the haul he had in his hands. "Midwife said it's gonna be a long night, so I figured I'd get some provisions."

"Give her our love, won't you? Tell her to push for us." Liv gave a false chuckle and Brandon frowned.

"Yeah, whatever. Why are you here though? The babies won't be born for hours."

I glanced over at Ryan, not entirely sure whether we should tell him. This was the happiest and scariest day of his life. He was going to be a dad. Did we really want to piss all over that and let him know two of his closest friends might be lying dead in the same hospital?

"You're right," Ryan answered for us all. "We couldn't stop thinking about you both and wanted to come and see how it was all going. But we'll head home and wait for you to call." He walked over to Brandon and patted him on the back. "Make sure you ring us as soon as it's all over, yeah? Oh, and keep your mouth shut. Stick to hand-holding and agreeing to anything."

Brandon laughed, but he was so dazed and confused he didn't give us a witty or sarcastic response, just nodded and said his goodbyes. We watched him leave, but we had no intention of going anywhere yet. Not until we had some answers. And then maybe tomorrow, or the day after, we'd let Brandon know what'd happened. Whatever that actually was.

—

We stayed in the waiting room for hours, alternating which one of us badgered the receptionists for news. After our thirteenth God-awful cup of cheap coffee, I saw Ryan bolt up from his chair and we all shot up too and followed him. Kian was walking down the corridor, clutching a bag from the pharmacy, and when he saw us, his shoulders dropped.

"Kian, mate. Are you okay?" Ryan hugged him, and when he pulled away the rest of us grabbed him into a gentle hug too.

"They're letting me go," Kian said in a raspy voice. "Shortage of beds and all that. My throat and chest are sore from the smoke, but they don't think there's any lasting damage. I was lucky. I managed to crawl over to one of the fire exits and get out."

"And Zak?" Emily asked quietly.

"I don't know. We got separated when the roof collapsed. He didn't follow me. He couldn't. I'm so sorry." Kian hung his head, and I could tell he'd started to cry, so we led him to the waiting area to give him more privacy.

"Is someone coming to pick you up?" Effy asked.

"I was gonna catch a cab outside. I didn't want to bother anyone," Kian replied.

"You should've called us. You know we'd come to you." Ryan said, putting his hand on Kian's knee and giving him a reassuring squeeze. Ryan stood up and went to grab his keys, but Effy picked hers from her bag and passed them to Liv.

"Liv, would you take my car and drive Kian home? I would take him myself but..." She looked back at me, but she didn't need to finish her sentence.

"Of course I'll take him." Liv took the keys and stood up. "Ring me if you hear anything, okay? I'll come straight back once I've dropped Kian off."

Just as Liv and Kian walked out of the doors, a doctor came in and called us over to join him in a quieter room attached to the side of the main waiting area. We knew then that this wasn't going to be good news.

"You're here for Zakary Benjamin Atwood, yes?" The doctor took a seat and looked each one of us in the eye.

We sat down with him, and Ryan spoke for us.

"We are. Is he here? Is he going to be okay?"

The doctor took a deep breath, resting his hands in his lap.

"He is here. He was brought in a few hours ago by our paramedics. His parents have been contacted and they're on their way, but they gave permission for us to speak to you about his condition."

"Which is?" Ryan sat forward, his hands shaking as he wrung them together.

"I won't lie to you, he's in a critical condition, and the next few days are going to be tough. He's got a big fight ahead of him. He has fourth degree burns––"

"And what does that mean? Speak English, doctor, give it to us straight," Ryan begged, cutting in.

"It means he's suffered some extensive burns that've gone through layers of his skin as well as the underlying tissue. Nerve endings have been destroyed––"

"Is he going to die?" Ryan was frantic. He just wanted the bare truth.

"I can't tell you one way or another at this point. Whether he survives or not depends on how he responds to our treatment. What I can say is, he's in the best hospital. Our burns unit is one of the best in the country. He's young and fit, so he has that on his side, and the burns are of a percentage that with good medical care can be treatable. As I said before, the next few days will be crucial. We'll be able to tell you more then."

"Can I ask a question?" Emily leaned forward as Ryan sat back in his chair looking totally defeated.

"Of course. I'll try my best to answer as clearly as I can," the doctor replied.

"Where are his burns? On which part of the body, I mean."

"His torso." The doctor pointed to his chest as if we didn't know what a torso was. "And his thighs are the worst affected areas. From what we can tell, something must've collapsed onto him. It pinned him to the floor."

"So, not his face?" Emily asked.

"There's some burns to the neck and lower part of his jaw, but no, not the face, as such. He was lucky in that respect."

"Nothing that's happened to him tonight is fucking lucky," Ryan snapped, and Emily glared at him for his momentary but totally justified outburst.

"It's not the doctor's fault," she hissed quietly. "Don't swear at him."

"I wasn't swearing at *him*, I was swearing at this whole fucked-up shit heap of a night." Ryan stood up and marched out of room, banging the door behind him, and we all just sat still, stunned into silence.

"I'm sorry, doctor." Emily started to apologise, but the doctor held his hand up and gave us a sorrowful smile.

"No apology needed. If we hear anything else, we'll let you know, but he's in surgery now and that's going to take a while. The best thing you can do is go home and get some rest. We should have news in the morning, after the surgery."

The doctor said his goodbyes and left. We stood up, feeling like zombies, and walked back out into the waiting area. Ryan was sitting in the corner, hunched over with his head in his hands, and Liv was next to him, staring blindly ahead of her.

"We can't do anything tonight," Emily said, taking the spare seat on the other side of Ryan. "Liv, do you want to come home with us? You can stop over, if you like? You shouldn't be alone. Not now."

Liv nodded and handed Effy her keys.

"If you hear anything, will you ring us?" Effy asked.

"Of course. We're all in this together," Emily answered.

Effy and I walked away feeling like we weren't entirely sure leaving was the right thing to do, but following our feet anyway.

"I don't think you should go back to Zak's on your own." Effy threaded her arm through mine as we walked at a snail's pace back to her car. "Come and stop at mine. My mum and dad will be asleep now. They won't mind."

I didn't have the energy to argue. And I certainly didn't want to go back to the apartment, not knowing whether Zak was going to make it or not. It didn't feel right.

"Are we gonna be okay?" I asked, feeling like a useless little kid again.

"We're gonna be strong for each other and we will get through this. Zak will pull through and we have Harper and Brandon's babies to look forward to. Hey… If anyone can survive a tough time like this, it's us."

"I don't know what I'd do if I didn't have you." I stopped as we reached her car and I held her, thankful she was here with me.

"Looks like fate brought us together at just the right time," Effy said, smiling sadly. "It knew we needed each other."

And we did.

I'd never not need her. She was my everything.

"Just promise me one thing, Finn. Promise me you'll talk to me. When it all gets too much... and it will... don't shut me out. Talk. About Zak, Alice, you, anything. I'm here and I want to help."

"I promise." I sighed. "And the same goes for you too." I tried to smile, but it was useless. And I wondered whether the weight of guilt was ever going to ease up. Most days, I already felt like I was drowning. Now the waves had grown so big I wasn't sure I even had the energy to tackle them anymore. But I was lucky. Luckier than I might've been if she wasn't here. She was the anchor, the buoy that kept me afloat. And there was one thing I was certain of... I wanted my happily ever after with her. I felt like we'd earnt it.

CHAPTER Twenty Six

FINN

One Week Later

Had it really only been a week since the fire? It felt more like a month. Granted, it had been the longest week we'd ever lived through, and we'd spent most of it at the hospital, alternating between trips to see Harper and the babies and sitting with Zak's parents, waiting on news.

We weren't allowed to see Zak. The risk of infection was too great, and only the immediate family were allowed limited access to the ward where he was. He was stable, for now, but his life had taken a drastic turn for the worse. It was going to take months, maybe even years for him to heal and start to live a normal life. The cheeky, fun-loving flirt that we all knew had died in that fire. In a way, a part of all of us died that night too.

The fire service confirmed what we all knew, it was arson. Someone had set fire to a pile of boxes that'd been stacked up in a room just off the main dance area. There were no witnesses and nobody came forward with any leads worth following, but we knew who it was, and the soldiers were marked men.

The police were keeping their investigation open for now. They'd interviewed us all, but we were cleared of any wrongdoing. They could've prosecuted us for the party and for endangering the people who'd come, but they didn't. Not yet, anyway. Maybe they thought we'd been through enough? Or maybe, police officer, Tom Riley, was back to pulling more favours for us behind the scenes? We didn't know, and we were too exhausted to question it.

As for me, I was still taking each day as it came. Knowing my uncle was gone didn't really make the demons living in my head disappear like I always thought they would've. Those fuckers had dug their claws in, set up camp for what they assumed was a lifetime, and they wouldn't leave. Not without a fight. I would have to work damn hard to get rid of them, but I was ready for it. I was ready to face my demons head-on to get through this and earn my peaceful future with the girl I loved. Peaceful being the operative word. The noises in my brain were dulling slightly, but I wanted the silence I'd projected over the years to reach my head. I craved the healing that Effy told me was possible. She'd looked into counselling and I was coming round to the idea, slowly.

I knew that one day I would have to admit what'd happened to me and Alice to someone else. Relive those years and face the truth to finally bury it. But that day wasn't today. Today, we were at Harper and Brandon's apartment, because Harper and the babies had been allowed to leave the hospital.

We all wanted to be here to help them settle the girls into their new home. Anything to put a smile on our faces, no matter how temporary that happiness was. We all needed a reminder that life could be good, and no matter what was happening in our own lives, the sun was still shining.

We all sat together in their living room, and considering what we'd all been through over the past few days, there was an unusual air of calm about the place. I supposed babies had that effect on people. Made them forget about the world for a while.

They were tiny, and so absolutely perfect. Brandon couldn't take his eyes off them and was loath to let anyone else hold them, but that didn't last long.

"I need to cuddle one of them. I didn't come all this way to watch you, Brandon," Emily joked. "I can see you any day."

"Okay, but be careful with her head," Brandon said, and Emily huffed out a laugh.

"I do know how to hold a baby." When she pretended to drop her as Brandon passed her over, it didn't go down well, and he gave her a wicked stare.

"I will be changing the godmother status if behaviour like that carries on," he said.

"You wouldn't? I mean... I was joking... I wouldn't––"

"Relax. We trust you," he butted in. "Like we could ever have anyone else. We want you, Ryan, Finn, and Effy. We'll have Zak too, but that might have to wait a while."

We all went silent, thinking about our friend still fighting for his life in the hospital. And what kind of life would it be when he did eventually pull through? The doctors might've said he was stable, but to us, that didn't mean shit. He was still hurting, and his life would never be the same again.

"I'd hunt you down if you chose someone else," Emily said, breaking through the tension that'd settled over us. Then she sighed and kissed the baby's head, sniffing her like she was fresh air. Why did women do that?

Harper passed the other baby to me and I sat still and stiff, feeling like I'd got a rod shoved up my back. I was scared to move in case I did something to hurt her, she was so delicate.

"So, who have I got here?" Emily asked in a sing-song voice.

"That's Phoebe. Phoebe Kate," Brandon announced proudly. "And over here with Uncle Finn is Esme Grace." Brandon hovered over me, stroking Esme's head.

"They're so tiny," Effy whispered, reaching over to stroke Esme and hold her little hand with her finger. "Tiny and perfect."

"With a perfect set of lungs on them at three a.m.," Harper joked back.

"Aren't you getting much sleep?" Emily asked.

"Not really. Brandon helps, but I'm feeding them myself, so there isn't much he can do."

"How was he at the birth?" Ryan asked, smirking at Brandon.

"He was amazing. I gave him some grief apparently, told him to never come near me again, but I honestly don't remember that. All I remember is his voice was the only one I could hear at the end. He got me through it." She glanced up at him as he went to stand next to her and bent down to kiss her. The love they had for each other was evident in both their eyes.

"It was the best day of my life. Well... so far." Brandon sat next to Harper and put her hand in his lap. "Which brings me to my next piece of news. I know we're all living through a shit time at the moment, but hopefully this'll cheer you up a little bit. If that's possible." He shrugged. "I asked Harper to marry me at the hospital, right after the girls were born. I couldn't not. I bloody love this woman and I want all of us to have the same last name... be a family." He kissed her hand as the room erupted into coos and quiet cheers so as not to wake the babies.

Effy shot up from her seat and went to hug Harper, and Emily sat close by with Phoebe in her arms, asking to see the ring. I noticed a look cross over Ryan's face, but he soon wiped it away and went to congratulate Brandon with a pat on the back. Seemed Brandon had beaten Ryan to that milestone too. Ryan still hadn't asked Emily yet. Said he was waiting until after the auction at the asylum, then he was going to make it all official with a proper proposal in the chapel. Doing it the way that he wanted, with his special touch.

"When Zak gets out of hospital, we can start planning

stuff. Sort out dates and everything," Brandon said, and the rest of us stayed quiet.

He was in his little family bubble, still on a high from the birth and thoughts of marrying Harper. Who were we to burst that? But we'd all spent long enough with Zak's family to know he wouldn't be out any time soon. Brandon didn't know the half of what had happened that night and how bad Zak's injuries really were. All he knew was he couldn't visit like the rest of us but he was on the mend. Eventually, when Brandon came back down to earth, he'd realise how bad it actually was.

"It'll be something for us all to look forward to," Emily replied, ever the hopeful, cheerfully optimistic one of our group.

The front doorbell sounded and Brandon went to answer it. Moments later, Liv walked in looking like she'd come dressed ready to go straight out clubbing later that night.

"Oh my God, they are gorgeous," she said, plonking herself onto the sofa next to Emily.

Emily passed the baby back to Harper and went off to make teas and coffees for everyone. Effy came back to sit next to me and I let her take Esme from my arms. She was a natural, and when I looked at her holding the baby and stroking her, it did something to me. Made my insides flip over thinking that one day that could be us. Our baby. Mine and Effy's.

After a while, Harper went off to the bedroom with the babies to feed them, taking the other girls with her. When she was gone, Brandon started to question us about the fire, the police investigation, and everything that had gone on over the past week. He knew, like we did, that the soldiers were more involved than anyone would let on, but we had to be clever about our next move. Exposing them wouldn't be easy, especially without Zak and his computer expertise.

"I've gotta say..." Brandon sat down and pinned Ryan with a stern look. "I don't think we should carry on with the events. Not after what happened."

Ryan wasn't in agreement and he folded his arms over his chest as he took a few deeps breaths before responding.

"What happened that night wasn't our fault." A few more steadying breaths and then he carried on. "I have a whole business plan set up. I'm not just gonna throw all that away. I've worked hard, we all have, and I'm not gonna stand by and watch that fall down the drain. Zak wouldn't want that."

He sat next to Brandon, wringing his hands, with a look of silent contemplation on his face. But his pleading wasn't over yet. "When we buy the asylum, it'll be different. It'll be a legitimate business. We'll run the parties from there and we'll have full control. I've worked hard on this; I'm not backing down just 'cos some punks from Brinton think they can fuck with us."

"But it's more than that though, isn't it?" Brandon argued back. "People were hurt. What's it gonna look like if we just carry on like that never happened?"

I could see both sides of the argument, but Ryan couldn't.

He was blinkered to any negativity coming his way.

"It'll show everyone that we're serious about what we do," he said through gritted teeth. "We have a reputation, a good reputation. This is what we do. It's what we're good at."

Brandon shook his head, disagreeing with Ryan, but when Ryan's mobile rang, he didn't get chance to say his piece. Ryan looked at the screen and shot up to answer it, walking over to the window as he did, keeping his back to us.

"Nigel. Good to hear from you. Are we all set for Tuesday?"

I knew the auction was on Tuesday, so this was an important call for Ryan, and when he stiffened as he listened to the guy on the other end, I knew it wasn't a courtesy call.

"What do you mean a better offer? I have the cash ready to go. Do the sellers know that?"

Brandon and I exchanged silent, knowing glances.

"This is bullshit," Ryan snapped. "What the fuck use are you as an agent if you can't sort this out? I don't care what papers are signed, that building is ours."

Brandon rolled his eyes and sat back in his chair. I felt for Ryan, but in the grand scheme of things, this wasn't affecting me like it was him. Maybe the asylum was a lifeline for him after the chaos we'd been embroiled in? We all had our ways of coping with what'd happened. But from the sounds of it, this was a non-starter.

"Can't you try to contact the new owners, see if they'll accept our offer?" Ryan waited a few seconds, and when Nigel didn't give him the response he wanted, he said, "Fuck you, asshole." And hung up the phone.

"So that's it? Deals off?" Brandon asked.

"There was no fucking deal. The vendors sold to someone else without even giving us a shot." Ryan banged his fist on the wall nearby, making us jump, but Brandon stayed quiet. He knew whatever he said would fall on deaf ears.

"That building is ours," Ryan stated, lifting his chin defiantly. "Finn's artwork is all over the damn place. I've spent hours renovating the chapel so I could ask Emily to marry me in there. I wanted it to be perfect. Now, I don't know if they're gonna knock the fucking thing down or what they're gonna do with it. It's fucking bullshit."

"I don't know what to say, man." Brandon shrugged, feeling at a loss for words like I did.

"I need to go there and find out what the fuck is going on," Ryan announced, just as Effy, Emily, and Liv walked back into the room.

Seeing Emily frown, Ryan filled her in on his phone conversation, but left out the details about his plans for the chapel. I guess he was still hopeful that he could do something to rectify that part.

"But what good will it do going down there?" Emily asked.

"I don't know," he snapped back. "But it'll make me feel a damn sight better. I can't just roll over and do nothing."

Ryan stood to leave and the rest of us blindly followed.

We couldn't let him face this alone, no matter what our own thoughts on it were. Brandon stayed behind with Harper and the twins, and we told him we'd keep him posted.

"Don't let him do anything stupid," he whispered to me before I left. "He's not thinking straight."

I nodded, but in reality, none of us were. We were all living in a daze of confusion. Our lives had been turned upside down and nothing was ever going to be the same.

CHAPTER Twenty Seven
FINN

When we pulled up to the old asylum, the front doors were wide open. We all parked, and Ryan stalked out of his car, banging his door shut and muttering to himself as he walked like a man on a mission. Emily followed not far behind, calling out, "Babe, calm down. If you go in there all guns blazing, you're gonna make matters worse."

"How could they be any fucking worse?" he shot back without breaking his stride.

Effy, Liv, and I kept quiet, making our way over the debris and rubble scattered along the path leading to the entrance. Music was blasting out so loudly that we all grimaced as we entered, letting our ears adjust to the level of noise. My artwork lining the corridors leading off the main entrance hall was still there, but now it was marked with crudely sprayed tags. All the subtle and intricate details lost underneath the amateur graffiti of some kids who probably broke in with nothing better to do than destroy what'd taken hours, days, months even to create.

"What the fuck?" Ryan looked around and then stormed towards the source of the music. "I was here a week ago and it didn't look like this. It's a fucking mess in here."

When we reached the doorway where the music was being played, we all stopped dead in our tracks.

"I wondered how long it'd take for you to show up." Adam Noble stood in the middle of the room, his stance cocky and self-assured as he folded his arms over his chest, tilted his head and smirked at us. The other soldiers were lazing around the room, smoking rolled-up cigarettes and drinking bottles of beer while their Rottweiler lay in the corner eating raw steak, slobbering and growling.

"Turn it down, Colton," Adam said without taking his eyes off us, and the music went from ear-splitting drum and bass to a quieter hum that matched the tension and adrenaline running through our veins.

The other soldiers just sat and stared at us, their eyes glazed over like zombies. Maybe those were more than rolled-up cigarettes they were smoking?

But what none of us could fathom was, what the hell were they doing here? This was Sandland, not Brinton. They were trespassing on our turf.

"I don't know what the fuck you're doing here but I came to speak to the owners." Ryan held his nerve and spoke clearly, even though I could see the tell-tale twitch in his neck that said he was close to losing it. "I think I might give the agents a ring. I'm sure the new owners wouldn't be happy to find out filth like you are squatting here." Ryan pulled his phone out of his pocket, but Adam just laughed back at him.

"And what makes you think we're squatters?" He took a few steps towards us, still grinning. "You are looking at the new owners of this building." He held his arms out and cackled. "Welcome to The Sanctuary."

We all stood there, stunned into silence. What the actual fuck was happening here?

"I don't believe it. How could you afford this?" Ryan frowned, glaring at Adam and waiting for the answer.

"Because of him." Adam nodded over to me and then winked. It took everything I had not to launch myself at him and wipe that smug smile off his face.

"We made a hell of a lot of money betting against Mathers," he announced proudly, and then he stared right at me again. "And your uncle might've donated some towards it too. Not that he had much choice. We cleared out his house and his bank account when we'd finished with him." He shrugged. "Call it pay back. We spent all night burying his body parts all over London. He owed us."

I felt sick to my stomach, but Ryan still wasn't buying it.

"No way," he snapped, shaking his head. "That's bullshit. I know how much this place was going for. You couldn't have."

"Why couldn't we?" Adam smirked and looked around at his fellow soldiers. "Because only the Renaissance men can put on events in Sandland? Because we're not as talented as you? We raised the money, made the deal, and signed on the dotted line this morning. You lose, Hardy. We win."

"This isn't over. I won't let this happen," Ryan shouted back.

"You've got no choice. And I would remind you that you're on private property... *our* property, right now, but arguing with you is so much fun. I love seeing how red your face is getting." Adam was having way too much fun poking Ryan. He was getting off on his anger.

"Just say the word and he's gone," Devon Brady piped up, but Adam held his hand up.

"And spoil all the fun? You need to watch this space, gentlemen. The Sanctuary is about to become the *hottest* place to be in Sandland." He winked, knowing his use of the word 'hot' would strike a knife into all of our hearts.

Ryan lurched forward to take out his own justice, but Emily stood in his way.

"We know what you fucking did, you no-good piece of shit. You started that fire at the factory. You hurt a lot of people, including our best friend." Ryan had lost it, but his anger only humoured Adam even more. Adam Noble fed off fury like Ryan's. He lived for it.

Eventually, Ryan stepped back, letting Emily's words that they weren't worth it penetrate through his anger.

"Better sleep with one eye open, Noble, 'cos I'm coming for you," Ryan hissed, pointing over Emily's shoulder.

"Do I look like I give a fuck? My last fuck burned along with your mate in the factory." Adam laughed at his own sick joke, then he looked right at me. "Times are changing. You're not the big men you think you are." And then he spotted Liv standing behind Effy. "Come for the private tour, sweetheart?"

"I've seen all I need to, thanks. This place had potential, but now it's full of shit." Liv glared back at him, not afraid to speak her mind. She could give as good as she got.

I expected him to laugh at her, but he didn't. Instead, he stared at her, studying her and contemplating his next move like the predator he was.

"I'm gonna enjoy showing you what happens when people talk back to me," was what he said next, but he didn't appear to be as confident in that moment as he had been seconds ago.

"Suck a dick," Liv shot back.

"That's your job, sweetheart."

Ryan had had enough, we all had, and he grabbed Emily by the elbow to pull her away. "Let's get out of here. I've seen enough."

"What? Don't you want to see what we did with the chapel?" Adam's words pinned Ryan to the spot, and I could see the rage brewing in his eyes. Noble had hit a very raw nerve.

"I swear to God, Noble, you are a dead man," Ryan said as calmly as he could.

"Good job I've got my own chapel for the funeral then, hey? Although, we have started to add our own touch to it. I mean, what better place to install the chains, cuffs, and other shit we're gonna use in there. Kind of like a crazy oxymoron; we're gonna worship all the fucking sins we can." Adam was pushing every one of Ryan's buttons and he knew it.

"Ryan, let's just go," Emily urged with desperation in her voice.

"Listen to your woman, Hardy," Adam called out. "Take me on and you'll regret it."

"Fuck you," Ryan spat and marched down the hall. This was a fight for another day. Nothing would be achieved from standing here arguing with them.

We turned to leave too, but Adam had to get the last word in.

"I'll be seeing you around... *Olivia*."

Liv stopped and spun back round to glare at him.

"Not if I see you first... *freak*."

And then she stomped off, leaving him cackling with laughter behind her.

"That guy is a fucking moron," Liv growled as she haphazardly picked her way across the uneven flagstones of the hallway and back out through the front doors. "I would say he gives me the creeps but that'd imply that I have actual feelings when I see him."

"Well, he creeps me out," Effy replied.

We hadn't told Liv about the blackmail, and even though she'd heard what Adam had said about my uncle just now, she either didn't care enough to ask about it or hadn't put two and two together. She did tend to live in her own world ninety-nine percent of the time.

"Liv, would you mind getting a lift back with Ryan and Emily?" I asked. "Only, I want to show Effy something."

Liv wrinkled her nose and looked over to where Ryan and Emily were standing arguing by his car.

"I guess I've got no choice." She opened her handbag and started rooting through it. "I'll put my AirPods in though. I don't want to listen to their lovers' tiff all the way home." And with that, she walked off, not even stopping to say goodbye.

"I need to get away from this place," I said, looking up at the building that now made my skin crawl. "I've wasted enough time on them. I want to move forward. Start living for me... and you."

"Me too," Effy replied.

I put my arm around her and we walked back towards her car.

"Where are we going?" she asked, narrowing her eyes and giving me a questioning look.

"I have another surprise for you. Something that I think might help give us a little hope in this shitty nightmare we've all been stuck in lately."

I didn't elaborate further. I didn't want to. I wanted to show rather than tell. We had a happily ever after we needed to start living, and right now, that's all I wanted to focus on.

CHAPTER Twenty Eight
FINN

We pulled onto the forecourt of Ryan's dad's garage, and I directed Effy to drive down to the rear where Sean had a few workshops. Ryan used the main one for his kit car business. But once, when I was talking to Sean about my art, he offered me the use of one of his spaces. The light in there was amazing, and it gave me a quiet place that I could call my own to escape the world and create whatever the hell I wanted.

"Have you bought a car?" Effy asked as we parked up and got out.

"Not quite. But I did buy some car parts." She frowned at me but I smiled, enjoying the fact that I could keep her on her toes.

I unlocked the padlock and pushed the doors open, stepping back to let Effy go first. When I heard her gasp, it made my whole body tingle with pride.

When I originally started working here, I thought I was going to create graffiti, maybe paint on canvas, but what happened surprised even me. I'd seen all the spare parts lying around the yard and most of what I'd used for my sculpture had been passed to me with no charge attached. They weren't ever going to be used again, and Sean seemed bemused that I wanted all his old crap as he called it. But to me, they were materials that I could bend, mould, melt down and reshape to create whatever the hell I wanted. A little bit like my life right now. I took what was used up and gave it new life, new purpose. Renaissance meant rebirth, after all, so really I was fulfilling my duty as a true Renaissance man.

My wishing well wasn't finished. I still had some areas of the roof that I needed to weld, and I had planned to inscribe something into the sheet metal that I'd used for the brick effect around the base. But after today, I felt that it was time to share it with Effy. Show her the lucky charm I was making for us both.

"Finn, this is stunning." She gasped, running her hand over the edge.

"I've always been fascinated by wishing wells," I told her. "When things got tough, back when Alice and I were growing up, I used to think to myself that maybe, if I could find a wishing well, I could make a wish and all the pain would go away. That's what my dumb childish brain told me, anyway."

"That's not dumb." She smiled her special smile meant only for me, and just like that, I didn't feel like such a loser anymore. "It's heart-breaking, Finn, but it's not dumb."

"I figured if I could throw a penny in, make that wish, it would all stop. But there are no wishing wells in Sandland.

There was *The Treacle Well* in our Alice in Wonderland books, but nothing we could use in real life. So, I've made my own."

"How is Alice?" Effy's face was a picture of concern and my heart swelled looking at how genuine she was and how much she really cared.

"She's staying where she is, up north with Danya. I said I'd take you there when everything dies down. Let you get to know her properly."

"I'd like that." Effy sighed.

"Me too." I pulled a penny out of my pocket and went to stand next to her. "I know it's not finished, but I thought we could do with a bit of good luck." I handed her the penny, placing it into her palm and closing her hand, then I held it tightly with my own. "Go on. Make a wish."

"Only if you make one too," she said, staring at me from under her long lashes.

I found another penny in my pocket and then stood behind her, wrapping my arms around her and breathing her in as I whispered, "Together. On the count of three. One… two… three…"

I couldn't help it. I watched her close her eyes and drop the coin in before I threw mine. The way she scrunched her nose up as she mouthed her wish was the cutest thing I'd ever seen.

"We were supposed to do it together." She pretended to look offended as she peered back at me from over her shoulder, but the light in her eyes gave her away. "What did you wish for? I wished——"

I covered her mouth and laughed.

"You're not supposed to tell me. It won't come true if you do."

Her eyes clouded over and seeing her face fall slightly made me pull her into me and hug her.

"I love you, Eff. And you don't need to tell me what you wished for, I already know." She leant back in my arms to look at me.

"You do?"

"Of course." I ducked my head down to whisper into her ear. "It's the same thing I wished for. And I'm going to enjoy making that wish come true every single day of our lives. You and me together. Always."

"Promise?" she asked, with love beaming in her eyes.

"That is a forever promise."

EPILOGUE

ADAM

There are three things that are certain in this life.

Death.

Taxes.

And the fact that if I want something, I will fucking get it.

And I want her.

She might think I'm the devil incarnate, but she ain't seen nothing yet. If she thinks the rumours are bad, she's gonna love the live action encore I've got planned.

I live for the fear, the thrill of the chase. And I'll chase her down to the ends of the earth with a smile on my face. She's in my sights now, and nothing is going to stop me.

Buckle up, Olivia. I'm coming––ready or not––to claim what's rightfully mine.

You.

The End

Thank you so much for reading.

If you enjoyed Finn and Effy's story, then please spread the word and leave a review.

The Soldiers of Anarchy, Book One.
Liv and Adam's story.

Rebels of Sandland, Book Four.
Zak's story.

Author Acknowledgements

Here it is! Another book written during a global pandemic, and what a rollercoaster it's been! I need to say a huge thank you to my family for letting me escape the crazy world we live in and indulge in the crazier minds of my characters. You are my rocks and I would be lost without you.

Next, I want to give a massive shout-out to my book besties, who have kept my sanity in-check and pulled me off the ledge more times than I care to admit. Lindsey, Ashlee, Lauren, and Robyn, you ladies are amazing. You make me laugh every day and I value your friendship so much. Thank you for always being there and for BETA reading Fractured Minds.

Robyn, the best PA ever! Thank you for being totally awesome and organising everything. Without you, I'd be lost. Your teasers are to die for and you work so hard to get our books out there. You're an angel, and I'm truly grateful for your hard work and friendship. If you aren't following her, then get to it. You'll find her at @books4days_with_robyn or @robynpa_

A special thank you to Lindsey Powell at Liji Editing, and Leanne at Irish Ink, for being utterly brilliant and polishing this story for me. I'm so glad I found you. You've helped to make my little book shine brighter. Thank you ladies.

To Michelle Lancaster, for taking the perfect photograph of my character inspiration for Finn, and Andy Murray, for being that inspiration. This cover is gorgeous! And last but not least, Lori Jackson, for designing a kick ass cover. You guys rock!

I will always be indebted to the hard work and support of all the bloggers and bookstagrammers on social media. Your posts and graphics are amazing and you always go above and beyond. Thank you for every single post, share and comment. It means the world. I wish I could list everyone, but the acknowledgements would be longer than the actual story! You all do such a fantastic job. Thank you so much.

To the indie author community, I love how encouraging, supportive, and utterly amazing you are. I feel proud to be a part of such an amazing community. #indieauthorsrock

Last but not least, to all the readers out there who've taken the time to download, read, and review my book. Thank you for taking a chance on me. I'm always immensely grateful for every read and review. Reviews are the lifeline of every author, especially us smaller indies. You guys make my day and make it all worthwhile.

Thank you for reading Finn and Effy's story. Stay tuned for more!

Lots of Love
Nikki x

For updates on my new releases and other news, follow me on the following links.

Instagram
Facebook
Reader Group
Twitter
TikTok
Bookbub

Printed in Great Britain
by Amazon